PENGUIN BO

MADAM PRIME N

Seema Goswami is a journalist, columnist and author. She began her career with the Anandabazar Patrika Group, working for *Sunday* magazine, before moving on to become the editor of *The Telegraph*'s weekend features. She currently writes a weekly column, Spectator, for the *Hindustan Times*' Sunday magazine *Brunch*, which has a large and dedicated following. She has also published two books, *Woman on Top* and *Race Course Road*.

# MADAM PRIME MINISTER

## SEEMA GOSWAMI

PENGUIN BOOKS

An imprint of Penguin Random House

PENGUIN BOOKS

USA | Canada | UK | Ireland | Australia
New Zealand | India | South Africa | China

Penguin Books is part of the Penguin Random House group of companies
whose addresses can be found at global.penguinrandomhouse.com

Published by Penguin Random House India Pvt. Ltd
4th Floor, Capital Tower 1, MG Road,
Gurugram 122 002, Haryana, India

First published in Penguin Books by Penguin Random House India 2021

ISBN 9780143455066

Typeset in Adobe Caslon Pro by Manipal Technologies Limited, Manipal
Printed at Replika Press Pvt. Ltd, India

www.penguin.co.in

*For my husband, Vir*
*As always . . .*

# 1

The applause began from the back of the hall and rippled its way to the front. Asha Devi put down the sheet of paper from which she had read out her oath of office and took in the scene in front of her.

The Durbar Hall of Rashtrapati Bhavan was a marvelous sight on any occasion. But today, it seemed particularly impressive, with the entire power elite of Delhi corralled into it. In the front row, on the right side of the aisle, sat her family.

Her mother, Sadhana Devi, shimmering in an ivory and black *chanderi* sari, her perfect features perfectly immobile, her eyes moist with the tears she would only shed in private. Next to her mother sat her sister-in-law, Radhika, an insincere smile plastered on her painstakingly contoured face as she clapped along with everyone else. Flanking Sadhana Devi was her younger half-brother, Arjun. Not for him the pretense of enthusiasm. His face was impassive and his hands were folded firmly and on his lap.

Next to Arjun sat the man whose job she had just taken— Karan Pratap Singh, her older half-brother, elder son and heir to their father, Birendra Pratap Singh. Karan had been chosen by their party, the Loktantrik Janadesh Party (LJP), to take over as Prime Minister after the shock assassination of their father but had only managed to hold the post for a few months.

To be fair, it hadn't really been his fault that his reign was the shortest ever for an Indian PM. Karan had made all the right moves. He had called a General Election within three months of Birendra Pratap's killing to capitalize on the sympathy wave engendered by his death. He had campaigned hard for the party, even as he held the country together in difficult times. But despite his best efforts, the election had thrown up a hung Parliament. And the intra-party negotiations that followed had elevated his half-sister, Asha Devi, to the post of Prime Minister.

At twenty-nine, Asha was the youngest PM ever in the history of India. But, as she stood at the podium, hands folded in a Namaste to acknowledge the applause, Asha didn't feel like celebrating this fact. All she felt was a deep and abiding dread as to what this moment would lead to. Her life would be changed forever, and she wasn't sure she was ready for that.

Adding to her disquiet was the fact that she felt like an imposter. She knew in her bones that she didn't deserve to be up here, being sworn in as Prime Minister by the President of India. She had neither the experience nor the skills that the top job in government required. She had never held a ministerial portfolio in her life. She was a first-time member of Parliament, having just won the family seat in Bharatnagar that her father had nurtured over decades.

And more to the point, she was also the reason why her party, the LJP, had performed so badly in the last General Election. If Asha's naked pictures hadn't been leaked to the media in the run-up to the last phase of polling, the final result of the polls would have been quite different. And it would have been Karan standing up here, basking in the adulation of the crowd.

But that hadn't happened. And now, contrary to all expectations, it was Asha who was on the dais, sitting on an ornate chair to sign her name on the document that made her the new leader of the country.

As she sat ramrod-straight, eyes lowered, she made an arresting picture in her pale pink chiffon sari, paired with a three-quarter-sleeved blouse and accessorized with a gold pendant of the symbol Om. Her hair was drawn back from her make-up-less face and twisted into a chignon that rested on the nape of her neck. But that severe style, which would have looked school-marmish on anyone else, made her classic beauty all the more apparent. Her eyes were pools of limpid brown, her generous mouth a pink slash across her peaches-and-cream complexion, bracketed by deep, delicious dimples.

Oh yes, Asha Devi was a bona fide beauty all right, thought Sukanya Sarkar, from her vantage point in the front row, across the aisle from the Pratap Singh clan. As leader of the Poriborton Party (PP), Sukanya had driven a hard bargain before agreeing to form a coalition government with the LJP (and assorted smaller parties). And part of that bargain was that Asha, not Karan, would be Prime Minister in the new dispensation.

Beaming beatifically at her new protégé, Sukanya looked back with satisfaction on a job well done. Not only had she managed to best her bête noire, Karan, by wresting the prime ministership away from him, she had also dug the knife in by anointing his half-sister, whom he loathed, in his stead. And, in the process, she had got herself a young, inexperienced Prime Minister, whom it would be simplicity itself to manipulate.

As Asha finished signing her name and got back on her feet, her eyes met Sukanya's. The smile that bloomed on Asha's face was the genuine article. She thanked the President, walked down the stairs and made her way straight to Sukanya. She bowed low in a Namaste but Sukanya was having none of that. She swept Asha into a hug that sent the assembled cameramen into a complete frenzy.

They made for an incongruous picture. Sukanya, looking even more plain than usual in her crumpled cotton sari, her unkempt hair bundled into a messy bun, stood only at a puny 5 feet 3 inches to Asha's 5 feet 11 inches (in heels) and barely came up to the new Prime Minister's chest. But even though Asha towered Amazon-like above her, there was no doubting that Sukanya was the power player in this new duo.

As if to reinforce that impression, Sukanya broke away from the embrace and taking Asha by the hand, led her across the aisle so that she could seek the blessings of her mother, Sadhana Devi, and the rest of her family. Asha bent down to touch her mother's feet and the photographers went wild again. By the time she had straightened up, Karan, Arjun, and Radhika were already moving towards the aisle, making their way to the exit.

Asha held on to her mother's hand, and followed them. It was a slow progress. Everyone within touching distance wanted to shake her hand and congratulate her. Those a little further off shouted out their greetings. As she stopped to acknowledge her well-wishers, Asha fell further and further behind the Pratap Singh family.

She shot a quick, anxious look to make sure that her mother was not alone. Once she saw that Radhika had taken charge of her, she turned back to acknowledge the greetings of the great and good of Delhi crowding around her despite the best efforts of the Special Protection Group (SPG) deployed for her security to maintain some sort of order. Asha cast one longing look at the exit, looming in the distance. And then resigned herself to pressing the flesh before she could make her escape.

She was now Prime Minister of India. And her time was no longer her own.

\* \* \*

Karan Pratap Singh fought hard to maintain an impassive front as he sat in the front row watching his sister, Asha Devi, being sworn in. This was meant to be his job, a post for which he had been trained relentlessly as his father's eldest son and heir. And yet, here he was, clapping along with the rest of the audience, trying to keep his real feelings from showing on his face, as his younger sister took on the title that was his birthright.

How on earth had it come to this?

But even as Karan asked himself this question, the answer was staring him in the face, if only he chose to turn it a few inches to the right. Sukanya Sarkar, the leader of the Poriborton Party, and the woman who had put paid to all his ambitions. It was her intransigence that had led to Asha occupying the seat he still considered his own. As he glanced across at Sukanya, smiling happily in her seat across the aisle, he felt that familiar wave of anger wash over him.

How smug the bitch looked as she nodded encouragingly at Asha! Not that Asha needed any encouragement. His half-sister, flush with success, was the very epitome of self-confidence as she bowed low in a Namaste to thank the Rashtrapati.

Just then, Asha turned and looked straight at him, a tentative smile breaking out on her face, almost as if she was seeking reassurance from a familiar face in the crowd. It took some effort but Karan managed an answering smile that briefly lit up his chiselled features that until then had looked as if they were carved out of granite. Maybe Radhika was right, he thought. Perhaps Asha, a virtual babe in the deep dark woods of Indian politics, would look to her elder brother for help and guidance. And he could run the government as before, albeit through remote control.

Almost reflexively, his eyes swivelled left to look at his wife, as she sat two seats away from him. She was wearing a serene expression, her mouth upturned in a slight smile. Her hair swished luxuriously around her shoulders, its golden strands reflected in her champagne-colour chiffon sari, as she turned around to catch his eye. Her smile grew wider and warmer as she looked at her husband, raising one eyebrow infinitesimally as if to ask if he was feeling all right.

Of everyone present today, only Radhika truly understood the effort it had taken him to be here, at the swearing-in of his sister. He barely had time to nod back at her before everyone in the audience was scrambling to their feet as Asha made her way down the dais.

Karan carefully arranged his face into a welcoming expression, preparing to congratulate Asha. But instead of heading to the side of the aisle where the Pratap Singh clan sat, Asha was striding purposefully towards Sukanya, who took a few steps forward to meet her halfway. The two women melted into an embrace, and the hall exploded with the flash of a thousand flashbulbs. Flushing angrily, Karan lowered the hand he had raised to greet Asha, hoping that nobody had seen it.

By the time Asha came across to greet her mother and her siblings, Karan's mood had darkened further. All he wanted was to get this ordeal over with. So, without even a perfunctory word of congratulation to the new Prime Minister, he turned to walk down the aisle, flanked by Arjun. Radhika followed close behind them, holding Sadhana Devi by the hand.

But even though his back was turned to Asha, there was no way that Karan could escape the fact that she was the woman of the moment. Cries of 'Asha ji, Asha ji' rent the air, as the power elite of Delhi scrambled to pay court to the new leader of the country. Karan quickened his pace as the assembled crowd parted to let him through. Clearly, nobody had any desire to waste time greeting the man whose glorious future now lay firmly behind him. They were all too focused on making the acquaintance of the woman who would rule India for the next five years to pay any attention to him, yesterday's man that he was.

Karan could feel Radhika and Sadhana Devi scrambling to keep up with his pace, falling behind with every step he took towards the exit. But at this point he couldn't have slowed down even if he wanted to. His feet were carrying him inexorably towards the main exit, and all he wanted was to make it there so that he could get into his car and be driven home to lick his wounds in the privacy of Race Course Road. He had had enough of being a public spectacle, of having his shame witnessed by the rest of the world.

As he got to the stairs, he saw the cavalcade of white BMWs crawl up the driveway. Karan breathed a sigh of relief. His getaway vehicle was here.

The lead car came to a halt and the SPG contingent took its customary places around it, one agent beside each door. Karan began walking down the steps, even as the SPG agent stationed at the back door stood to attention.

He had gone half-way down when he felt an urgent hand at his elbow pulling him back. Karan looked back in exasperation only to see that it was Radhika, shaking her head embarrassedly at him. 'What?' he exploded, all his pent-up anger and frustration finally boiling over. 'What's the matter?' Radhika shook her head again and pointed mutely behind her, where Asha was making her way to the entrance.

That's when it hit him. The motorcade that had dropped him to the swearing-in was no longer his motorcade. It was now Asha's, and it was waiting to drive her to South Block so that she could make her first appearance at the Prime Minister's Office (PMO).

Burning red with humiliation, Karan stepped back to make way for his sister. And without even a glance in his direction, Asha slid into the back seat of her car and was driven away.

As he stood, waiting for his car to come and pick him up, Karan realized that everybody around him had noticed that little drama. And he was sure that by the evening, it would be the stuff of legendary Delhi gossip. Ten years from now, they would still be talking about the time Karan Pratap Singh tried to get into his sister's prime ministerial cavalcade and had to be stopped by his wife.

He had thought when he sat down to watch Asha take the oath of office that the day couldn't possibly get any worse. But it just had.

* * *

Manisha Patel, star anchor of the All-India Television News Network (AITNN) channel, was watching Asha Devi's swearing-in along with her panel. Everyone was miked and ready so that when the feed cut back to the studio, they could effortlessly switch to analyzing the historic scenes they had just witnessed. India had a woman Prime Minister yet again. And this one was just twenty-nine years old!

Manisha cast her mind back to when she had been twenty-nine. What had her life been like then? Oh yes, she had been struggling hard to be taken seriously in a newsroom dominated by men. She had been fighting for the right to be deployed to cover the unrest in Kashmir, over the objections of her executive editor who believed that this was no job for a woman. And she had been coping with the overweening arrogance and overpowering jealousy of a boyfriend who could not believe that his girlfriend was actually refusing to back off from stories that he considered his own.

Asha would be up against the same kind of male chauvinism in her own life now, thought Manisha, as she watched the new Prime Minister step down from the podium and fall into an embrace with Sukanya Sarkar. Well, she wouldn't find a better role model than Sukanya when it came to negotiating her way as a woman in a world run according to the rules set down by men.

As the ceremony at Rashtrapati Bhavan wound to a close, the feed cut back to the studio. As the voice in her earpiece counted down, Manisha checked out her shot in the monitor above her teleprompter. She felt a flash of irritation as she saw that the make-up guy had again gone berserk with the foundation, turning her at least four shades fairer than she was in real life. In her preternaturally pale face, her black, kohl-rimmed eyes gleamed like two alien beings in a milky galaxy. Oh well, it was too late to do anything about that, she shrugged mentally, as she flicked her highlighted hair into place so that it framed her face, and swiveled towards the camera, a bright smile on her face.

'Hello and welcome! As we've all just seen, India has a new Prime Minister, the first female PM since Indira Gandhi. And just like Indira Gandhi, Asha Devi too comes to office as a surprise candidate, an untested commodity who has been elevated to the top job because of some peculiar circumstances.'

Turning to her first guest, Nandini Kashyap, a veteran of TV panels such as this one, Manisha threw the discussion open with a gentle first question. 'What do you think, Nandini? Do you see Asha emerging as an Indira Gandhi-like figure? Or do you think she will be revealed to be the *"gungi gudiya"* that Indira never was, being manipulated from behind the scenes by her brother, Karan Pratap?'

Nandini laughed uneasily. She had spent many years cultivating Karan Pratap as a source and was reasonably close to him and his wife Radhika. She knew it wouldn't be politic to praise Asha too much. On the other hand, Asha was the new Prime Minister, and it wouldn't do to be less than enthusiastic about her prospects.

'You know Manisha,' she ventured after a beat, 'I think we should give Asha the benefit of the doubt. She is a woman of substance, a woman who doesn't let anything get her down. Look how she came back from the photo scandal that would have destroyed any other woman politician. She is stronger than she looks . . .'

'Yes, that may well be true,' interrupted Manisha, 'but that doesn't answer my question. Do you think Karan Pratap will allow her to function as Prime Minister or will he be running things from behind the scenes?'

'I wouldn't put it like that,' responded Nandini cautiously. 'I think Asha will welcome any inputs that her brother may have. After all, she is very inexperienced when it comes to government. This is her first job, you know. So, I think she will be happy to accept help wherever she can find it.'

Dhruv Sahai, spokesman for the LJP, could not contain himself any longer. 'Manisha ji, can I make one point? Please give me just a couple of minutes. Without any interruptions, please.'

Manisha suppressed her irritation at his unctuous request. Anyone would think she ran one of those debate shows in which the anchor never let anyone else complete a sentence. But rather than remonstrate, she just nodded permission.

'I'm sorry Manisha ji, but I think you are completely missing the point. Asha ji and Karan ji are family. They are brother and sister. Of course, they will help each other. Of course, they will advise one another and listen to the advice given to them. That's what family does. I don't think the media should read too much into it if Karan ji helps Asha ji in any way. Nor should you try and create trouble between the two by pitting them against one another.'

'It's not the media's job to support the government, Mr Sahai,' snapped Manisha, finally losing her patience. 'It is our job to question it. And that's exactly what I am doing.'

Turning to Lokesh Bharadwaj, the spokesman of the main opposition, the Samajik Prajatantra Party (SPP), she asked, 'So, how does it feel, seeing the woman your party tried so hard to destroy taking the oath of office to become Prime Minister of India?'

It was a needlessly provocative question. But Manisha thought that she had the right to phrase it that way given that the former leader of the SPP, Jayesh Sharma, had been directly implicated in the leaking of those naked pictures of Asha. Given that background, she thought this was fair comment.

Bharadwaj obviously disagreed. Putting on his most outraged expression, he spluttered as he mounted his defence, 'Manisha ji, I am so disappointed in you. I never thought that you would become one of those anchors who sensationalize everything.'

'How am I sensationalizing anything? I'm saying what every person in this country knows to be true,' countered Manisha.

'No, you are saying what some people believe to be true,' Bharadwaj shot back. 'And that doesn't make it true, by the way. Nobody has produced any proof of the involvement of the SPP in the photo scandal. And until you can prove such allegations, you should not make them. This is nothing short of libellous!'

At the mention of the word 'libel' and with the threat of a lawsuit hovering in the air, Manisha decided to take a different tack. Turning back to Dhruv Sahai, she asked, 'Do you think the LJP will look back on this day with regret or with happiness? After all, you were pretty much forced into making Asha Devi the PM by Sukanya Sarkar. And what does it say for your party that you were held hostage by the junior partner in your coalition?'

It was now Sahai's turn to splutter with indignation. And so it went, yet another day in the highly charged, acrimonious world of TV news discussions in India.

Across town, in the studios of News Tonight Network (NTN), Manisha's rival network, the debate was even more bad-tempered than usual. Gaurav Agnihotri, the head of NTN, had been angry and upset ever since the last few BARC ratings had come in. For the first time in a year and a half, his show had slipped from the number one position. In its place was the interview that Manisha had done with Asha Devi after the photo scandal broke. Since that breakthrough, Manisha's prime time show's TRPs had nearly doubled. And now there were weeks when she beat him—by a whisker but beat him nonetheless—to the number one slot.

Shot through the professional rivalry were his complicated personal feelings about Manisha. The two of them had met as young reporters, while working in Doordarshan, and had quickly fallen in love—and in bed—with one another. The relationship had been doomed from the very outset. Competing for the same stories, neither of them willing to concede ground to the other, their affair had soon deteriorated into shouting matches followed by make-up sex. Soon only the shouting matches remained while the sex (make-up or otherwise) slipped off the table.

The end of their love story had been as messy as it was inevitable. And since then, both Manisha and Gaurav had gone on to build impressive careers at their respective networks. To this day they hadn't as much as exchanged a 'hello' since their explosive break-up, though each kept an eagle eye on the other's career trajectory.

That said, Gaurav's current mood of anger and resentment wasn't primarily aimed at Manisha. Its target was Asha, who had chosen Manisha over him. No doubt, he told himself, it was because she feared Gaurav's aggressive questioning, while she was sure that Manisha—out of some stupid sense of female solidarity— would lob softballs at her. And that's exactly what Manisha had done, going with a gently-gently approach that had allowed Asha to rehabilitate herself in the court of public opinion. She hadn't even pressed the point about why Asha had chosen to pose for such revealing—even obscene—pictures for her then fiancé, Sunny Mahtani!

Now, rumour had it that the two women had become good friends, exchanging text messages and phone calls several times a week. And if his sources in AITNN were to be believed, the first interview that Asha gave as Prime Minister would also go to her favourite anchor, Manisha Patel.

Well, Asha had made her choice. Now she would spend the next five years paying for it. Gaurav would make it his personal mission to ensure that she didn't even have a honeymoon period as Prime Minister. He would be chipping away at her image every day, beginning today.

Shrugging off these angry thoughts, Gaurav tuned back into the discussion swirling around in the studio. One of the

panelists was droning on about how amazing it was to have a
fresh young face as Prime Minister. This was an opportunity
for the country to start afresh, a way to reboot, to do away with
the old and usher in the new. It was amazing how many clichés
the man could employ in just a couple of sentences.

It was time to show these losers who really ran the show
in the studio of NTN. Cutting into his guest's monologue,
Gaurav interjected, 'Just how stupid do you think the people of
India are? Do you think all of us are idiots?'

The panelist stammered out a response, but was not
allowed to get beyond a few words before Gaurav interrupted
yet again.

Turning away from his guest to face the camera, and raising
his voice even more, Gaurav continued, 'Ladies and gentlemen,
this is what is wrong with this country. We have yet another
member of a political dynasty taking over as Prime Minister,
and we are being told that this is the start of a fresh, new
chapter in the history of India. Well, let me tell you that it is
nothing of the sort. The Asha Devi administration will provide
nothing more than a continuation of the failed policies that
were introduced by her father, Birendra Pratap Singh and then
reinforced by her brother, Karan Pratap Singh.'

The LJP spokesman could no longer sit silent, while this
diatribe raged on. 'I'm sorry Gaurav ji, but you are being very
unfair to my party, and to Asha ji. She has just been sworn in as
the Prime Minister. How can you write her off like this without
even giving her a chance? You are being most unfair!'

'Unfair? Did you just call me unfair?' Gaurav thundered, his
slightly pudgy face turning red even as his salt and pepper curls
reverberated with rage. His eyes gleaming angrily through his
rimless spectacles, he turned the full force of his wrath on the
hapless LJP spokesman.

'How dare you, sir? How dare you? Just because this channel doesn't worship the Pratap Singh family like some others I don't wish to name, you think you can accuse us of being unfair? We are the only channel in this country that is completely fair. We are the channel that asks tough questions of everyone in the country. And we will ask those same questions of the new Prime Minister whether you like it or not. More importantly, we are the only channel that puts News Over Views.'

As usual, Gaurav managed to capitalize the three words that were the calling card of NTN: News Over Views.

The LJP spokesman lost his temper as well at this. 'It's not your questions we object to. It's the fact that you have already made up your mind about Asha Devi and the new government. And we all know it's because she chose to speak to your rival channel rather than to you.'

Gaurav went ballistic. 'We all know why she chose not to speak to me,' he sneered. 'It's because she knew that I would not give her the easy ride that some other anchors of the Lutyens' media would.' Gaurav took care to mispronounce 'Lutyens' as always, to reinforce just how much of an outsider he was in that rarified world. Having grown up in Patiala and gone to college in Chandigarh, Gaurav was not a fully paid-up member of the closed group that was the Lutyens' elite. And he lost no opportunity to point this out, to reinforce his anti-establishment credentials.

Mindful of the voice in his earpiece, Gaurav turned to his camera again to wrap up. 'I would like to end the show today by issuing a challenge to the new Prime Minister. Asha Devi, if you have the courage of conviction, then have the guts to appear on this channel. Come on my show to face all the questions the nation wants to ask. And give us the answers we are looking for.'

Gaurav paused for a moment to draw out the suspense. And then ended the show with his trademark line. 'Thank you for staying with us, ladies and gentlemen. And thank you for voting for News Over Views by watching NTN. We'll see you again, tomorrow, same time, same place. Goodbye.'

# 2

This was the third meeting of her Cabinet in three weeks. And Asha Devi felt the same dissatisfaction she had experienced the first time round as she glanced around the conference table. The faces ranged around her were a visible reminder that though she may be Prime Minister, this was, by no means, her government. At least, it wasn't her government alone. It owed as much—if not more—to her coalition partner, Sukanya Sarkar.

The Poriborton Party (PP) chief had struck a hard bargain, scoring two of the four big ministries in the Cabinet (and many other less important portfolios). The defence ministry had been bagged by the PP as had been the external affairs ministry, though Asha had stood her ground and retained the key home ministry for the LJP.

Asha felt a small glow of satisfaction as she turned to look at her home minister. Savitri Shukla had always been something of a backroom girl in the LJP, working low-profile jobs, first for the party and then for the government. As Birendra Pratap's power minister, she had won his confidence with her quiet but steady competence and her complete antipathy for the limelight.

When the time came to nominate a home minister, Asha had thought long and hard about whom she could trust implicitly in the party. And the more she thought about it, the more Savitri ji (she no longer thought about her as Savitri Aunty even in the privacy of her thoughts) seemed like the right choice. Shukla had enough administrative experience to take on the job of home minister and yet she wasn't high profile enough to put anyone else's nose out of joint. She was the soul of discretion and her loyalty to Birendra Pratap, and now his daughter, was beyond doubt. And Asha needed a family loyalist in the ministry that would oversee the investigations into her father's assassination.

Feeling Asha's eyes upon her, Savitri Shukla looked in her direction and smiled. In her starched and neatly pinned-up cotton sari, Savitri looked like the archetypal Indian housewife, complete with a sensible bun nesting on the nape of her neck. But Asha knew that behind that maternal manner and portly figure lay a sharp and astute political brain that was belied by the slightly befuddled manner Savitri always affected. Asha was sure she would need that sharpness and agility of mind sooner rather than later.

She abandoned these thoughts to pay attention to what Defence Minister Prabha Saraf was saying. The Poriborton Party had run its election campaign on an anti-corruption plank and it wasn't ready to let that go now that it was part of the government. So, at every Cabinet meeting, Saraf brought up the L'Oiseau arms deal, arguing that the government should be seen to be pursuing it with even greater zeal.

Asha had no problems with that. If anything, she was more committed than anyone else at the table to bringing former defence minister, Madan Mohan Prajapati, to justice. He wasn't just the man behind the L'Oiseau deal but also the man behind her father's assassination. So, if anyone wanted Madan Mohan behind bars and facing the death penalty, it was Asha.

So, Asha had no problem with pursuing the guilty in the L'Oiseau deal. What she did have a problem with was the righteous indignation with which Prabha always brought up the topic.

What did the woman think? That nobody was aware of her background? That nobody knew that her industrialist husband's fortune was based on a series of dodgy deals? (Though, admittedly, none of them had anything to do with the defence ministry.) And that it was this tainted money that powered Saraf's political career? The blatant hypocrisy struck Asha anew every time Saraf started on her holier-than-thou diatribe against corruption.

'I really think that we should let Sagar Prajapati turn approver if he agrees to testify against his Uncle,' Saraf was saying now. 'That is the best way to get some resolution in the case.'

Asha felt that familiar hot haze of anger rise up within her. Her body seemed to respond viscerally whenever anyone mentioned Madan Mohan Prajapati, the man her father had appointed as defence minister, and her own mentor when she first stepped into politics in her own right after her father's assassination. She hadn't known then that Prajapati was not just corrupt (he was the man at the end of the money trail of the L'Oiseau deal, though it was his nephew, Sagar, the moneyman, whom the French had arrested) but that he was also the man who had ordered the hit on her father once Birendra Pratap confronted him about his corruption.

Controlling her emotions with an effort, Asha responded coolly. 'Yes, Prabha ji, the CBI is already working on that. As soon as the extradition process is over and Sagar is back in India, that will be our first order of business.'

Turning to the external affairs minister, Aroop Mitra, Asha asked, 'Where are we on the extradition process, Aroop da? By now we should have had Sagar in custody. What is taking so long?'

Aroop Mitra turned to give her the full benefit of his aristocratic visage. A full-blooded bhadralok from one of the oldest families in Calcutta, he had been nominated as external affairs minister by Sukanya Sarkar. The joke was that he was the only person in the Poriborton Party to speak English with an English accent, and hence, had got the nod for this plum portfolio. And even though Asha had initially balked at accepting another PP luminary in a top ministry, she had to admit that she had been pleasantly surprised by Mitra. He was the voice of reason in every Cabinet meeting, his sonorous tones calming things down whenever matters grew a little heated.

It was with the same absence of passion that Mitra brought her up to speed with the progress in the extradition case against Sagar Prajapati, assuring the entire Cabinet that the man would be back in India in a matter of weeks.

It was left to the human resources development minister, Aditya Deva, an old LJP hand, to bring up the other case that was at the top of Asha's mind: the investigation into the assassination of her father, Birendra Pratap. The two arms dealers, Gopi Goyal and Akshay Trivedi, who had facilitated the plot, had provided rock-solid evidence against Madan Mohan. But the defence minister had departed the country's shores before he could be arrested, and was now untraceable. There had been regular 'sightings' of him in locations as far apart as Sao Paolo, Montenegro and Johannesburg, but every single time the news had turned out to be false.

Today as well, Asha had no real progress to report. The investigative agencies were working every lead they had, but information on Madan Mohan was as scarce on the ground as the man himself. Asha's eyes immediately went to her younger half-brother, Arjun Pratap Singh—now commerce minister in her government—as she made this lack-of-progress report.

His was a quiet presence at this table. But no matter how rarely Arjun spoke, Asha was always hyperaware of him. Looking at him now, wearing the regulation white kurta pyjama that all politicians wore as a default uniform, she could see no traces of the wild party animal who had driven their father crazy with his drinks and drugs lifestyle.

Birendra Pratap's death had sobered his younger son up. As had, Asha suspected, her photo scandal to which Arjun had reacted with anger and contempt. But beneath all that, Asha could sense that there was an element of 'There, but for the grace of God, go I.'

And if anyone was the prime object for a sex scandal, surely it was her younger half-brother, who had spent most of the last decade partying away with his gang of noted homosexuals. And even though Arjun had never admitted to being gay, he had never quite been in the closet either. Rumours of his homosexuality had been rife all through Asha's growing up years, fanned by Arjun's flamboyant and verging-on-camp personal style. And though Arjun took care to be seen in public with beautiful young women from time to time, the fiction didn't really hold.

But there was little evidence of that former life in the man who sat morosely a few seats down the table. Asha could see the tightening of Arjun's lips that signaled that he wasn't happy at the slow pace at which the investigation into their father's death was progressing. But then, neither was she. But the truth was that they were up against a brick wall, unless someone, somewhere, could find out where Madan Mohan had gone to ground. And given Prajapati's resources and sphere of influence, this was a near-impossible task.

Then, it was time to discuss the last item on the agenda. Finance Minister Alok Ray, who had been chafing at the bit all through the meeting, finally cleared his throat and began speaking about his pet project: the proposal to abolish income tax on anyone below thirty years of age.

Asha could tell by Arjun's irritated expression that he didn't think much of this proposal and that made her perversely more open to it. She set aside the papers on the Birendra Pratap assassination case and leaned forward to listen carefully to Ray.

In a room full of standard-issue netas, Alok Ray, with his rangy build and clean-cut features, stood out like a horse among mules. Not for him the politician's uniform of white kurta pyjama. Ray still stuck to his investment banker look: an elegantly cut suit, which made the most of a lean but muscular figure that was not the product of endless hours in the gym but the consequence of many years spent hiking and rock climbing in the Himalayas. In a concession to the new world he found himself in, Ray had eschewed the tie and exchanged his button-down shirts for ones with Chinese collars. Even so, he looked less like an Indian politician and more like an Iranian diplomat, an impression strengthened by his dark, closely cropped beard, fair complexion and mop of springy black hair.

Having made his fortune in investment banking, Ray had spent some years running his own hedge fund before being headhunted for a top job with the International Monetary Fund (IMF). That's where he had come to the notice of then Indian Prime Minister, Birendra Pratap Singh, who had lured him back to India with the job of Governor of the Reserve Bank of India (RBI).

Ray, who had just split from his American wife of many years, and didn't have any children to hold him back, had grabbed the opportunity with both hands. It wasn't just that he wanted to give back something to the country that had given him so much, he also needed a change of scenery to recover from the bruising divorce battle he had been through. So, at the age of forty, Ray had arrived back in India, the country he had left as a college student, to take over the RBI—and had lost no time in proving the naysayers (who found him too young and raw for the job) wrong.

Now, two years later, he found himself ensconced in the Cabinet as finance minister.

As even Ray would concede, this wasn't because of any great skill or accomplishment on his part. He had just happened to be in the right place at the right time. When Asha and Sukanya were tussling over who would be the new finance minister, his name had been thrown in the ring as a 'neutral' candidate. As a non-political technocrat, it was pointed out, Ray would not be part of either the LJP or the PP camp in government. And given his stellar performance as RBI governor, there was little doubt that he would make a better finance minister than many of the other names in the fray.

Asha had accepted the idea only too readily, given how highly her late father had thought of Alok. Sukanya had been resistant at first, but had melted at her first one-on-one meeting with the man, quickly thawing under the wattage of Ray's charm. And it didn't hurt that Ray —having shrewdly taken the measure of the woman—had conducted the entire meeting in their mother tongue. Speaking in Bengali always put Sukanya at ease, and it wasn't long before she was positively purring with contentment as she discussed the state of the economy with Alok.

At the end of that hour-long meeting, Alok Ray had got his 'Sukanya di's' nod to be India's new finance minister.

Whether he would have the same success in getting his fiscal agenda through Cabinet was another matter entirely. The proposal that nobody under the age of thirty should pay income tax had met with fierce pushback from his fellow ministers. And with every intervention, Ray's temper was rising. Honestly, he thought to himself, as yet another minister droned on, how could you possibly discuss economics with an illiterate and innumerate bunch like this?

His exasperation must have shown on his face because he saw Asha smiling wryly as she caught his eye. Almost involuntarily, his face relaxed into an answering smile. Arjun, who had caught this little interlude, looked even angrier than usual. Interrupting the civil aviation minister, who was holding forth in his usual whiny style, Arjun demanded, 'And in any case, what is about thirty that makes it the right cut-off age? It seems completely arbitrary to me. Why not make it thirty-five? Or even forty? What's so special about thirty?'

The entire room swiveled across to look at Alok. What was so special about thirty?

But his response was lost to posterity as there was an urgent knocking on the door. Before anyone could answer, the door burst open, propelling Arunoday Sengupta, the National Security Advisor (NSA) and Madhavan Kutty, the Principal Secretary (PS), into the room.

It was left to Kutty to break the silence that followed. 'I'm sorry to interrupt, Madam Prime Minister,' he said, addressing Asha. 'But we have to brief you right away.'

* * *

It had started off as just another Wednesday afternoon at the Kautilya Mall. The ladies who lunch were out in full force; Chanel, Dior and Hermès bags at the ready, all set to do a bit of light shopping followed by some not-so-light lunching.

Those who had had the good sense to make a reservation were seated in the basement restaurant, trying the delights served up by the nine kitchens on offer. Those who had made the rookie mistake of just turning up in the belief that a table would be magically conjured up for them had been duly turned away and were now settling down—with very bad grace—at the café in the atrium, which everyone knew was equivalent to restaurant Siberia. And those social X-rays who didn't let a morsel pass their mouths in the middle of the day were doing a desultory trawl of the shops, picking up a pair of earrings here, a designer kurta there, paying with wads of cash that made clear that demonetization had been a complete farce.

It was at exactly 2.37 p.m. that the two Range Rovers drove into the mall. The security guards at the outer gate waved a languid hand, signaling them to stop for a security check. But instead of stopping, the drivers of both cars accelerated and drove right through the barriers. Within seconds they were at the inner gate of the mall, where the five men in each vehicle (including the drivers) got out, AK-47s in their hands.

Just for a second the guards thought that the armed men might be the security detail of one of the politicians who often visited the mall. That belief was shattered along with the silence of the afternoon as a fusillade of shots rang out, killing all the guards in attendance. Two women, who had been standing on the porch, waiting for their cars to arrive, hit the floor the moment they heard the shots. But it was to no avail. The terrorists turned their guns on them, hitting them as they lay prostrate on the ground.

The ten men then peeled off into two groups of five, one group sprinting down to the basement entrance, while the other entered the main gate and locked it shut.

By now, all the women—and it was mostly women, if you discounted the male sales assistants in the shops—inside the mall had heard the firing. The sound of high-pitched screaming filled the air as the ladies ran for shelter. Some dodged into the shops that lined the atrium, others sprinted into the toilets at the far end of the mall. Some dived under the tables at which they had sat, others sheltered behind the counter of the open kitchen.

They found cover wherever they could and waited. But there were no more shots fired. Instead, the men, all of them wearing camouflage much like army officers, and with balaclava masks over their faces, fanned out through the mall, forcing everyone out of the shops and into the open space in the middle, where they made them lie face down.

It was only in the basement restaurant that the terrorists faced any resistance. Shouting, 'Down. On the ground,' they walked through the restaurant, five abreast, using the butts of their rifles to hit anyone who dared look up at them. But they were barely halfway through the room when shots rang out from under one of the tables, hitting three of them square in the chest.

It made no difference to their progress. In fact, such was the quality of their body armor, the shots barely slowed them down. They just raised their rifles and began firing back, aiming at the table from under which the attack had come. When there were no further answering shots, one of the men upturned the table. Underneath it lay four men, all of them wearing grey safari suits, and all of them indisputably dead. But the terrorists were taking no chances. One of them stood over the prone men and pumped in a few more bullets for good measure.

By then, the screaming of the women had reached a crescendo. 'Quiet,' shouted one of the men. 'Stay quiet and you won't be harmed. Make one more sound and you will all be dead.'

The silence fell almost immediately. Four of the men fanned out to the corners of the room, their guns at the ready to deal with any resistance. The fifth one began walking through the room, roughly yanking up the heads of the women on the ground, taking a good look at their faces and then letting them fall back. He had gone through three rows, before he suddenly paused at one woman. Taking his phone out of his pocket, he checked to see that the face in front of him matched the one on his screen. Once he was sure of that, he yanked her roughly to her feet.

'We've found her,' he called out triumphantly to the others. 'Here she is.'

Radhika Singh swayed slightly on her five-inch Manolo Blahnik stilettoes, staying upright with difficulty. As daughter-in-law to one Prime Minister and wife to another, she had been trained by the SPG on how to cope with a kidnapping. But all of that training fled her mind as sheer terror took over. Shaking with nerves, she struggled in the grip of one of the men, even as another took plastic ties and tied her hands behind her back. The two men wrestled her on to a chair and once she was seated, they secured her legs to the chair. Only when she was completely trussed up did they address her.

'Are you Radhika Singh?' asked one.

Radhika, who had had just caught sight of her SPG detail lying dead on the ground a few tables away, began sobbing uncontrollably, her cries nearing hysteria as the truth of her predicament came home to her.

When she didn't answer, one of the men stepped forward and slapped her hard across the face. 'Shut up and answer,' he said, his Kashmiri accent apparent in every word of English. 'Are you Radhika Singh?'

She nodded mutely, her eyes wild in her petrified face, which had turned as white as the linen dress she was wearing. Nodding in grim satisfaction, he roughly removed Radhika's silk scarf from around her neck and stuffed it in her mouth.

One of the men whipped out a rolled-up piece of cloth from one of the pockets of his camouflage uniform. He unfurled it to reveal the black flag of ISIS. Tacking it on the wall behind Radhika, he took up position beside her, his AK-47 pointing menacingly at her head. One of his companions took up an identical position on her other side.

Once they had composed their macabre tableau, they signaled to one of their companions to begin shooting. Holding his iPhone aloft, he gave them the thumbs up to begin.

The man on the left began speaking. 'Bismillah al Rahman al Rahim . . .'

* * *

Four minutes later, the video dropped on Twitter. Asha had just dismissed the Cabinet, asking only the members of the Cabinet Committee on Security (CCS) to stay back to be briefed on the terror strike by Sengupta and Kutty, when one of her aides rushed in, holding his phone aloft. Wordlessly, he handed it to her after pressing play.

Asha could feel her insides melting with fear as she saw her sister-in-law, Radhika, a bruise flowering on the left side of her face, sitting bound and gagged between two gun-toting masked men, with the black flag of ISIS in the background. It took her a few seconds to recover sufficiently to focus on what one of the men was saying.

It began with the standard spiel on the atrocities that the Indian forces had committed in Kashmir. The usual exhortations of 'azaadi' followed but Asha couldn't hear them over the silent scream issuing from her sister-in-law's terrified face.

But even as she focused on Radhika's expression, it was two other faces that Asha was actually seeing —those of her young nieces, Kavya and Karina. At ten and six, they had already experienced the violent death of their grandfather. There was no way she was going to let them suffer any more loss; and most certainly, not of their mother. No matter what it took, she vowed to herself, she would bring Radhika back.

Asha forced her attention back to the video, as the terrorists began enumerating their demands. They wanted the release of twelve terrorists who had been arrested in Kashmir six months ago as part of an anti-terror drive. These men had to be taken across the line of control and handed over to Pakistani authorities. Once that was done, they wanted a helicopter to land on the roof of Kautilya Mall so that they could fly to an unspecified destination across the border.

If these demands were met, they would release Radhika Pratap Singh. If they weren't, they would start killing the hostages, one woman every half hour. The government had exactly six hours to act before the killing started.

As the video cut out, Asha handed the phone back to her aide, who silently backed out of the room. Turning to the others ranged around the table, she asked, 'What do we do? What strategy do we have in place to deal with something like this?'

The ministers who were part of the CCS turned to Sengupta. As National Security Advisor, this was his area. Sengupta paused for a moment, straightened his tie and began, 'Well, Prime Minister, the Indian government's policy was laid down by your late father. And he decreed that we should not negotiate with terrorists. Doing so just puts a target on the back of every politician and his or her family . . .'

'Don't be ridiculous,' Asha snapped, her nerves finding expression in anger. 'Of course, we negotiate with terrorists. How many militants did we let go in exchange for Rubaiya Sayeed, the then home minister's daughter? And didn't foreign minister Jaswant Singh fly to Kandahar with three hardcore terrorists to exchange them for the passengers of IC 814? Don't give me this nonsense about not negotiating with terrorists.'

Sengupta, who had never before been subjected to Asha's temper, immediately retreated into the safety of semantics. 'Well ma'am, that was in the past. I am only telling you what the current position of the Indian government is, as was laid down by Birendra Pratap ji. Of course, in the real world, we would have to compromise on occasion to ensure the safety of our citizens . . .'

Alok Ray, first-time minister and a novice when it came to the workings of government, cut in to ask, 'Who exactly is in charge of negotiations? Is it the Intelligence Bureau? Or is it R&AW?'

Kutty answered, 'Well, that depends. In the Rubaiya case it was the IB. And in Kandahar it was R&AW. I think we need to get inputs from both. And of course the NIA will play a central role.'

Ray nodded. Even he, a newbie in matters of national security, knew that the National Investigation Agency—set up in 2008 by an Act of Parliament—was the nodal agency when it came to investigating terror attacks all across the country.

As if on cue, an aide came into the room to say that a secure video link had been set up with IB Director Suresh Shastri, R&AW Chief Anil Bhalla, and the NIA director general, Balvinder Singh. But before they could begin briefing the Prime Minister, the door opened yet again.

Asha looked up impatiently, irritated at yet another interruption. But her annoyance died the moment she saw a disheveled Karan enter, escorted by an ashen Arjun.

Instinctively, she got to her feet and met Karan half-way down the room. And seeing the naked despair on his face, it seemed entirely natural to hug him close, rubbing his back in long, repetitive strokes like you would to soothe and calm an inconsolable child.

It was as if a dam had burst at Asha's touch. Karan began sobbing, his shoulders shaking with the strength of his emotion. Asha hugged him tighter before finally letting him go. 'It's going to be okay, bhaiyya,' she said, struggling to control her own tears. 'We will get her back.'

Karan collapsed in a chair, holding his tear-stained face in his hands. Arjun sat down in the empty place next to him. Defence Minister Prabha Saraf raised her eyebrows at this. This was a meeting of the Cabinet Committee on Security. Only the Prime Minister, the defence minister, the home minister, the finance minister and the external affairs minister were entitled to be here. Neither Karan nor Arjun had the right to attend.

She shot a quick look around the room. Nobody else seemed at all concerned about the interlopers in their midst. Saraf thought for a moment of taking a stand against this irregularity. And then, looking at Karan's devastated face, decided to let it be. There were some things that were more important than rules and regulations.

Asha called the meeting to order and the bureaucrats began briefing in turn. Information was rather thin on the ground, Shastri conceded reluctantly. There had been no chatter on the usual channels about such an attack being planned. Anil Bhalla chimed in to add that R&AW had been equally in the dark. It was left to Singh, the head of the NIA, to explain that the National Security Guard (NSG) had already been deployed around the mall, with its commandos ready to storm the place at a moment's notice if needed. Additional army units had also been requisitioned and would be in place in a couple of hours at the earliest.

The moment he heard this, Karan stiffened. Sensitive to his response, Asha immediately said, 'Please keep all security forces on standby. They must not engage with the terrorists. We have to try and resolve this peacefully if possible. God alone knows how many casualties there will be if there is a pitched battle in that enclosed space.'

Turning to Sengupta, she asked, 'Do we know anything about the group that is behind this? Has anyone taken responsibility?'

But it was Shastri who responded. 'Ma'am, nobody has claimed responsibility so far. But it's clear from the accent of the hostage taker in the video that these men are Kashmiris. We are running the faces of those on camera through our facial recognition software but with those masks in place it will be hard to get a match.'

Karan could not stay quiet any longer. 'Aren't you missing the point?' he burst out. 'That is an ISIS flag behind my wife!'

'Yes sir,' responded Shastri. 'But that doesn't necessarily mean anything. The Islamist movement in Kashmir routinely uses these flags to scare the population. It doesn't mean that any of these men are actually part of ISIS. They are probably just some boys from the Valley.'

Savitri Shukla made an exasperated noise. As home minister, she felt this inadequate briefing reflected badly upon her. So, it was with some asperity that she said, 'Mr Shastri, surely as IB chief you can do better than that? Even we can make these kinds of educated guesses. We need you to give us facts not suppositions.'

Kutty intervened to save the hapless Shastri from the wrath of his new boss. Turning to Asha, he said, 'Madam Prime Minister, it's no point discussing who or what is behind this right now. We simply don't have that information as yet. But we need to discuss how we are going to handle this. How do we respond to the demands of these terrorists? That's what we need to decide.'

Asha nodded in agreement but there was no doubt in her mind. She would give in to any demands so long as it got Radhika back. It didn't matter if people dismissed her as a weak Prime Minister. Or if the media attacked her for releasing dangerous men just to save her own sister-in-law. All she cared about was getting Radhika home safe and sound. Nothing else mattered.

First off, Asha made clear, the NSG and the army were to stand well back. She didn't want any trigger-happy commando jeopardizing the safety of the hostages. Next, they needed to establish direct and continuous contact with the terrorists inside the mall. Once that was done, she wanted to be patched through so that she could speak to Radhika and make sure that she was well. Only after she was sure that her sister-in-law was okay would she even begin to negotiate on the terrorists' demands.

As Kutty nodded and busied himself with making phone calls to make that happen, Asha directed the home minister to get in touch with the J&K government to see how soon the terrorists that the men wanted in exchange for Radhika could be released across the Line of Control in Kashmir. Savitri Shukla made rapid notes and then excused herself from the meeting, heading back to the home ministry to supervise operations from there.

The rest of the CCS sat listening intently as the IB director, R&AW chief and the head of the NIA took them through the rest of the briefing, droning on about the various terrorist outfits that could be behind this operation. And then, finally, this pretense at an intelligence briefing was over, with nobody any wiser as to who was holding Radhika Singh—and about 200 other women—hostage.

Asha dismissed the others and withdrew to her office, followed closely by Karan and Arjun. And there, the three Pratap Singh siblings sat in troubled silence, awaiting further developments, each of them dreading how this day would end.

# 3

Radhika Pratap Singh could feel the plastic restraints around her hands and legs tightening every time she moved. And yet, she could not stop squirming around to find a more comfortable position on the chair to which she was tied.

Her captors, after recording their video, had retreated to the far side of the room, leaving her alone with her terror. Despite herself, her eyes kept going to the table, beside which her entire SPG detail lay dead. And every time she looked at those poor men tasked to protect her, men who had died in that endeavor, her tears came afresh.

Radhika was convinced that she was next. There was no way the Indian government would agree to the conditions set by the terrorists. And even if Asha allowed her familial loyalty to prevail over settled policy, there was no guarantee that the terrorists would keep their end of the bargain.

What was to stop them from gunning her down once their comrades had been freed by the Indian state? What if the commando forces that were no doubt deployed by now, jumped the gun and stormed the mall in the hope of saving the hostages? All of them were more likely to die in the crossfire than be saved by their rescuers.

There was no good way for this to end. The only thing that remained to be decided was how she would die. Would she be lucky enough to get a bullet to her head? Would she get a knife sliced across her throat? Or would she be decapitated on camera like she had seen on some of those gruesome ISIS videos on YouTube?

All Radhika hoped for was that her daughters be spared the knowledge of how she died. That they would not, at some point in their lives, stumble upon a clip of their mother being butchered on camera. That they would not have to cope with those nightmares at least. Their lives would be difficult enough without that trauma.

The thought of Kavya and Karina growing up without her brought on a fresh bout of tears. She would never get to see them with their first boyfriends, she wouldn't get to plan their weddings, to pamper and spoil their children while they complained about how grandma broke all the rules.

And all those dreams she had had about growing old with Karan would remain just that—dreams. Radhika couldn't begin to imagine how her husband would cope without her. He couldn't even look after himself. How would he manage to look after their two motherless daughters as well?

But she tried to console herself, he would have Amma and Asha to help him. Both her mother-in-law and sister-in-law doted on those kids. They would do right by them when she wasn't around.

Radhika's reverie was broken by one of the terrorists coming up to her and thrusting a phone in her direction. 'Talk,' he barked gruffly at her, removing the scarf that he had stuffed into her mouth.

Radhika took a deep breath and croaked a low 'Hello' through her parched throat.

'Radhika,' she heard Karan say, his voice tight with tension and fear. 'Are you okay? They haven't hurt you, have they?'

'No, no, they haven't,' Radhika replied, tamping down on the tears that threatened to come once again. 'I am okay,' she said, trying to sound as reassuring as she could.

As Karan's voice dissolved into tears, Asha took over. 'Bhabhi, please don't worry,' she said. 'We will get you out of there. Please stay strong. This will be over soon.'

Before Radhika could respond to this, however, the terrorist holding the phone snatched it away and held it up to his ear. 'Okay,' he said, 'now you've spoken to her and seen that she is fine. You have another five hours to meet our demands. If you don't do that, then you will be responsible for all the killings that follow.'

Saying that, he disconnected the call, slipped the phone back into his pocket. Then, with his one free hand (the other still wielded that AK-47), he scrunched up Radhika's scarf and over her protests jammed it back into her mouth.

After a few muffled cries, Radhika subsided back into silence. But this time round, it was a silence imbued with hope. Her family was looking out for her. Maybe this wouldn't end so badly after all. There would be no bullet in her head or a knife across her throat. Maybe she wouldn't lose her head on camera.

Maybe, just maybe, she would make it back home alive.

* * *

Gaurav Agnihotri had conducted his own investigation into the terrorist attack at Kautilya Mall from his vantage point in his TV studio and, in less than an hour, had come to the conclusion that it had been masterminded by the ISI. There was no way some rag-tag militant outfit had planned and executed this operation. The Kashmiri boys fronting it had been trained by those shadowy figures that ran the Pakistani military operation in Rawalpindi.

So, how should India respond? There was no question in Gaurav's mind. The only way out was full-on war with Pakistan.

'Ladies and gentlemen,' he thundered, his bloodshot eyes conveying his anger to the millions watching. 'This is the time to show the world that India is no longer a soft state. That we do not negotiate with terrorists. We destroy them. This is the time for the Prime Minister to show some spine. But does Asha Devi have it in her to do that? Can she put the interests of the nation above the life of her own sister-in-law?'

One of the panelists felt impelled to intervene at this point. 'Gaurav, it is not as simple as that. And it is not just Radhika Singh's life that is at stake. There are as many as 250-odd people held hostage inside the mall, most of them women. I don't think the Prime Minister has any option but to try and resolve the situation peacefully.'

'Peacefully?' exploded Gaurav, 'Peacefully? Are you serious? How on earth can you even suggest that? The government needs to respond with the full force at its command. We need to get our commandos to storm the mall and get the hostages out. Sure, there will be some collateral damage but that is a price worth paying.'

The former R&AW officer who was on the panel had been shaking his head all through Gaurav's little outburst. 'What you call "collateral damage" is the murder of Indian citizens. And let me tell you, if the NSG or the army engages in a gunfight within that confined space, you will probably end up with 50 per cent of the hostages dead or injured. That is more than 100 people. No force in the world will accept those kinds of odds.

And no government in the world will take a risk like that, no matter how "soft" or "hard" it is.'

'See, that is the problem,' sneered Gaurav. 'We are too frightened to strike back. If it had been Israel, they would have stormed the mall, killed the hostages and rescued the terrorists by now.'

The R&AW man smiled. 'You are right about that. They would have killed the hostages all right. Though I am not sure they would have "rescued" the terrorists.'

Gaurav flushed bright red. In his keenness to make a point, he had misspoken. But surely it was clear that he meant 'kill the terrorists and rescue the hostages'. There was no need for this asshole to draw attention to his mistake in that snide manner. Making a mental note to tell the guest coordinator never to book him again, Gaurav turned to the rest of his panel to take the discussion forward.

Today was not his day though. Not one person on his handpicked panel would go along with Gaurav's thesis that the only way to respond to the hostage crisis was by escalating the situation to full-on war. Everyone else agreed that the government needed to tread softly, and deal with this situation as discreetly as possible. Long-term plans to annihilate Pakistan could wait.

Manisha Patel had been at lunch when the hostage crisis began. She was meeting an old college friend who was visiting from the States for a spot of sushi at Megu, the Japanese restaurant at the Leela. But the moment news of the attack flashed on her Twitter feed, she abandoned both her friend and an excellent nigiri platter to hotfoot it to Kautilya Mall.

She got there in ten minutes; so she had to wait another five for the OB van to arrive. But half an hour into the hostage crisis, Manisha was up and broadcasting from a few hundred metres away from the mall, having managed once again to be the first on the scene.

By the time the other camera crews got there, the secure perimeter around the mall had been widened, forcing Manisha to move further down the road. The security forces would not allow the media to get any closer. And all the news channels had been instructed to defer telecast by a few minutes so that the movements of the commandos outside the mall were not revealed to the terrorists in real time.

Manisha had no problem with this. In fact, she was glad that some lessons had been learnt from the 26/11 terrorist attacks in Mumbai in 2008 when news crews had been allowed to broadcast live from right outside the Taj Mahal and Oberoi Hotels, and Chabad House in Colaba. As a result, the terrorists who had been holed up at these locations and were in constant touch with their handlers in Pakistan had got instant information about every move the commando teams were making.

This hadn't just hampered the rescue efforts but had also resulted in heavier casualties for the security forces. The media had been made the villain of the piece then but, thought Manisha, at least part of the blame lay with the authorities who hadn't bothered to issue guidelines that the TV crews and press reporters could follow.

There had been much soul-searching after that terrorist attack, and ever since then the Information and Broadcasting Ministry had come down heavily on those channels that flouted guidelines and allowed live telecast of such attacks. After a couple of channels had their licenses suspended, the rest had hastily fallen in line. So now, there was a modicum of discipline and a measure of control on how such episodes were covered.

The studio cut back to Manisha even as she was trying to get some information from a source in the NSG on her phone. Hastily hanging up, she composed herself and began her report.

Not that she had anything new to say. She had already filed one dispatch ten minutes ago giving the information she had gleaned from her sources in IB and the NIA that the government was all set to make a deal with the terrorists. That Karan Pratap had been part of the CCS meeting that had been addressed by the IB, R&AW and NIA chiefs. That Asha had got in touch with the J&K government to see how the transfer of the terrorists in custody could be expedited to ensure the release of the hostages.

Nothing had changed in the ten minutes since her last telecast. Nor had there been any new developments. And yet the beast of 24/7 television wanted some fresh meat from her.

Scrambling to come up with something new, Manisha found herself falling back on the reporter's worst enemy and best friend: speculation.

'What is the latest development, Manisha? What can you tell us about what is happening behind you?' asked the anchor's voice in her ear.

Nodding furiously, Manisha began, 'Well, the latest is that the Pratap Singh family has closed ranks. They have decided to go ahead and concede all the demands of the terrorists so that they can secure the safety of Radhika Singh.' Manisha paused for a beat before continuing. 'And of the other hostages, of course.' The pause should be enough to signal her skepticism that Asha Devi was motivated by anything other than family ties.

'But I am told that there is some disquiet among the security forces about the government's decision to release the twelve men who have been named by the terrorists. These are not minor militants; they are terrorist masterminds. Wasim Khursheed, for instance, is in prison for an operation that resulted in the death of twelve army men. Wajahat Drabu is responsible for blowing up a police station that resulted in the deaths of twenty policemen . . .'

The anchor interrupted at this point, sounding impatient at having to sit through a laundry list of terrorist atrocities. 'Yes, yes, these are terrible people. But really, what choice does the government have? You can't allow these terrorists to butcher 200 women. Do you know how the negotiations are proceeding on that score?'

How the fuck would I know that, Manisha fumed to herself. I have been stuck here for the last half an hour, relying on a dodgy phone connection to get whatever information I can. How the fuck would I know that?

But of course, she said nothing of the sort. Adopting a suitably solemn vein, she began, 'I think the home minister and the R&AW chief are heading the negotiations. But from what I have been able to gather, there should be some resolution soon . . .'

'Sorry to interrupt, Manisha, but there is some breaking news,' the anchor hyperventilated into her ear. 'We have just been told that the Jihad-e-Azaadi has released a statement taking responsibility for this terror strike.'

Well, that made sense, thought Manisha. The Jihad-e-Azaadi was the latest terrorist outfit to crop up in Kashmir. In a matter of months since its inception, the JEA had earned its place in the alphabet soup that made up militancy in Kashmir. And over the last couple of years the JEA had been conducting militant strikes, sponsored first by the Lashkar-e-Tayyaiba and then by Jaish-e-Mohammad. Six months ago, however, the JEA had openly aligned itself with ISIS, projecting itself as the sub-continental arm of that terrorist network.

Until today, however, the JEA had dealt in small-potatoes kind of operations: a small IED blast on a highway; an ambush on an army truck as it moved through difficult terrain; an assassination of a senior police officer.

The Kautilya attack was in a different league, though. Precise and perfectly coordinated, it was clearly being conducted by operatives who had been trained for the job by men who had military experience. And Manisha had no doubt that this training would have been imparted by Pakistani military officers who ran the terrorist camps across the Line of Control in Kashmir.

The ISIS flag was a red herring. It was the ISI, the dreaded Inter-Services Intelligence of Pakistan, which was behind this operation. Of this, she had no doubt.

This was not good news for the hostages or for the commandos hoping to rescue them. The men holding Radhika Singh and 200-odd women hostage were not some young boys from the Valley, bent on making a statement. They were military-trained and battle-ready. And they would not go down without a fight.

Maybe it was best that Asha Devi's government arrived at some sort of compromise with them.

* * *

Back in the Prime Minister's office in South Block, that is exactly what Asha was trying to do. But it was proving more difficult than even she had feared. The Jammu and Kashmir chief minister was reluctant to release three of the twelve men that the terrorists wanted freed. These were hardened terrorists, he argued, who would wreak havoc in the future if they were released. He was willing to let the others go, albeit with reservations. But releasing these three men was out of the question.

As the hours ticked away and the deadline imposed by the terrorists got closer and closer, Asha was getting more and more frustrated. But it was Karan, who had finally got his emotions under control after speaking to his wife, who came up with the solution. Trying to reason with the CM, he told Asha, would not work. He would simply go public with his misgivings and that was the last thing they needed at this time. The best way to co-opt him was to 'incentivize' him in some way.

What on earth did that mean, asked a bewildered Asha.

Never mind about that, Karan assured her. She didn't need to know the details about such stuff. In fact, it was better if she didn't have a clue. After all, as Prime Minister she needed to have deniability in this matter. As did the rest of the Pratap Singh clan. So, she should just task Madhavan Kutty with this job, and let him get on with it. Kutty had a longstanding friendship with the Chief Secretary of the state, he would use that connection to get the CM on board.

While these negotiations were in play, Asha spent her time on the phone with Savitri Shukla, who was coordinating the release of the terrorists, the modalities of freeing the hostages and the transport arrangements for the hostage-takers.

Then, just as things were beginning to fall into place, the Pakistanis threw a spanner in the works. The Pakistani Prime Minister called up Asha on the hotline to protest that they did not want to be involved in this whole mess. Pakistan did not want the prisoners crossing over to their territory, and nor did they want to offer safe passage to the militants. His country had had enough of being seen as a terror hub and a safe harbor for terrorists. And if he agreed to let the prisoners and terrorists into his territory it would perpetuate the narrative that Pakistan was a perpetrator rather than a victim of terror, just like India.

When all arguments failed to convince him, Asha fell back on an emotional appeal. How would he feel, she asked the Pakistani leader, if it was a member of his family who was being held hostage? Would he not do everything within his power to ensure her release? Why couldn't he see that that was just what Asha was trying to do? She had to agree to all the demands of the terrorists—no matter how unreasonable—if she wanted her sister-in-law back home. And one of those demands was safe passage to Pakistan.

In the end, after much begging and pleading, the Pakistani Prime Minister agreed to take in the prisoners who would be released and the terrorists. But only if Asha made it clear to the world at large that they had agreed to do this at the pleading of India. The Indian government would have to put out an official statement to that effect so that there were no misunderstandings on that score. The Pakistanis were fed up with being seen as a sanctuary state for terror and would only cooperate if it was made clear that they were acting purely out of altruistic motives.

It was only thirty minutes before the deadline imposed by the terrorists—and after many conference calls between the Army commanders in Srinagar, the IB director, the R&AW chief and the NSG commander—that the logistics were finally in place.

The prisoners would be released from Srinagar jail and flown to the Line of Control in a helicopter along with an army escort. There, they would wait until all the hostages had been released in Delhi; only then would the freed men be allowed to cross the border at a designated spot and go over into Pakistan Occupied Kashmir (POK).

Meanwhile in the capital, the ten terrorists would make their getaway in a military helicopter that would land on the roof of the mall, and spirit them away across the border, landing in a destination that was still undisclosed.

This was the bit that Karan did not like. What was to prevent these killers from dragging Radhika on board with them and taking her across the border to Pakistan? After all, what better guarantee against being shot down by the Air Force than the presence of the Prime Minister's sister-in-law on board?

Asha, who shared his reservations, damped down her own fears and decided to go with the judgment of the foremost intelligence and security officers of the government. These men had been trained for these situations, they knew what they were doing, and their brains were not clouded by emotion like hers was.

But despite her efforts to calm herself down, Asha could not bring herself to watch the live footage of the rescue operations that was beamed across to PMO by the NSG. She could feel Karan and Arjun tensing up as the feed began live-streaming, but she kept her eyes firmly shut. It was almost as if she felt that looking at the events unfold—even on a video link—would jinx things.

It was only when she heard the whirring of the helicopter that told her that the terrorists had taken off from the roof of the mall that she opened her eyes and looked at the screen.

And there, on the roof, her arms and legs still trussed up, lay a tiny figure in a white dress. Even as Asha watched, her heart beating so hard that she was sure the others in the room could hear it, she saw a posse of camouflage-clad men run on to the terrace. They threw a security cordon around the woman sprawled on the floor, while one of them took out a knife and cut her restraints.

With a sigh of relief, Asha saw Radhika stagger to her feet. She could see her sister-in-law's shoulders heaving as she broke down in tears. One of the men threw a thermal blanket around her and bundled her off the terrace and into the mall.

Only then, as the figure of her sister-in-law disappeared off the screen, did Asha allow the tears she had been holding in for so long to come tumbling down her cheeks. Turning to Karan, she saw that he was weeping as well. She put a consolatory arm around him and he gathered her into a fierce embrace. 'Thank you, Asha, thank you for bringing my wife back home.'

Then, to Asha's surprise, she felt another pair of arms enveloping the two of them. Arjun held his brother and sister close as all three of them wept unabashedly. Asha could not remember a time when she had felt so close to her half-siblings. After a lifetime of being on the fringes of this family, of being treated as an interloper, she was finally being embraced as a sister.

Of course, this closeness had come at a price. And even as she luxuriated in the embrace of her brothers, Asha knew that she would pay for this moment for months and years to come. This incident would come to define her prime ministership. And mark her as a weak leader who had caved in when she should have stood firm.

But none of that mattered, she told herself. What mattered was that Radhika was safe and sound. That Kavya and Karina had their mother back. No price was too high to pay for that.

# 4

By the time the alarm went off at 5 a.m., Satyajit Kumar had already been awake for half an hour. But he'd stayed in bed, mulling over a problem that had kept him awake half the night. What was the right amount of time to wait before attacking the Prime Minister for putting family over country? Was one week a long enough interval? Was a fortnight more appropriate? Or should he wait even longer?

If there was one thing that Kumar was good at, it was waiting. After all, he had spent nearly half his life doing just that: waiting.

In his 30s, Kumar had been widely tipped to take over the leadership of the SPP but had narrowly lost out to his fellow Young Turk, Girdharilal Sharma. Kumar had made his peace with the defeat, going on to become a strong and faithful number two to Sharma in the party. But when Sharma succumbed to cancer, and Kumar thought it would finally be his turn to get the top prize, the party decided to give the top job to Gyanendra Mishra, an old Sharma loyalist, who would keep the seat warm until Girdharilal's son, Jayesh, was old enough to occupy it.

Once again, Satyajit Kumar had been obliged to put on a brave face and accept working under a new party president. But canny politician that he was, he had made the most of a bad deal and negotiated a return to his home state, Bihar, to lead the party in the next Assembly election. His return had galvanized the somnolent state unit into action, and his homespun wisdom and rustic wisecracks had electrified crowds on the campaign trail. Against all the odds, Kumar led the SPP to an improbable victory in Bihar and was duly installed as chief minister.

There, the undisputed king of his little fiefdom, Kumar had gone a little crazy. Setting up corrupt deals and hoovering up kickbacks, Kumar had soon amassed a personal fortune that would keep his next seven generations in clover. But all the money in the world could not help him win another term as Bihar chief minister.

And that was just fine with Kumar. He had had enough of being stuck in Bihar, far away from the centre of action in Delhi. So, he had lobbied for and got a Rajya Sabha berth and settled down to being an elder statesman for his party, and a dial-a-quote politician for all the TV news channels. Nobody gave a soundbite quite like Satyajit Kumar and soon his TV persona gave him a higher profile than he might otherwise have had.

Kumar would have been quite content with this existence, but circumstances had recently given him a fresh lease of life. After SPP leader, Jayesh Sharma, had been personally implicated in the release of Asha Devi's naked pictures, the party had been scrambling around for a new party president. There were a handful of young dynasts who had been vying for the post, but none of them could cobble together enough support to get the top job. Just when things were getting too messy with factional fights breaking out in each state unit, the party's parliamentary board had decided to come up with a 'compromise candidate', an elder statesman who would be acceptable to all.

After mulling over a few names, they had decided to offer the job to Satyajit Kumar. He had accepted with alacrity, pushing the party to make the announcement before it changed its mind. And so, a good three decades after he had first tried for the job, Satyajit Kumar was the president of the SPP.

So yes, you could say that Kumar was very good at waiting. Or, conversely, that waiting had proved to be good for him.

As the alarm sounded on his mobile phone, Kumar turned it off before it woke his wife, snoring gently by his side. He quietly slipped out of bed and into the bathroom to brush his teeth. And then, still in the crumpled white cotton pyjama kurta he had slept in, he stepped out of his bedroom through the side door, walking down the lawn towards the back garden.

He heard them before he could see them. Bleating piteously, they came scrambling up to the gate of their enclosure, pushing each other aside to be the first to greet him. He opened the gate and went on his knees to pat them on their gnarly heads.

Other people had dogs, cats, or even cows. Satyajit Kumar had goats.

It had started when he was a young politician looking to set himself apart from the others in the field. Watching a programme on Mahatma Gandhi one day, which had shots of him milking his goats, it had come to him in a flash. That is what he would do: keep goats in his backyard, and milk them every day. It would reinforce his image as a rural leader, a son of the soil, who had not let the evil ways of the city spoil him.

But what had started as a conceit had soon become a habit. And now he couldn't conceive of a life without his beloved goats.

Settling down on a plastic stool, Kumar placed a steel bucket under one of the goats' udders and began milking. There was something about that rhythmic pull and squeeze that relaxed him, that allowed him to think about the problems plaguing him without being distracted. Truth be told, Kumar came up with some of his best ideas while he was filling the bucket with goat milk.

Not to mention that it also made for great visuals when he gave interviews to the media. Over the years, Kumar had made a habit of calling journalists over at milking time and talking to them as he went about his business. His party trick was to fill a glass with freshly squeezed milk when he was done and hand it over to the hapless hack in question.

'Udderly, budderly delicious', Kumar would grin, in his Bihari-accented English, taking great delight in the discomfiture of those journos who were repulsed by the idea of drinking goat's milk fresh from, well, the goat.

'*Arre bhai, aap shehri log* goat cheese *toh khaate hain. Toh* goat *ka dudh bhi pi lijiye na!*' (You city people eat goat's cheese all the time. Drink some goat's milk as well) he would chortle, refusing to take no for an answer.

But today, as he squeezed and pulled, pulled and squeezed, Kumar was on his own, using this quiet time to come up with a strategy to take on the Prime Minister. He built it up in his head, he turned it over and over to examine it from all angles, made a few tiny adjustments, and then finally, he was satisfied with his plan of action.

Asha Devi would not know what had hit her when he was finished with her.

\* \* \*

It was now a week since the Kautilya terror attack. And Asha had kept to her resolution of not watching any of the Indian

TV channels. That, she was convinced, was the only way to preserve her sanity.

That didn't mean that she didn't know what the media was saying about her. Asha knew full well that she was being dismissed as a pushover, a softie, a tender-hearted but essentially ineffectual woman, a weak leader who could not be trusted to keep India safe. And she also knew that she needed to change this narrative—and change it quick.

And the man who would help her do that was joining work today. Nitesh Dholakia, her father's trusted private secretary, who had been on sabbatical all these months to look after his cancer-stricken wife, had agreed to come back to work with her now that his wife had passed away.

Nobody knew how to work the media like Dholakia did, how to generate the right headlines; and Asha would be relying on him to do just that. She had set aside an hour to discuss strategy with him this afternoon and was looking forward to a fresh perspective from a man who had seen it all.

But before she headed out to the PMO, she had to see her mother. Even though the two of them shared the house at 3, Race Course Road, given Asha's mad schedule, it was a massive effort to make time for her mother during the day or the evening. So, mother and daughter had fallen into the habit of having breakfast together every morning, because that was the only uninterrupted time they could spend with one another.

Sadhana Devi always had breakfast in bed. Or more accurately, in her bedroom, at the small round table set against the window that looked on to the back lawn. As Asha stepped into the room, she cast an apprehensive eye on the table. Amma, who feared that Asha was not eating properly, had begun to order very elaborate breakfasts in order to tempt her daughter to have more than a piece of toast and coffee in the morning.

Today, she had outdone herself. The table groaned under the weight of a platter of idlis and medu vadas, a big bowl of poha, a plateful of aloo parathas, some fluffy pooris and aloo *subzi* and a stack of pancakes for good measure.

Honestly, whom did Amma think she was feeding? A platoon of the Indian Army?

But looking at her mother's hopeful face as she pulled out a chair to join her at the table, Asha could not bring herself to berate her. If this was what brought her joy, putting together a frankly ridiculous breakfast buffet for her daughter, well then that's what Amma would do every day for as long as she liked. And Asha would play along, sampling just a little bit from every dish on display.

Today, however, Asha was in luck. Help was on its way and knocking on the door. Even before Sadhana Devi could say 'Enter', the door opened to reveal Kavya and Karina, still in their pyjamas, being held back by a wan-looking Radhika, who asked quietly, 'Is it okay if the girls join you for breakfast, Amma?'

Sadhana Devi nodded, a delighted look on her face. There was nothing she loved more than feeding people. And nobody demolished a breakfast buffet with quite as much alacrity as her granddaughters.

Asha got up to add a few more chairs to the table and said gently to Radhika who was making to leave, 'Why don't you join us Bhabhi? I haven't had a chance to talk to you in a while.'

It wasn't as if Asha hadn't tried. She had spent many hours in 7 RCR, where Karan and his family lived, trying to coax Radhika out of the near catatonic state into which her sister-in-law had retreated after being taken hostage in the terror attack. But no matter how much effort she made, Radhika remained sealed off in her own private hell, replying to remarks at random, her eyes glazing over as she retreated into a space where no one else was allowed entry.

It had been a difficult week for everyone. Even though the adults had tried their best to shield them from the truth, the kids had soon found out what their mother had gone through. Neither of them had said very much, but ever since the attack they never strayed very far from Radhika, gravitating back towards her every few minutes as if to reassure themselves that she was still okay. They refused to sleep in their own room, snuggling between their mom and dad every night. But even that didn't stop the nightmares that had them waking up screaming in the early hours of the morning.

Between looking after his wife and consoling his children, Karan had had his work cut out for him. For the first time in her life, Asha was actually worried about her brother. Like their father, Karan tended to internalize his grief, his fears, his tensions. The only person he had ever opened up to or leaned on was his wife. But now that she was the one who needed support, he had bundled up his feelings and locked them away in a hard-to-reach compartment of his heart.

Asha had tried her best but she could not get through to him. He was enormously grateful for her decision to save his wife no matter what the cost. In fact, he never stopped relaying his gratitude, much to her embarrassment. But that's as far as it went. It didn't matter how hard she pushed; her brother refused to open up and tell her what he was going through.

Clearly, Karan wanted to preserve the image of the strong man that he had always believed himself to be. And Asha was terrified that this show of strength would prove to be his ultimate weakness.

But those thoughts would keep for another day. This morning was about Radhika and the kids. So, Asha put her worries about Karan aside and applied herself to coaxing a smile out of her sister-in-law and her nieces.

It was hard going but she finally got Kavya and Karina giggling as she related the story of one of her more outrageous escapades at boarding school. Radhika smiled along but Asha could tell that she wasn't really paying attention.

Finally, as Asha drained her coffee and got up to leave, she leaned down and asked Radhika to walk her to the porch. Radhika looked startled at the request but got up and followed her out of the room after a moment's hesitation.

Once they were finally alone, Asha said bluntly, 'Bhabhi, I am worried about you. You don't seem yourself at all.'

Radhika's lips cracked open in a smile that didn't quite reach her eyes. 'No, I'm fine, Asha. Really, I am. I'm just a little tired because I didn't sleep too well.'

'Have you slept at all since the attack?' asked Asha.

Radhika paused and then said quietly, 'Not really. It's been difficult. Especially since the girls can't sleep through the night either.'

'Bhabhi,' said Asha, returning to a theme she had been harping on for days now, 'you really should see a therapist. You've been through a very traumatic experience. You need to talk about it to a professional . . .'

'I'm not doing that,' Radhika cut in sharply. Then, softening her voice, she added, 'Don't worry about me, Asha. I am fine. Well, I will be fine. But you've got to let me deal with things in my own way—and in my own time.'

Asha shot a glance at her watch and bit off her reply. She really needed to get going. This discussion would have to wait.

\* \* \*

Nitesh Dholakia was back in his usual office at PMO. As he settled down in his swivel chair, resting his head on the white towel that had been placed on its back in the true tradition of Indian bureaucracy, his eyes fell on the picture frame that occupied pride of place on his desk. It was the same picture that had accompanied him through every office he had ever worked in. It featured his wife, Neelam, in her red wedding sari, her hair festooned with flowers, sitting on the stone staircase that had led to their first government house.

He still remembered the moment he had taken this picture. Their simple court marriage had taken all of ten minutes to solemnize. And then, they had partied all night long with family and friends. It was well into the early hours of the next morning when they had finally driven to their first-floor government flat on Satya Marg. There, Neelam had collapsed on the stairs to take off her heels before she climbed up the staircase. And as she sat slumped, looking happier than he had ever seen her look, Nitesh had snapped a picture of her laughing face.

Memories like these were all he had left of her now. Neelam had been diagnosed with cervical cancer a year or so ago, and when the disease progressed more rapidly than anyone had expected, Dholakia had taken a leave of absence from his job as private secretary to Birendra Pratap Singh to look after her. While he was away from PMO, Birendra Pratap had been assassinated, Karan Pratap had taken over as Prime Minister, and then the election that followed had propelled Asha Devi to the top job.

Meanwhile, Neelam had struggled bravely in the face of an implacable disease. And by the time she finally succumbed to it, Nitesh was almost grateful to see her go, so unspeakable had been her suffering. It was only after her funeral, when he came back to an empty house—they had never been able to have children—did the reality of her departure hit him. And then, the grief was like a punch to his stomach, leaving him breathless and in actual physical pain. The very idea of living in a world without Neelam was unthinkable.

And yet, here he was, less than a month later, back at work, at his old job, this time working for the daughter rather than the father. Partly it was that he could not rebuff Asha, when she came asking for help. He felt he owed her father that much. And partly it was that he knew he needed to get out of the house and do something before his sorrow drove him mad.

Staring at the picture of his dead wife on his desk, Nitesh asked himself if this was a good idea. Did he really need to spend every day looking at a face that produced a piercing agony in his heart? On the other hand, how could he possibly exile Neelam from the place she had always occupied in his office? Or indeed, in his life?

Dholakia's ruminations were interrupted by the arrival of his PA. The SPG had called ahead to say that Asha Devi would be arriving in PMO in the next five minutes.

By the time the prime ministerial cavalcade drove up to the sandstone building in South Block, Dholakia was already positioned at the main entrance to greet his new boss and walk her up to her office. In his hand was a file with her schedule for the day, neatly typed out, and annotated in his own hand.

First on the list was a call with Poriborton Party chief, Sukanya Sarkar. She had been phoning incessantly over the last week, getting more and more querulous with every call. Did Asha not realize that the government was getting a bad rap because of its handling of the terror attack? Was she aware that people were dismissing her as a soft touch because she had capitulated to the terrorists' demands in a matter of hours?

Didn't she see that the government had to take some stern steps to correct that impression?

Today, Asha was ready to brief Sukanya on the 'stern steps' she had decided upon. In her meeting last night with the service chiefs, she had been briefed on a proposed surgical strike on terrorist training camps run by the Pakistan Army across the border in Pakistan Occupied Kashmir (POK). Satellite imagery showed that training activity in two of the camps nearest the Line of Control had picked up over the last few weeks. And the army feared that this meant that another terrorist strike was in the works. The only way to deal with this was to take preemptive action by striking the two camps simultaneously and obliterating them completely.

The operation would be undertaken jointly by the army and the air force, Asha explained to Sukanya. Military choppers would air-drop commandos at the Line Of Control and would provide air cover as they went in around three kilometres beyond the Line of Control to destroy two training camps and three terror launch pads. It was estimated that the operation would be over in an hour and would, with luck, wipe out the Pakistani presence in that sector.

'What about our own casualties?' asked Sukanya. How many men could they lose by mounting such an enterprise?

The service chiefs had assured Asha that the last such surgical strike had resulted in the death of some thirty-odd terrorists and a handful of Pakistani army officers while the Indian side had suffered no casualties at all. But Asha could not begin to take such an optimistic view of events. They could lose a significant number of men, she warned Sukanya, never mind the army chief's assurances. And they had to be prepared for that.

Sukanya, who had the politician's trick of ignoring bad news when it did not suit her to listen to it, paid no attention to this. She was more interested in how the announcement would be made by the government. The press release, she insisted, must specify that the decision to conduct the surgical strikes had been taken jointly by Asha Devi and Sukanya Sarkar.

Asha agreed and hung up with a wry smile. With every passing day she was becoming more and more familiar with the cynical opportunist behind Sukanya's 'woman of the people' image. And every such incident left her more disillusioned than ever with the state of Indian politics.

Meanwhile, the Cabinet Secretary was waiting in the antechamber with a clutch of files that she needed to weigh in on. Asha got up from behind her large desk and moved over to the sofa on the far side of her office. Settling down in her usual place, and hastily gulping down the cappuccino that had gone quite cold while she spoke to Sukanya, Asha gestured to Dholakia to ask the CabSec (as he was called in government speak) to enter.

Kalpesh Mishra arrived looking as if the woes of the world were upon his shoulders. And as he took her through the many matters that required urgent attention, Asha realized that he was right to look so burdened.

There was a fresh snag in the extradition proceedings of Sagar Prajapati. Sagar, who had been arrested by the French for his role in the L'Oiseau arms deal, had challenged his extradition to India in the International Court of Justice at the Hague, pleading that the conditions in Indian jails were far too terrible to warrant sending him back to serve his sentence back home. The government was hopeful of winning the case when it was finally heard next week, but this meant a further delay in getting Prajapati back to India. Only once he was back in India, undergoing what Mishra euphemistically referred to as 'sustained interrogation in custody', would they be able to build an airtight case against Madan Mohan in the arms deal case.

And then, there was the investigation into her father, Birendra Pratap's assassination, in which the prime suspect was again Madan Mohan. But despite the efforts of police forces across the globe to trace the former defence minister, there was still no sign of him. The government had, however, tracked down three more Swiss bank accounts linked to Madan Mohan and had frozen them with the cooperation of the Swiss government. Mishra hoped that cutting Madan Mohan off from his source of funds would help in smoking him out. But Asha, who had a better idea of just how vast Mohan's black money holdings were, was not very optimistic.

There was one piece of good news in today's briefing, though. Satellite imagery had picked up the ten freed terrorists as they were escorted into a hideout in Pakistan Occupied Kashmir. With technical help from the National Security Agency (NSA)—the premier American agency when it came to collecting intelligence by monitoring phone calls, and tracking activity on the Internet—the NIA had been keeping a tab on all the calls made in and out of that building and its vicinity.

Two days ago, they had finally had a breakthrough. One of the phones in use in that building had been used to make a phone call to a mobile phone in Delhi. The Delhi number had been traced to a Kashmiri student who was studying in Jamia Millia Islamia and living in Jamia Nagar, near the University. The phone of the student was now being tapped and the investigators hoped that it would help them break open the case.

Why didn't the IB just pick up the student in question and bring him in for interrogation, asked Asha. Wasn't that a better way of dealing with this than allowing him to go about his life normally? What if he suddenly upped and ran? What if he slipped across the border as well? Why risk losing such a valuable lead?

Kalpesh Mishra was his usual bureaucratic self, humming and hawing as he went into his 'On the one hand' and 'On the other hand' routine. Asha bit down on her impatience and decided to consult with Madhavan Kutty and Arunoday Sengupta instead before coming to a final decision. Relieved at having shifted the responsibility to someone else, Mishra nodded gravely and acquiesced.

Dholakia saw him to the door and then came back and sat down on the armchair opposite Asha to discuss their media strategy over the next few months.

'Okay,' said Asha wearily, 'Let's start by discussing where I am going wrong.'

But Dholakia was not interested in conducting a post-mortem of her media performance. What was done was done, he said, dismissing the past with a wave of his hand. Now, it was time to focus on the future and how she could build a relationship with the media, how she could better control it, and how she could use it to further her own interests.

In order to do all this, the first thing she needed to do was build relationships with the editors and anchors who decided how stories were covered in newspapers and on television.

'Stop right there,' said Asha, holding up her hand as if to ward off a blow. 'I have zero interest in building relationships with editors and anchors. I don't trust these people as far as I can throw them.'

'Trust?' asked Dholakia. 'Who said anything about trust? Trust doesn't enter into the equation. You are never to trust them. You just have to use them for your own purposes.'

And with that, Nitesh Dholakia laid out his masterplan for Asha to rewrite the narrative about herself in the media.

Operation Outreach, as he termed it, would begin with her having regular Friday evening meetings with a small group of editors and anchors, not more than six at a time. These meetings would be held on a strictly off-the-record basis. The media invitees could ask her any questions they liked and she would answer them as honestly as possible. But they would have to give an undertaking that nothing they discussed would ever appear in the public domain.

But, asked a frustrated Asha, how exactly would that help her? She needed more positive coverage of her prime ministership. She needed to recover her image in the mirror of public opinion. How would staying off the record help?

The idea, explained a patient Dholakia, was to launch a charm offensive. The aim was to make these media people feel privileged because they had been given special access to the Prime Minister. If they felt that she was seeking them out and being honest with them, they would be seduced into giving her the benefit of the doubt. And if they felt more warmly towards her privately, they would treat her with more kindness on the front pages of newspapers and on prime-time TV.

But that, explained Dholakia, was only step one. There were at least three other things she needed to do on a priority basis to improve her media coverage. Today, however, he was only prepared to discuss one of them: the interview she had to grant a news anchor to discuss the agenda for her government.

Who would she feel most comfortable talking to?

There was just one name on that list. Manisha Patel, the woman who had conducted the interview with Asha in the aftermath of the scandal involving her naked photos with such empathy and deftness of touch. If she was going to speak to anyone, it would be Manisha.

Dholakia, who had watched the interview and admired Asha's performance, nodded in agreement and promised to set it up soon. And then it was time for her to go into another meeting.

As Asha Devi was rapidly discovering, a Prime Minister's work was never done.

# 5

It was exactly two weeks, six hours and fourteen minutes after the terror strike at the Kautilya Mall that the news broke. Prime-time news, which had the attention span of a gnat, had moved on from that story days ago. Which is why it came as a complete surprise to both Manisha Patel and Gaurav Agnihotri when their 9 p.m. debate shows were 'crashed' into because Doordarshan was running an 'address to the nation' by Prime Minister Asha Devi.

In a matter of seconds, the Doordarshan feed was being carried across all channels, with the legend 'Breaking News' emblazoned over it. TV screens across the country cut to a single image: that of the new PM, wearing an expression as sober as her black sari, seated behind an imposing desk on which the Indian tricolour occupied pride of place. Asha's kohl-rimmed eyes gazed straight into the camera as she read her speech off the teleprompter.

Just moments ago, she announced, the Indian army and air force had jointly conducted a surgical strike against Pakistani terrorist training camps across the Line of Control in Kashmir. The raid had resulted in the utter destruction of two camps and three staging posts, from where terrorists were launched into the Valley. While the number of Pakistani casualties had yet to be determined, the Indian side had suffered no losses.

The operation had lasted around an hour and ten minutes and had been a complete and unqualified success. The camps in which the Kautilya Mall terrorists had been trained had been obliterated off the face of the earth.

'Let this be a warning to all those who seek to do us harm,' said Asha, her eyes flashing with something between anger and resolve. 'If you raise your hand against us, it will be struck down. If you seek to terrorize our people, we will hunt you down and destroy you. If you dare to target our country, you will face complete and utter annihilation.

'Let this be a warning to all those who seek to do us harm,' she reiterated, her voice hardening even further. 'India is no longer a "soft" state. We will not hesitate to take the hardest of measures to defend our people and our borders. And no power on earth can stop us from doing so. Jai Hind.'

The moment Asha finished her speech, the feed cut back to the studios. As the camera cut back to Manisha Patel, her face reflected the sheer incredulity she had felt on hearing the Prime Minister speak. Who would have thought that a Prime Minister who had rolled over so easily and released hardened terrorists to secure the release of her sister-in-law would change course in a fortnight's time and take a major step like this?

Recovering quickly, Manisha set her features in a neutral expression as she welcomed her viewers back to the studio. Fortunately, the discussion she had planned for today had been on border security after the number of skirmishes on the Line of Control had increased in recent weeks. So, her panel of guests comprised an ex-army general, a retired R&AW officer, and two journalists who had been on the security and intelligence beat for decades. So, it would not be difficult to discuss this unexpected development with some lucidity.

But in the absence of any more information than the Prime Minister had chosen to give, nobody in the studio knew what to make of this surgical strike.

How would Pakistan react to this infringement of its de facto border? Would the situation at the LOC, already very tense in the aftermath of the Kautilya terror strike, deteriorate even further? What if the Pakistanis retaliated in kind and did the same sort of surgical strike in the border areas of Rajasthan, J&K or even Punjab? Could two nuclear power neighbours really afford to raise the stakes like this without something catastrophic happening as a consequence? Would world players like America and China allow that to happen without intervening in some manner? And would that make things better or worse?

Manisha fired off these questions to her 'expert commentators' even as she listened to the voice in the ear as her director attempted to feed her additional information he was gleaning from the wire services.

Her panel was evenly divided between those who believed that this was a masterstroke of Asha's and those who were convinced that this was her greatest blunder. The first group saw the surgical strike as a symbol of India's readiness to act against her enemies, no matter what it took. 'It's about time we took some direct action instead of just compiling and sending dossiers that the Pakistanis can sneer at,' said the jubilant former army man.

The second group was consumed with misgivings. Asha Devi, they believed, had upped the ante without considering the consequences. What if the Pakistanis stepped up their attacks? After all, it was their avowed strategy to destroy India with a thousand cuts. What would the Prime Minister do then? She could hardly order a full-scale invasion of Pakistan without half the world jumping down her throat. So, had she thought things through when she sent Indian forces beyond the Line of Control?

Each side was convinced of the efficacy of its argument. And neither side was prepared to concede an inch. So, inevitably, the debate grew more and more acrimonious, until Manisha was compelled to go for a break so that she could restore some order to her panel.

There was no such ambiguity among Gaurav Agnihotri's guests, though, carefully hand-picked as they were to ensure that only the most rabid 'nationalists' got on. All of them were ecstatic at the thought of India finally having the guts to teach those evil Pakistanis a lesson they would remember for the rest of their lives.

Strangely enough, it was Gaurav—jingoistic flag-waver though he was on all such occasions—who was not prepared to cover Asha Devi with praise for the surgical strike. As far as he was concerned, it was too little too late. The Prime Minister should have stood firm against the terrorists to begin with.

'And what is so "daring" about this "surgical strike", anyway?' Gaurav asked, making air quote signs as he spoke. 'Any army officer serving in Kashmir will tell you that they do this sort of thing all the time. Every day, our brave troops go across the Line of Control to seek and destroy the staging posts of the Pak terrorists. So, why all the fuss about this "surgical strike"?'

The retired army general on the panel, who had winced every time Gaurav made his air quote sign, intervened at this stage. 'Gaurav, you are correct when you say that this sort of thing has been done routinely for years. But this time, as I understand it, the forces have penetrated deeper into Pakistan-controlled territory and inflicted far greater damage.'

But Gaurav Agnihotri was having none of that. While a surgical strike was well and good, he thundered, when was the Prime Minister going to clamp down on the terrorists operating with impunity in the Valley? The Indian army lost officers and jawans every single day while the terrorists suffered minimal casualties. When would that imbalance be rectified? Was Asha Devi even capable of doing that, asked Gaurav, the scowl on his face giving away his true feelings.

Clearly, Gaurav still hadn't forgiven Asha for giving that interview to Manisha Patel. And as his panelists got a measure of the anchor's feelings about the PM, they too began backing away from effusive praise of Asha. By the time the show ended, the consensus had changed completely, as Gaurav summed up in his sign-off.

'Ladies and gentlemen,' he thundered, 'the Lutyens media may be taken in by all this hype about a so-called surgical strike. But let me tell you, all this is just a hoax to pull the wool over your eyes. If there was such a strike—and the government has not provided any proof of that—then it came much too late. What is the point of destroying terrorist camps after the terrorists have destroyed you?'

Gaurav paused to catch his breath. There were two high spots of colour on his cherubic cheeks, while his salt-and-pepper curls looked more disheveled than ever. 'If the Prime Minister really wants to take on Pakistan,' he went on, 'there are many things she can do. To start with, why doesn't she get Dawood Ibrahim back from his hideout in Karachi? Everyone knows the palatial villa he lives in. Why don't Indian security forces take out his house one night? Or even rendition him to India to face justice?

'But we all know that this government lacks the guts to do anything like that. So, they try and fob us off with symbolic gestures like this so-called surgical strike. Well, Madam Prime Minister, let me tell you that we Indians are not fools. And you should not treat us like fools either.

'That's all the time we have tonight. Thanks for watching. And thank you for choosing News Over Views.'

* * *

Satyajit Kumar was livid. His meticulously crafted plan of painting Asha Devi as a pushover, a soft touch who had no idea how to be Prime Minister, was unraveling even before he could deploy it. Even to his jaundiced eyes, Asha had come across as a strong leader, as she calmly announced the news of the surgical strike to the nation. So, her performance must have gone down like a dream in the rest of the country.

Kumar's wife, Pratima, cast a worried look at her husband. She didn't like the way his face turned red the moment he was annoyed about anything. His blood pressure was too high, but nothing would induce Kumar to go on a diet or even take the occasional stroll around the impeccable lawn of his Lutyens bungalow. But she knew better than to remonstrate with her husband. Satyajit Kumar didn't like being told that he was getting older and unhealthier.

Pratima made a mental note to tell her daughter to raise the subject with her father when she came by for lunch the following day with the grandkids. Sunanda was their only child and the proverbial apple of her father's eye. She was also the only person who would get away with remonstrating with him about his unhealthy lifestyle.

The bearer came in with a tray of the green tea they always drank after dinner. But even before he could set it down, Satyajit Kumar was on his feet. 'I'll have my tea when I get back,' he told his wife brusquely. 'I have a meeting with some party leaders now.'

The outhouse of his bungalow had been converted into an office complex. And that's where Kumar headed, his head overrun with thoughts of what might have been. By the time he had covered the short distance, however, he had shrugged them off and was all set to come up with a fresh game plan.

The conference table in his office seated eight, but there were only four people around it now. There was his number two in the party, Ram Lakshman Yadav, an old Jayesh Sharma loyalist whom he had promoted for the sake of continuity. Flanking him were the two senior-most general secretaries of the party. And seated opposite them was his own private secretary, Jayant Jha, who had been his dogged lieutenant for a couple of decades now.

Satyajit Kumar lowered himself into the chair set at the head of the table with an audible sigh (clearly the weather was beginning to turn, judging by the twinge in his joints) and brought the meeting to order. Asha Devi's surgical strike had dealt a death blow to their original plan.

Their entire strategy now had to change. So, did they have any ideas? How could they target the Prime Minister?

The silence in the room was finally broken by Kumar himself. '*Itna sannata kyun hai bhai?*' (Why is there so much silence?), he asked, referencing a popular line of dialogue from the film *Sholay*. This prompted a few weak smiles, and even a couple of laughs as the men in the room acknowledged Kumar's attempt at humour.

And then finally, Jha said hesitantly, 'Satyajit ji, I think we have no option but to go easy on our criticism of Asha Devi—at least, in the short term. This surgical strike will make her very popular with the people. And if we attack her at this time, we could risk being labeled anti-national.'

Yadav, who had been nodding approvingly all along, chimed in, 'I agree completely with Jayant ji. If the Prime Minister is moving against Pakistan, then we need to support her. We can't be seen to be playing politics with the security of the nation.'

Satyajit Kumar, wily old politician that he was, knew that both men were right. And with the adaptability of a man who thought nothing of changing his mind when the facts changed, he was willing to concede ground on this one. He would not take on Asha Devi on the surgical strike, even though he believed it was a cosmetic venture that would play well on TV screens but not change anything on the ground level. But, for the moment, he was content to keep his doubts to himself, and go along with the flag-waving jingoism that would soon overtake the country.

What he was not willing to do was to let Asha Devi ride the wave of patriotism and establish herself as a strong and stable leader. She was heading what was, at best, an unstable coalition. There had to be a way to destabilize her government; or, with a bit of luck, bring it down.

One way to do that would be to open a channel of communication with Sukanya Sarkar. It was only a matter of time before the notoriously fickle leader of the Poriborton Party became disillusioned with Asha Devi (just as it was inevitable that Asha would get tired of Sukanya forever throwing her weight around). And when that happened, the Samajik Prajatantra Party and its leader, Satyajit Kumar, would be ready and waiting to provide an alternative.

The SPP general secretaries were dubious about this. They had been part of the negotiations when the party's former leader, Jayesh Sharma, had tried to put together a coalition government with Sukanya Sarkar. They had witnessed the bond that quickly formed between Sukanya and Jayesh, whom

she had known and loved as a child. And they had also seen
the visceral disgust with which Sukanya had repulsed Jayesh
after he was shown to be involved with the leaking of Asha's
naked pictures.

Why would Sukanya Sarkar entertain overtures from the
party that had let her down so spectacularly?

'For one very simple reason,' responded Kumar snappishly.
'That was Jayesh Sharma's SPP. This is the SPP of Satyajit
Kumar. We don't pull stunts like that. And Sukanya ji has
known me long enough to know that.'

Kumar and Sarkar had, in fact, a chequered history going
back to the time that the young Sukanya had joined the SPP after
earning her stripes as a student union leader. She had quickly
become a favourite of the then party President, Girdharilal
Sharma (father of Jayesh Sharma), and rapidly climbed up the
ranks. But when Girdharilal soured on her, becoming fed up of
her mercurial temper and constant rages, it was Kumar whom
Sukanya had turned to for succor.

To his credit, Kumar had tried his hardest to patch things
up between Girdharilal and Sukanya. But it was too late for
that. Girdharilal had already turned his attention to his new
protégé, a young Dalit leader called Didi Damyanti, and was
giving her the same prominence in the party that Sukanya had
once enjoyed.

It was only a matter of time before a livid Sukanya left the
SPP, despite Kumar's best efforts to try and keep her within
the fold, to form her own regional outfit, the Poriborton Party.
But in the decades that followed, the two of them had kept
in touch, meeting on occasion to catch up on their lives and
following each other's careers at a distance.

Kumar was sure he would count on that friendship to
improve relations between the Poriborton Party and the SPP.

And if he could succeed in doing that, then Sukanya would see him as the natural alternative if things went wrong with her coalition with Asha Devi's LJP.

He just needed the right opportunity and the right occasion to reach out to her. And luckily for him, there was one coming up in a matter of weeks. Sukanya's nephew, whom the childless leader treated as her son and heir, was going to get married next week in Kolkata and Kumar was invited. That's where he would re-establish contact with his old friend, take a measure of her feelings for Asha Devi and her commitment to the coalition with the LJP.

Of course, it was early days yet. Even Sukanya Sarkar would not be mad enough to bail on a government she had helped install in a matter of months. But at least Kumar could remind her that if she ever needed another option, he was right there to provide it.

* * *

Her heart was still thumping with the adrenaline rush of her live address to the nation when Nitesh Dholakia came into her office to inform her that all the members of the Cabinet Committee on Security were waiting for her in the adjoining conference room. Taking a moment to gather her thoughts and finish the rapidly cooling cup of cappuccino placed before her—sometimes she felt she could measure her life in cups of half-drunk coffee—Asha put her briefing papers together and went next door to start proceedings.

Asha wasn't looking forward to this meeting. She had gone against established principle and not consulted the CCS before ordering the surgical strike. Nor had she done its members the courtesy of informing them about the strike in advance. They had arrived at South Block thinking that they were convening for another regular CCS meeting. It was only when they got here that the news of the surgical strike had been broken to them.

Asha had good reason for keeping this information to herself. The only way of keeping secrets in a place as leaky as Lutyens' Delhi, she knew full well, was to keep the circle of trust really tight. And she had yet to build that kind of trust with the members of the Cabinet Committee on Security, especially the ones who didn't belong to her party.

The atmosphere was tense as Asha walked into the conference room. Even before she could take her seat at the head of the table, a visibly bristling Prabha Saraf began voicing her discontent. She was the defence minister of the country, she informed Asha in angry tones. How could the Prime Minister go over her head and order a surgical strike without keeping her in the loop?

Asha had a certain sympathy with her point of view. And she may even have been placatory towards her if Prabha hadn't pushed her luck even further.

'There is a certain protocol when it comes to government,' she said to Asha, loftily. 'There is something called the dharma of coalition government. You have to take your allies along when you make major moves like this. You can't make these decisions unilaterally.'

It was the patronizing tone that got Asha riled. She'd never taken kindly to being talked down to by anyone and she wasn't going to start now that she was Prime Minister of the country.

'What makes you think that I have taken this decision unilaterally?' she snapped. 'I have kept Sukanya ji in the loop all through. She is the leader of your party. And she has been on board with this decision from the very beginning. If she chooses not to take you into her confidence, then you should take this up with her instead of lecturing me about the "dharma" of coalition government.'

Saraf's hackles had begun to subside at the mention of Sukanya Sarkar's name. But they rose yet again at this rebuke in front of the whole CCS. But before she could say anything to inflame matters further, her PP colleague and external affairs minister, Aroop Mitra, laid a calming hand on her forearm.

Turning to Asha, Mitra said, in conciliatory tones, 'We understand, Asha ji. If you have discussed the matter with Sukanya di, then that is all that matters. She is the final decision maker in our party. If it was fine with her, then of course, it is fine for us.'

But Saraf wasn't going to let it go so easily. Shrugging off Mitra's restraining hand, she began again, though in softer tones. 'Yes, I agree with that. But as defence minister, I feel that I should have been taken into confidence. There is a chain of command in such matters. And we should adhere to that.'

Now it was home minister Savitri Shukla's turn to play peacemaker. 'Prabha ji,' she began, a soft smile on her matronly features, 'this is not the time to stick to niceties such as protocol and all. The country is facing a crisis. Madam Prime Minister had to act decisively. And she did just that.'

But even this mild intervention got Prabha Saraf agitated. 'Who is saying that the Prime Minister should not have acted decisively? Not me, certainly. All I am saying is that it was possible to do this after taking the CCS into confidence. Any Prime Minister who had any understanding of how government works would have done that.'

Finance Minister Alok Ray had been silent so far, with just his tightening lips bearing witness to his exasperation. Conscious of his status as a newcomer to politics and the government, he usually sat silently at these meeting, restricting himself to listening and learning. But this last remark from Saraf tipped him over the edge.

'Someone like Atal Behari Vajpayee, you mean?' he asked Saraf, a slight smile playing on his lips.

'Exactly,' she replied triumphantly, walking right into his well-sprung trap. 'Atal ji would never have done anything like this.'

'Except that he did exactly that,' pointed out Alok. 'When the Vajpayee regime conducted nuclear tests, the only two people in government who knew about that decision were Atal ji and his National Security Adviser, Brajesh Mishra. George Fernandes, the defence minister at the time, was not told about the tests in advance. Even the number two in the government, Lal Krishna Advani, was informed about them at the very last moment.'

Prabha Saraf tried to interject at this point, fairly spluttering with rage. Ray raised a magisterial hand and continued to speak as if he had not been rudely interrupted. 'Sometimes it is necessary to maintain secrecy in matters of national security, Prabha ji. And that's exactly what the Prime Minister has done. As members of the CCS, we should congratulate her on a job well done on a day like this. Don't you agree?'

Finding herself in a minority of one, Prabha Saraf beat a strategic retreat. 'Yes, yes, of course, we should congratulate Asha ji. The surgical strike has been a resounding success and has shut the mouth of all our critics.'

Before she could add any caveats to this praise, Asha jumped in. 'Thank you so much, Prabha ji,' she said, flashing a dimpled smile. 'I am so very grateful for your support.'

But the support that Asha was truly grateful for was that which had come from a truly unexpected quarter, Alok Ray.

He was not someone who owed her any personal loyalty. He did not have any special equation with her, having met her one-on-one less than half a dozen times. And yet he had stuck up for her, and done so in a manner that wasn't just forceful but also calming enough to defuse the situation.

Asha turned her head in Ray's direction to express her thanks to him. Feeling her gaze upon him, he looked away from Prabha Saraf and towards her. The expression in his eyes as they met hers was hard to describe. There was a flash of humour, a tinge of triumph, and a smidgen of sympathy. It was almost as if he was telling her, without speaking a single word, that he understood how tough her job was—and that she could count on him to always have her back.

But the feeling that rose unbidden in Asha's heart as she smiled back at him was not just gratitude. She realized, with a start, that it was mixed with another feeling that she hadn't experienced for a long time: desire.

The moment that thought rose in Asha's head, she vehemently pushed it away. Desire was not her friend. Desire was what had almost ended her political career. Desire was what had almost destroyed her life. She was done with desire after what her last boyfriend, Sunny Mahtani, had done to her.

She had met Sunny after she moved to London (exiled there by her father, who was exasperated by the scandals revolving around her in Delhi) and had almost immediately fallen in love with him. The two of them—the daughter of the Indian Prime Minister and the playboy heir to his father's multi-billion-dollar empire—had quickly gained the approval of both families and a wedding was soon looming on the horizon.

But as Sunny's corrosive jealousy and controlling nature became more and more apparent, Asha began to question her choice of life partner. And then had come that cataclysmic afternoon, when they were both attending a society wedding at an English country house, when Sunny had forced her into having sex—slapping her across the face when she resisted.

She had broken up with him after that, refusing to listen to any of his pleas asking for forgiveness and another chance. But Sunny had had his revenge when she came back to India and joined politics after her father's assassination. He had sent all the naked pictures she had posed for during their relationship to her political rivals in the SPP. The pictures had been duly leaked in the run up to the election, torpedoing the LJP's chances of getting a simple majority in Parliament, and nearly destroying Asha's own career.

No, desire had done her enough damage. It had no place in her life now. She was all about duty now.

Asha looked away from Alok Ray, nodded a curt dismissal to her ministers, and walked next door to her office for her next meeting.

# 6

Sagar Prajapati, nephew and bagman of former defence minister, Madan Mohan Prajapati, and prime accused in the L'Oiseau arms deal case along with his uncle, was not in the habit of flying commercial. During his long and chequered career as an arms dealer and middleman working on behalf of Madan Mohan, Sagar had travelled the world in fancy private jets, complete with butter-soft leather seats and an on-board shower to ensure he arrived fresh at every destination.

So, it was entirely fitting that he was being flown back to India in a private plane.

There were a few differences, of course. This time around, he was not the only passenger on board. There were several burly men in ill-fitting suits flying with him. This time around, there was no champagne on tap or caviar canapés for the asking. Instead, he was served simple dal chawal with one oily subzi in an aluminum foil dish, along with some mineral water.

And then, there was the small matter of the handcuffs. They had been slapped on to his wrists from the moment he exited the car at Paris airport to make the short journey across the runway to the plane. And they had remained in place throughout the flight, except for short intervals when he needed to use the loo or eat or drink something.

It was all quite unnecessary of course. Needless drama, he called it in his head.

After all, he was hardly likely to escape even if he had the full use of his hands. And if he did manage to escape, where on earth would he go? His accounts had been frozen, his uncle had abandoned him and gone to ground, and he didn't have a friend in the world he could count on. So, how far could he realistically get?

The PA system on the plane sputtered to life and the pilot announced that they had begun their descent into Delhi. Sagar felt his spirits sink even further as he envisaged the media scrum that would greet him at the airport. His picture in handcuffs would be broadcast across the nation—no, across the globe. His humiliation would be laid bare to the watching world as he was frog-marched off to prison. The prime-time debates that would follow would damn him as a common criminal with every sound bite.

His thought chain was interrupted by a loud thud, as the aircraft made a rather hard landing. And then, it was time to disembark and head out to face the baying Indian media, which would have his head for lunch and feast on the rest of his carcass for dinner.

It was perhaps fitting that he heard them even before he saw them. The shouts got louder still as they hoved into view. 'Sagar, Sagar, Sagar,' the chants began, as they tried to get him to look into their cameras so that they would get a full-face shot. But Sagar had been briefed by his lawyer to keep his head down and his eyes on the ground as he exited the airport. 'Whatever you do, don't make eye contact with the media,' the Frenchman had intoned in his heavily accented English.

And Sagar Prajapati would have been well advised to do just that. But as he was pulled along by the two burly IB men escorting him, he tripped and fell forward. As they jerked him upright, his eyes involuntarily followed the motion of his body and looked up.

His blood ran cold as he saw the man in the front row of the amassed media. He had the regulation DSLR in his hand, but he wasn't focused on taking pictures. He was more concerned with making eye contact with Sagar. And as their eyes met, the man made a quick slashing motion across his neck.

It was in that instant that Sagar Prajapati finally put a name to the face. This was Bhupendra Rathore, his uncle's enforcer. The man tasked to break fingers and smash heads by Madan Mohan Prajapati. The man who made sure that anyone who went against the former defence minister lived to regret it. Or, more accurately, did not live to regret it.

Wherever in the world his uncle was, he was still sending orders to his thugs. And he was also sending a message to his own nephew. If Sagar stepped out of line, his head would be on the block. And no power in the world could save him.

* * *

Like the rest of the world, Asha had missed this little interplay between Sagar Prajapati and Bhupendra Rathore. Watching from her office in South Block, along with Nitesh Dholakia, she could barely recognize the man she had grown up around in the shamefaced pale shadow who was being hustled, handcuffed, through the airport.

Sagar had been brought up by Madan Mohan Prajapati as his own son after his father (Madan Mohan's brother) had passed away. The teenage Sagar had been sent off to Europe to study and then set up in business by his uncle. And once Madan Mohan became defence minister, Sagar had been promoted to his moneyman, taking kickbacks and bribes on his uncle's behalf, and looking after the money through various secret accounts set up in such tax havens as the Bahamas and Dubai.

If only Baba was alive to see this, rose the wistful thought in Asha's heart. As Prime Minister, her father, Birendra Pratap Singh, had trusted Madan Mohan Prajapati implicitly as his right-hand man. So, his shock must have been immense when he discovered that his defence minister had been making money on all the deals conducted by his ministry.

Asha still didn't know the details of the confrontation that had ensued between the two men. All she knew was that it had led directly to her father's death. Madan Mohan had used his contacts in the arms business to stage the assassination of Birendra Pratap with a poison pen at an election rally. By the time the investigation had identified Madan Mohan as the prime conspirator, he had already left the country. And he remained untraced to this day.

But, at least now, his nephew was in custody even if it was on an entirely different charge. Sagar had been directly implicated in the L'Oiseau arms deal, with some of the kickbacks and bribes being traced to an account in Dubai that was linked to his firm, PP Consulting. After a long and tangled legal battle, he had finally been extradited to India.

'That must be a relief for you, Madam Prime Minister,' said Nitesh, as the visuals from Sagar's arrival at Delhi airport flashed on the television. 'Now that he is back home, we can finally file charges in the L'Oiseau case.'

Asha nodded absently, her attention still focused on the TV images. Would Sagar ever flip on his uncle? Would he really turn approver in the L'Oiseau case? Everyone in government seemed to be sure that this would happen. But Asha herself was a lot less optimistic. She knew the control that Madan Mohan had always exerted on his family. And she was sure he was still pulling their strings from wherever in the world he was.

The scene on the TV screen before her abruptly changed as the AITNN feed cut back to the studio. Manisha Patel was in the anchor's chair, but not looking her usual impeccable self. Her blusher was applied in a rather slapdash manner and her highlighted hair was pulled back into a high ponytail. But then, as Asha knew well, Manisha was not a morning person. So, she must have rolled in late to office, which didn't leave her much time in the make-up chair.

'Welcome to our special broadcast,' said Manisha, her mouth a grim line. 'We have breaking news for you at this hour. Sagar Prajapati has been extradited from France and brought back to India. His plane landed at Delhi airport a few minutes ago and he is currently being transported to CBI headquarters. He will be presented before a magistrate later today and is expected to be moved to Tihar Jail while his case is tried.'

As Manisha went on to give a potted history of the L'Oiseau case to her viewers, Asha changed channels until she arrived at NTN.

No surprises here. Gaurav Agnihotri was in the anchor's chair and in full-on fulmination mode. 'Ladies and gentlemen,' he was thundering as Asha tuned in, 'one of the thieves who stole money from the people of India has finally been brought back to face justice. But the government still doesn't have a clue as to where the prime suspect in both the L'Oiseau deal and the Birendra Pratap assassination is.

'Where is Madan Mohan Prajapati? Why can't our investigative agencies trace him and bring him back to justice?'

Asha muted the TV and turned her back on it. For once she found herself in agreement with Gaurav Agnihotri. It was a novel feeling, and not one that she particularly cared for.

Her train of thought was interrupted by a knock on the door. Suresh Shastri, director IB, was here for his weekly meeting with the Prime Minister. Dholakia got up and shook Shastri's hand and then made to leave.

But Asha waved a hand and gestured that he should stay. Despite himself, Dholakia felt rather gratified at this mark of favour. Traditionally, the IB chief delivered his weekly brief to the Prime Minister with no other officials in the room. That he was being asked to stay was an indication that Asha Devi's trust in him was absolute. This fact would not be lost on Suresh Shastri, who would now treat him with greater respect. And once word of this went across the bureaucracy, so would every other bureaucrat.

Shastri's briefing on the L'Oiseau case had been overtaken by events so he junked that. Instead, he brought the PM up to speed on the progress in the Kautilya terror attack case.

He reminded the Prime Minister that satellite surveillance of the Kautilya Mall hostage-takers after they were released had traced them to a building in Pakistan Occupied Kashmir (POK). Over the last few weeks, all calls coming in and out of the building had been monitored by the NIA (National Investigation Agency) with some technical assistance from American intelligence. Around three weeks ago, one such call had been made to a Kashmiri student, Suhail Geelani, living in Jamia Nagar.

The IB had kept Geelani under watch ever since and tapped his phone and bugged his apartment. It now had sufficient evidence to prove that Geelani was the head of a sleeper cell that had been activated by the Jaish-e-Mohammad to provide ground support to the terrorists of the Jihad-e-Azaadi (JEA) who carried out the Kautilya attack.

'So, what are we doing about this?' cut in Asha, growing impatient with the slow pace of Shastri's storytelling.

Shastri looked a bit put out at being interrupted mid-flow. But gathering himself again, he went on to brief the PM about how the agencies wanted to wait until all the parties were together in Geelani's apartment before they planned a raid.

But how will you know when that happens next, asked Asha.

The tapped phone calls, explained Shastri, had revealed that a meeting was scheduled for the next morning. A SWAT team had been assembled by the NIA and would be in place before all the players gathered in a decrepit building in Jamia Nagar. And if all went well, every single member of the sleeper cell would be in custody by noon tomorrow.

Finally, some good news, thought Asha, as she bid Shastri goodbye. She checked the time on her phone. She had a ten-minute break before her next meeting. Just enough time for a quick cappuccino, to give her a caffeine fix to get through the rest of the day.

* * *

Satyajit Kumar had missed his goats enormously. And going by the enthusiasm with which they greeted him, it was clear that they had missed him too. But the two days he had spent in Kolkata had been well worth it, he thought, as he settled down on his plastic stool to begin his usual early morning ritual of milking them. At the very least, they had given him some clarity on how he should proceed next.

Kumar had been invited to attend the wedding reception of Sukanya Sarkar's nephew and had flown in a day ahead hoping to network with some of his Poriborton Party contacts before he met with Sukanya herself. Over endless cups of tea, he had chatted and gossiped with some old hands of the PP trying to suss out the lay of the land. Was Sukanya still as keen on Asha Devi as she had been a few months ago? Or had disillusionment set in—as it usually did with Sarkar?

The conversations he had had over that day had been illuminating. By the evening, it was clear to him that the Sukanya-Asha relationship was still in its honeymoon stage. There was no breaking them apart just yet. The euphoria that the surgical strike had created and the burst of positive publicity that followed had driven up Sarkar's personal popularity ratings sky-high. And canny operator that she was, Sarkar was well aware that Asha Devi's standing with the public would have improved tremendously as well.

So, there was no way that Sukanya was going to do anything to jeopardize her equation with Asha Devi any time soon. Going against a weak and inexperienced Prime Minister was one thing. But only a very foolish politician would take on a Prime Minister who was perceived as both strong and popular.

So, when Satyajit finally got to speak with the PP leader on the sidelines of the wedding reception, he had played along as Sukanya sang the praises of Asha Devi. Oh yes, she had surprised him too with her decisive action. Yes, she was growing into her role every day. And so on and on and on until he had completely exhausted the bag of clichés he always lugged around for just such an occasion.

On the flight back to Delhi, Kumar had mentally written off Sukanya Sarkar as a potential ally, in the short term at least. And it was with a certain inevitability that his thoughts turned to her sworn rival and implacable enemy—Didi Damyanti.

Now party leader and unquestioned supremo of the Dalit Morcha, Damyanti had—like Sukanya Sarkar—started her career with the Samajik Prajatantra Party (SPP). The two women had started off as friends, working together as young leaders to shore up their party's prospects. But as the competition between them heated up, relations soon deteriorated. It all came to a head when then SPP leader, Girdharilal Sharma, chose Damyanti over Sukanya to lead the youth wing of the party.

Sukanya had already been sulking because she felt that Sharma favoured Damyanti over her (which he did, preferring Damyanti's discretion and charm over Sukanya's constant temper tantrums). So, being passed over for the leadership of the youth wing was the proverbial last straw for her. Sarkar had promptly resigned from the SPP, leaving to found her own provincial outfit, the Poriborton Party.

Damyanti's victory had been rather short-lived, though. When Sharma had refused to project her as the chief ministerial candidate for Uttar Pradesh, she too had left to start her own party, the Dalit Morcha. It hadn't been easy going but by sheer dogged persistence, Damyanti had finally won the chief ministership of UP, then lost it to a wave of anti-incumbency. But undaunted by this reversal, she had worked hard to revive her party at the grassroots, ditched the arrogance that had led to her being dubbed Devi Damyanti, and won the state back five years later.

More importantly, Damyanti had managed to increase the footprint of her party in the last General Election, increasing her tally of MPs to an impressive fifty-five (just five less than the PP, which had won sixty seats).

At the moment, the government was being run by a coalition of the LJP (with 190 seats) and the PP, which gave them a head count of 250, with the shortfall being made up by smaller parties and independents. But Satyajit Kumar believed that with 184 MPs, the SPP wasn't completely out of the race for power. And if he couldn't peel away Sukanya Sarkar and her sixty MPs from Asha Devi, then he would try his luck with Didi Damyanti and her band of fifty-five.

Coalitions like the one run by Asha and Sukanya were inherently unstable. All it would take was the defection of a few smaller parties and a couple of independents for a no-confidence motion against them to succeed in Parliament. And once the government was defeated on the floor of the house, it would be simplicity itself to get a major chunk of the PP or the LJP to cross the floor without falling foul of the anti-defection law (which held that if two thirds of the elected representatives left, it triggered a split in the party, and the MPs would not have to resign their seats).

But those plans could wait. Satyajit Kumar's immediate target was the Bihar Assembly elections, which were to be held in three months' time. With his instinctive understanding of the demographic divides in the state and his razor-sharp grasp of the electoral arithmetic that would come into play, Kumar knew that an SPP and Dalit Morcha alliance would be an unbeatable one—the LJP simply wouldn't stand a chance against their combined might.

The two parties together would have around 45 per cent of the vote. And if they could decide on a pre-poll alliance and do the right kind of seat adjustment, the best-case scenario was that they would sweep the polls and end up with a two-thirds majority in the Assembly. And even in a worst-case scenario, the alliance would prevail with a simple majority, winning at least 125 of the 243 seats.

But the trick was in getting Damyanti to agree to a pre-poll alliance that would give the SPP a fair chunk of the seats in play. The Dalit Morcha leader was notorious for driving the hardest of bargains, haggling her allies down to the bare minimum by leveraging her infamous unpredictability and unstable temperament as tools in the negotiations, and emerging as the major player in any coalition. Satyajit Kumar needed to have all his wits about him when he finally sat down to negotiate with her.

He mulled over the best way to deal with her, as he began milking the last goat of the day. Pull, squeeze. Pull, squeeze, Pull, squeeze.

As always, the rhythm of milking his goats put Kumar in the meditative state in which he did his best thinking. And by the time he was done, he knew his best bet would be to approach Damyanti as a junior partner. The SPP could afford to play the supporting act in the state so long as it led to the first electoral defeat of the Prime Minister after the General Election. He would sublimate his ego to ensure a loss for the LJP, which would strike a devastating blow at Asha Devi's image.

And in any case, Kumar consoled himself, he was used to playing the long game. And in the long game, he would prevail over Didi Damyanti. Of that, he had no doubt.

* * *

It was finally time for Asha's last meeting of the day. She signed the latest lot of files that had been placed before her, and then left her desk to take up position on the sofa on the far side of the room.

Of late Asha had taken to meeting her ministerial colleagues in this more informal setting rather than seated at her desk. Having them face her across a forbidding expanse of table felt like a power move: a way to distance herself from them; a device to exert her power and assert her status. And while this worked well with bureaucrats, whom Asha wanted to intimidate with the power of the Prime Minister's office, she didn't think this was suitable for her fellow ministers.

There was a short, sharp knock on the door, and Nitesh Dholakia popped his head in to announce that Alok Ray had arrived. A minute later, the finance minister was walking through the door, stylish as always in his collarless shirt and hand-made suit.

Asha felt a telltale flush rise from her bosom, as she remembered that brief moment of lust she had experienced when she last saw Alok Ray. She pushed that memory away as she half-rose from her seat to greet him. But Alok waved her down. 'No, no, don't get up. I have it on excellent authority that women should never rise to greet men.'

There was something about that phrasing that reminded Asha of her father. Birendra Pratap had had that same joshing style, the same dry sense of humour. And, as they did with every stray memory of Baba, the tears came rushing up into her eyes. Asha blinked furiously trying to push them right down, and hoped to God that Ray hadn't noticed. But she realized that her efforts had been in vain as he leaned across the coffee table to hand her an immaculately starched white handkerchief.

And just like that, through her tears, Asha found herself giggling. Was this man for real? Who on earth carried around a handkerchief in this day and age? It was such an old-fashioned gesture that Asha felt as if she had been transported back in time. And that she was living in one of those Regency romances she had devoured so hungrily in her teen years.

She raised her head to see Ray gazing at her, a look of incipient panic on his face. No doubt he thought that the Prime Minister had gone hysterical with grief. And that he didn't know quite how to handle the situation.

'Are you okay, Prime Minister?' he asked anxiously. 'We can always do this later . . .'

'No, no, I am fine,' said Asha, finally getting a grip on herself. 'It's just that the handkerchief set me off. I mean, I don't know any man who still carries a handkerchief in his pocket.'

A boyish grin split Alok Ray's bearded face, and his brown eyes twinkled with humour. 'Well, you have to blame my mother for that. She drilled it into my head as a child that I must have a clean handkerchief on me at all times. And I've never fallen out of the habit ever since.'

'What a good son you are,' Asha exclaimed. 'Your mum must be so proud!'

'She was,' responded Ray quietly. 'She passed away when I was fifeen. Cancer.'

'Oh God! I am so sorry Alok. I didn't know,' said Asha.

'No reason why you should, Prime Minister,' he said, waving away her contrition.

'It's Asha,' she replied. 'Please call me Asha. Whenever you say Prime Minister, I keep looking around, waiting for my father to respond. For me, he will always be "Prime Minister" no matter who occupies the actual chair.'

The tears rose again, and this time Asha let them come. Somehow it seemed okay to share her grief with Alok now that she knew that he too had experienced the untimely demise of a parent. Losing your mother at fifteen? What must that do to a young boy? It didn't bear thinking about.

As she asked him about his mother, Alok found himself getting a bit teary as well as he recounted some of his fondest memories of her. That led Asha to remember some of her own favourite anecdotes featuring her father.

And then, much to her surprise, Asha—who never revealed her private self to outsiders—found herself confiding her inner-most feelings in Alok. How she still hadn't come to terms with the fact that she hadn't been with her father when he died. How her last conversation with Baba had deteriorated into a slanging match, and how much she regretted that. How she hadn't had time to really mourn her father because she had plunged head-first into electioneering soon after his death. And how her grief still overtook her at times, striking out of the blue to fell her as she went about her day.

Alok understood exactly how she felt. He had been at boarding school when his mother had finally succumbed to the cancer that had turned her into a shadow of her former self. He had arrived at home the following day to find her laid out on the floor, covered in marigold garlands, as family members lined up to pay homage. The grieving son did not get as much as one private moment with his dead mother before he was asked to light the pyre that would consume her body in flames.

As Alok related this story, his voice quivering with emotion, his body language changed from that of a confident master of the universe to that of a vulnerable young boy. Watching this transformation, Asha was overcome by a sudden urge to reach across and hug him. But the moment the thought popped up in her mind, she pushed it away. She really didn't know him well enough to make a physical overture like that. And what if he misinterpreted it as some sort of come-on?

Asha knew that her reputation had taken a hell of a knocking after her naked photos had been released to the media. 'Slutty Savitri' was just one of the cruel, taunting nicknames that had been attached to her. Ever since then, she had become hyper-aware of her behavior around men. She chose to greet them with a namaste rather than shake hands. She made sure that she did not laugh too much or too loudly at their jokes. And even though the entire world had seen her naked body by now, she restricted herself to wearing saris with conservative blouses in public.

No, hugging Alok Ray was out of the question. But as they finally began discussing matters relating to the finance ministry, Asha felt happier and lighter than she had in years.

It took her a moment to analyze that feeling after Alok Ray left. It wasn't just catharsis at finally having been able to talk about her feelings about Baba. It wasn't just relief at sharing her experiences with someone who understood. The lightness she felt was because she had finally found a friend.

Or, if she was being honest, someone who had the potential to be more than a friend. But after the disastrous end of her last relationship, the last thing Asha wanted was to put herself out there again. Not to mention, that it would be totally inappropriate to become involved with one of her own ministers.

In any case, she told herself with a shake of her head, there was no evidence that Ray had the slightest sexual interest in her. Or if he did, he was enough of a professional not to show it and make her feel uncomfortable. The best thing Asha could do was follow his lead. She needed a romantic involvement right now about as much as she needed a hole in her head.

And of the two outcomes, the latter seemed far more likely.

# 7

Jamia Nagar was still asleep when the surveillance team got into position at both ends of the narrow street on which Suhail Geelani lived in a second-floor flat in a run-down building. The bulletproof vests they wore were well-hidden by their quilted jackets, as were the pistols they had tucked into their trousers, where they sat snug against their backs.

There were two teams of four, sitting in two shabby cars, taking care to be as inconspicuous as possible. Not that they were too worried about attracting unwanted attention. This was a neighbourhood in which nobody asked too many questions or even took notice of anything out of the ordinary. It was best that way. See no evil, hear no evil, and you would not someday be asked to testify in court against a neighbour, a friend, or even a family member.

So, in Jamia Nagar, people tended to mind their own business. And secure in that knowledge, the advance party sat quietly, keeping their eyes peeled on the building midway down the street, the one with the bright red door, which led to Geelani's flat, up two steep flights of steps.

They were in radio contact with the SWAT team huddled in a truck a couple of streets away, and with the snipers who had been stationed on four of the buildings adjoining the one housing Geelani. All of them sat patiently, waiting for the arrival of the five other members of the sleeper cell. Only after every one of them was in the flat would they storm the building and take everyone into custody.

To some younger members of the surveillance team, all this *bandobast* seemed like overkill. All they had to do was to take six men into custody. They had the advantage of surprise and superior firepower. Not to mention that their targets were pretty low-down on the terrorist food chain and would not exactly be trained for hand-to-hand combat.

A small police party could have taken the whole cell, they thought, and got back home in time for breakfast. There really was no need for all this *dramebaazi* (theatrics).

But those among them with longer memories knew just why this massive operation had been mounted to capture this sleeper cell. They still remembered the bad publicity that had ensued after the Batla House encounter, which had gone down just a few blocks away from where they were stationed.

This was soon after the Delhi serial bomb blasts in 2008. A group called the Indian Mujahideen (IM) had claimed responsibility, and soon after, the police had received a tip-off that a small group of IM members were hiding in a building called Batla House in Jamia Nagar. A Delhi police special cell team had been dispatched to the location to pick up the members.

More than a decade later, there was still no clarity on how things had gone down in the raid. But by the time it ended, two members of the IM had been shot dead, two had escaped, and only one had been taken into custody. But in the firefight that had broken out, the police officer leading the team had been shot dead. Apparently, he had taken off his bullet-proof vest before the raid because it was a hot day—and perhaps because he didn't anticipate that there would be any resistance from the IM members—and that proved to be a fatal mistake.

So given this background, it wasn't surprising that the authorities were taking no chances this time around. The Jamia Nagar operation would go smoothly, no matter how many men—both in plainclothes and uniform—they had to throw at it. And every single one of them would be in body armour—and armed to the teeth.

It was exactly 6.03 a.m. when the first man arrived for the meeting. He drove up on a decrepit scooter, parked it quickly, and scuttled into the building without even removing his helmet. But that mattered little. The surveillance party could identify him by the number of his scooter alone.

After that, the arrivals picked up. By 6.10 a.m., all five men were present and accounted for. That made six in total, if you included Geelani, whose flat they were meeting in.

It was at 6.15 a.m. when the go-order came. The surveillance team members stayed in their cars but pulled out their guns, ready to provide supporting fire as the SWAT team ran quickly down the road and into the building, with just two members staying at the main entrance to stand guard.

The idea had been to strike with overwhelming force so that the men inside surrendered immediately and without even thinking of offering resistance. And in any case, the reasoning went, these were low-level operators who had just been brought in to provide logistical support. They were not trained fighters with heavy artillery at their command. So, how much of a fight could they really put up?

As it turned out, the answer to that question was: a lot.

Far from being a low-level support staffer of the JEA, Geelani was actually one of its best bomb-makers. His specialty was crafting suicide belts for young men to strap on as they went forth to seek *shahadat* (martyrdom) for their cause. And as it happened, today he had a few of those tucked away, awaiting delivery to Kashmir.

By the time the SWAT team had climbed up one floor, the noise of their heavy boots had given them away. By the time they reached the door of the apartment, four of the men inside had strapped on their suicide belts. The moment the door was rammed open, one of the men threw himself on the SWAT team member who entered and blew himself up, taking down the next six men in line.

Barely had the men further down the stairs realized what was happening, when two other terrorists had rushed down the stairs, detonating themselves as they ran. The fourth man blew himself up in the flat, taking Geelani and his other colleague with him—along with all the evidence that could have been collected.

It was all over in less than three minutes. And by the end of it, the entire sleeper cell was gone—along with all the intelligence it could have provided. And as many as twenty-odd SWAT team members lay dead, with several others so badly injured that it was only a matter of time before they added to the death toll.

As security operations went, this one had turned out to be an unmitigated disaster. And things were only going to get worse from this point on.

* * *

The harsh ringing of the telephone woke Asha up at 6.25 a.m. Disoriented for a moment, she fumbled for her iPhone to put off her morning alarm. But no, the sound was coming from the red handset by her bedside. And it was never good news when this line rang.

She snatched up the receiver and breathed 'hello' into it. It was Suresh Shastri, director of the IB, on the other end. The Jamia Nagar raid had gone badly wrong. The men of the JEA sleeper cell had strapped on suicide belts and blown themselves and everyone around them to eternity. They were all dead—as were around twenty members of the SWAT team that had gone in. And given the severity of the injuries of those wounded, the death toll was bound to go up.

By the time Shastri had finished his little recital, Asha was wide awake, every new detail adding to her anger and despair. The raid had been planned painstakingly over weeks. How could things have gone so wrong?

'How come nobody knew that he had all this stuff in his flat?' she asked sharply. 'Hadn't we bugged his apartment? Did nobody check to see what kind of arms and ammunition he had in there?'

Shastri was shamefaced. No, nobody had seen anything untoward in the flat when the bugs were put in. It was possible that these suicide belts had been moved in at a later stage, being stored there before being sent to Kashmir. Or else they had been hidden so cleverly that they escaped the attention of those searching the flat.

Asha had her doubts about both these theories. The most likely explanation, she thought (but did not say) was that the men who had gone in to plant the bugs hadn't bothered to make a thorough examination of the flat. They had just planted the bugs, done a cursory round of the premises and left.

And that single mistake had resulted in the deaths of twenty men—or more.

Asha swallowed the silent scream of frustration rising in her throat and attempted a more reasonable tone. 'Has the news hit the media as yet?' she asked. 'Are there any reporters on the scene now?'

No, said Shastri. The media had still to make their way to Jamia Nagar. And in any case, the security forces had thrown a wide cordon around that area, so nobody would get close to the burning building.

That was all very well, said Asha. But what about the locals? These days every single person had a camera phone and there could be hundreds of pictures of the incident by now. How would they control those?

Shastri assured her that phone signals were being jammed in the area and internet services had been suspended. So, nobody would be sending out pictures or videos any time soon.

Once things had calmed down a bit, they would send officers door-to-door, confiscating phones and deleting any images and videos stored on them.

Asha had her doubts about whether any such operation would work. In this age of social media, all it needed was one image or video to make it on to a digital platform for things to go viral. She knew this from bitter experience from the time her naked pictures had been leaked on the net. Despite the best efforts of her brother Karan, who had the entire machinery of the Indian government behind him as Prime Minister, it had been impossible to pull every image from the Internet. And she was sure that in some dark corner of the web, her naked pictures still lived on, available for every pervert to pleasure himself to.

Not happy with the direction her thoughts were taking, Asha pushed herself out of bed as she hung up on Shastri. This was not the time to fixate on her own problems. The security operation she had depended on to push the investigation into the terror attack forward had instead set them back enormously. Instead of garnering vital intelligence and generating positive headlines, it had turned into a veritable shit show.

Now it was time for some damage control. Asha picked up her phone and dialed Nitesh Dholakia. If anyone knew how to salvage a situation like this, it was her personal secretary.

* * *

Ashraf Mehdi had woken early that morning so that he could revise his notes for an exam he was giving later in the day. He brewed a strong cup of tea and walked across to his desk, which was set against the window that looked down on the street below. He stood behind the sheer curtains for a moment to take his first sip, when something caught his attention.

There was something off about the scene that was stretched out before him, two stories below on ground level. It took him a moment to work out what that was. And then his eyes homed in on the two cars that were strategically parked on either end of the road. He had never seen them here before.

And why were the men within them making no attempt to get out or drive on. What could they possibly be doing parked on the street corners like this?

Ashraf's mind immediately went to a dark place. Was this some sort of terrorist attack? Would these cars be blown up by the men inside them when there were more people around to kill and maim?

Then he shook his head, admonishing himself for these flights of fancy. He had clearly watched too many episodes of Homeland last night. His mind was fried. He was seeing terror strikes when all he had before him were two groups of probably blameless men sitting around in cars. He really needed to get a grip on himself.

But despite that little internal scolding, his misgivings persisted. To settle his nerves, he picked up his phone from the desk and parting the curtains slightly took two pictures of the street, capturing first the right side and then the left.

The early morning light had made the otherwise grimy scene look rather picturesque, in a gritty, Fellini-esque sort of way, thought Mehdi, a student of filmography. On an impulse, he opened the Facebook app on his phone to upload the shots he had taken. He was still thinking about the caption when the street below him suddenly exploded into activity.

An entire column of men in camouflage and body armour was sprinting down the street, two abreast, their guns raised, ready to fire. Almost without thinking, Ashraf switched to Facebook live mode and began videoing the events unfolding on the street and streaming them on his account.

The SWAT team stopped at the building opposite his and began running up the stairs. Ashraf zoomed in as far as his phone would allow him to and caught sight of the men through the windows at the end of each stairwell, their faces hidden behind heavy helmets. It was, thought Ashraf, almost like a scene out of Criminal Minds or NCIS.

It was clear now that the second-floor flat, across the street from his apartment, was the target of the security forces. The men leading the charge were positioned directly in front of the door, ready to ram it open. Instead, it flew open on its own to the sound of a loud explosion.

Ashraf let out an involuntary cry of horror, but it was lost in the screams that were emanating from across the street. Even though his hands were shaking, he kept his camera lens focused on the events unfolding before him. He could see at least six men from the security forces lying on the floor, dead or wounded. It was difficult to tell from this far.

Ashraf was just zooming out to get the entire building in his frame when there was another explosion. This one came from halfway down the stairwell. He scrambled again to go into close up so that he could get the flaming staircase into focus. But before he could do that, there were another explosion further down the stairwell. And then, came the final blast, which blew away the entire frontage. The interior of the building now lay exposed to his camera, with dozens of men lying dead and wounded, while fires raged all around them.

Ashraf focused on the fire and smoke coming out of the building for a minute, ignoring the shouts and shrieks at ground level. Then he slowly panned down to the street, where the men who had been sitting in the cars were now running ragged, their weapons at the ready, while those SWAT team members who were unhurt were trying to help their wounded colleagues.

By now, as was inevitable, a group of curious onlookers had gathered, and were being pushed back by plainclothesmen and uniformed cops. It was into this scene of complete and utter confusion that a line of ambulances drove in. The wounded men were quickly loaded into them, and in a matter of minutes, the ambulances had driven off, sirens blazing.

It was only then that Ashraf realized that his legs were trembling with the shock of what he had seen. He had managed to distance himself from the events unfolding before his eyes by filtering them through his camera phone. That layer of separation had allowed him to film those tragic scenes without actually processing what he had been witness to. It was only now that the enormity of what he had seen struck him.

It hadn't been the terror strike of his imagination. But the reality was just as bad.

Sitting down heavily at his desk, he looked down at his phone to check his video feed, almost as if to reassure himself that the events he had seen had really happened, that they weren't just a figment of his overwrought mind. But the images were all too real, and Ashraf began replaying his video to get a better sense of how things had gone down. In the first instance, he had been too focused on recording everything on his phone to make too much sense of what he was shooting.

But he could hardly focus on his video for the emojis darting across the screen as people reacted to his story. Ashraf's eyes floated down to the counter to check how many people had watched his live story. He was shocked to see that he had already clocked 357 views, with hundreds of messages scrolling across his page. And it wasn't even 6.30 a.m. yet. This would probably end up being the most-watched thing he had ever shot.

That was certainly true. But what Ashraf Mehdi didn't quite realize in that moment was that this Facebook live feed would make him famous forever after.

* * *

Manisha Patel had never been a fan of Facebook. She had opened an account in the early days, hoping to connect with old friends and family scattered across the world. But soon tiring of the endless boasting—not to mention the never-ending supply of baby pictures—she had quietly deleted her account and exited the service.

So, she wouldn't have been aware of Ashraf Mehdi's live feed for hours if it hadn't been for a young intern who had just joined her crew. Sanchita Mishra had just passed out of Jamia, where she had been one year senior to Ashraf Mehdi, who was now in his final year. But even though she didn't know him very well, she had accepted his friend request when it had popped up on her phone a few months back.

The reason why Sanchita ended up watching Ashraf's live feed in real time, though, was her mother. Arti Mishra did not believe in taking cabs to the airport. If she had a flight, she expected either her husband or her daughter to drive her. That was the absolute least they could do, given how much she did for them.

Today, her father was out of town, so it had fallen on Sanchita to chauffeur her mom to her early morning flight. And to her credit, Sanchita was dressed and ready to go at 6 a.m. But when her mother re-opened her bag yet again to conduct another last-minute check to make sure she had everything she needed in her hand luggage, Sanchita got bored and began scrolling through her phone. Twitter was still asleep so she opened Facebook.

'Ashraf Mehdi is live,' said the announcement on her screen. Intrigued by why anyone would be live streaming video at six in the morning, Sanchita clicked on the link. And then froze as she saw the Jamia Nagar disaster—as it would soon be dubbed by the media—unfold in front of her horrified eyes.

Initially it all seemed like a video game, with those uniformed men in full body armour running down the road and then rushing up the stairs of the building, their weapons drawn. But the flash of the first explosion that sounded like a bomb had gone off made it all too real for Sanchita. This was followed by two more explosions in quick succession, with people screaming and shouting in the background, making it clear that this was a real-life horror, not one of the games that her brother spent so much time playing on his laptop.

And then came the final blast that lit up the screen with yellow-red flames and tore a hole in the building, exposing its innards to the world—and to Ashraf's camera.

It was a shocking scene. And it grew more surreal as the feed panned back to ground level, where the survivors were picking up the dead and placing the wounded in ambulances that arrived so quickly that they must have been waiting for just such an eventuality.

Sanchita's breathing had grown more and more ragged as she watched the traumatic scenes play out. She gasped with shock when her mother entered the room with a cheery, 'Okay, I am finally ready to go. Sorry about that . . .'

Arti broke off as she saw the expression on her daughter's face. Sanchita looked as if she had seen a ghost. 'What happened beta? Is everything okay?'

'No, no, it's not,' said a pale and shaking Sanchita, handing over the phone to her mother so that she could see Ashraf's feed as well.

'I'm sorry Mum,' she said, 'But you're going to have to call an Uber. I'm probably the first journalist to see this story. I need to call this in before the other channels find out.'

Her mother nodded mutely as Sanchita began scrolling through her phone for Manisha's number. Everyone knew that Manisha Patel liked to sleep late into the morning. But just this once, Sanchita was sure, she would not be upset to be woken up.

It took a groggy Manisha a few seconds to grasp the gravity of what Sanchita was saying. And then she was out of bed and logging on to her computer before she remembered that she did not, in fact, have a Facebook account. Thinking quickly, she asked Sanchita to run the video on her laptop, record it, and email the file to her. After that, she was to get in touch with Ashraf Mehdi and try and persuade him to come to the AITNN studio to talk about what he had witnessed. If she couldn't get through to him on the phone, she was to drive to Jamia Nagar and track him down to his house. Manisha would be arriving there with a crew within the next half hour.

But before any of that happened, they had to send the link to the video to the producer of the morning news bulletin. It was imperative that they run those images before anyone else.

And that's just what they did, with the legend 'Breaking News' playing all over it. They only had first-mover advantage for about ten minutes. After that, all the other news channels discovered Ashraf Mehdi's Facebook account and were plundering his feed.

But in those ten minutes, Gaurav Agnihotri went mad with jealousy and anger. How on earth had AITNN managed to swing this scoop? How could their reporters have known that this obscure student from Jamia was going to run this Facebook live feed? Did they have prior information of the raid? Had they tipped off Ashraf Mehdi to record this? Had the security services leaked to Manisha Patel? What other privileged information was Manisha being fed by her sources at IB?

Gaurav's mind was running wild with conspiracy theories. But putting those aside for a moment, he quickly got dressed and headed for the NTN studio. He needed to anchor the coverage of this disaster himself. He couldn't trust it to the early-morning anchors.

By the time Gaurav got to his studio, Manisha was already in Jamia Nagar, broadcasting her first piece to camera from outside the cordon that the security forces had set up. Gaurav felt his temper rise again as he saw her on one of the screens on the video wall. How on earth did she manage to be the first on the scene every single time? He could swear that the woman was a witch.

Or, more accurately, another word that rhymed with that.

# 8

Asha had barely hung up on Nitesh Dholakia when the internal intercom line rang beside her bed. She picked it up, already irritated at the thought of having to deal with another domestic drama involving her mother on a day like this. But it was her brother's baritone that greeted her on the phone.

Karan Pratap Singh was the lark of the family, always up at 5.30 a.m. to do a bit of yoga or a spot of cardio in his home gym. Today, he had clambered on to the treadmill at 6 a.m. after a quick cup of coffee, turned on the TV and tuned into AITNN. He enjoyed watching the morning shows because the discussions on them were more good-natured and even-tempered than the debates on prime time.

But even before the first segment was over, the morning show feed cut out and the screen cut back to a studio where an anchor sitting behind a desk said the two words that Karan had come to hate the most: Breaking News. Every time he heard that phrase, he muttered to himself, 'Breaking news? Yeah, mission accomplished. You broke the news all right!'

Today, however, was that rare day when that phrase was both apt and accurate rather than another instance of hyperbole. The screen filled with the view of a street down which uniformed men were marching down two abreast. As Ashraf Mehdi's Facebook live began streaming on his TV, Karan's feet automatically came to a halt. He was about to be thrown off the treadmill when he had the presence of mind to hit the emergency stop button.

He did all this without once taking his eyes off the TV screen, which was now awash with red and yellow flames as the house that had been raided was set ablaze by a series of blasts. Karan watched open-mouthed as the operation that Asha had told him about only last night went completely south.

As the final explosion blew away the front of the building, Karan scrambled off the treadmill and reached for the intercom. Dialling Asha's bedroom number, he was fully prepared to be the one to wake her and give her the news. But her punchy hello made it clear that she had been up for a while.

'Hi Bhaiyya, all okay?' she asked, her reflexive concern for Radhika overshadowing everything else that was going on.

'No, it isn't,' Karan responded tersely. 'Switch on the TV and turn to AITNN. I'll wait.'

Asha groped for the TV remote which was lost somewhere in her bed sheets. She finally found it and turned the TV on to AITNN and froze as she saw the raid being relayed on live television.

How on earth had this happened? How had this TV channel managed to get hold of this footage? Was there a leak in the IB or the NIA? Had AITNN been tipped off by sources in one of these agencies?

But as she tuned into the commentary, Asha realized that it was nothing of the sort. This was a live video that had been streamed on Facebook by a man who lived across the street on which the raid had taken place. Talk about being in the wrong place at the wrong time, she thought bitterly.

It was only a matter of time before this video was run across every news channel in the country. So much for IB officers going door-to-door and deleting pictures and videos from people's phones. Not that she had ever thought that would actually work.

Asha suddenly realized that Karan was still holding for her on the intercom. Picking up the phone, she said, 'Yes, Bhaiyya, I just saw it . . . What do I do now?'

The moment the words were out of her mouth, Asha regretted them bitterly. The last thing she wanted was to retreat to an infantile state in which she couldn't cope with the challenges of her job and depended on her big brother to rescue her. She was the Prime Minister of India, for God's sake. She had a staff to assist and advise her. She had the resources of the entire government at her command. She didn't need to go crying to her Bhaiyya for help.

But it was too late now. Karan had hung up the phone, promising to be with her in five minutes. And when he arrived at Number 3, still in his tracksuit, Asha's spirits sank further. Karan was accompanied by Arjun, who was still rubbing the sleep from his eyes.

Good God! A family meeting? That's all she needed on a day like this. Tamping down on her resentment, Asha pressed the bell to order coffee for everyone, when much to her relief Nitesh Dholakia entered the living room. At least now she would not be outnumbered, she thought.

Further reinforcements were on the way as well. By the time the coffee arrived, so had the National Security Adviser, Arunoday Sengupta, and Principal Secretary, Madhavan Kutty; and the post-mortem into the Jamia Nagar disaster began in full earnest.

The consensus that emerged held the IB squarely responsible for the failure of the operation. The Intelligence

Bureau operatives who were shadowing Suhail Geelani should have worked out that he wasn't a low-level operative. And that the sleeper cell he headed wasn't just composed of people tasked with logistical support. This had been a well-armed and highly motivated group. And it had taken down some twenty-odd members of the security forces. And as if that death toll was not high enough, many residents of the building had also perished in the blasts that destroyed it.

'Well, ma'am, some sort of collateral damage was always on the cards,' Sengupta pointed out to a fulminating Asha. 'In operations like these, that's always the risk you take.'

'Collateral damage?' Asha exploded, her pent-up nerves finally giving way. 'Is that what you call it when innocent people are caught up in a badly botched operation like this? You're talking about people's lives here. Don't try and camouflage it with mealy-mouthed phrases like "collateral damage".'

Karan laid a restraining hand on her arm and asked the question that had been plaguing Asha for an hour now. How did the security forces not know that the cell had suicide belts tucked away for just such an eventuality? Had no one thought of doing a sweep of the flat in all the time it was under surveillance?

The sheepish silence that followed was an answer in itself.

Asha shook off her impatience and asked Dholakia to call a meeting of the Cabinet Committee on Security in South Block in half an hour. She wanted the chiefs of IB, R&AW and the NIA in attendance—and she wanted some explanations.

While the bureaucrats headed off to execute her order, the Pratap Singh siblings sat in the living room of Number 3 for another few minutes, watching the TV coverage of the Jamia Nagar attack, switching through channels to get a sense of the story as it developed. And as anchor after anchor railed against the security agencies for this disaster, blaming them for rushing blind into this kind of operation, it was clear that the narrative that was being built was going to damage the government's reputation even further.

And the buck, as always, would stop at the desk of Madam Prime Minister, Asha Devi.

\* \* \*

Manisha Patel was in a foul temper. First off, the cordon set up by the security agencies was so wide that she couldn't even see the building where it had all gone down from where she was positioned. She had been determined to do her pieces to camera with that flaming building in the background. Well, that wasn't going to happen now.

The second irritant was the fact that they could not trace Ashraf Mehdi. Sanchita Mishra had been calling him ever since she saw his Facebook live feed, but the phone just kept ringing before being switched off. And they couldn't go to Mehdi's house to locate him either, because it lay within the security cordon that the media could not breach.

So, there was no way she could get hold of her star witness. And there was no way she could get near ground zero. She may as well have been broadcasting from the studio for all the difference it had made coming to Jamia Nagar to do her 'on-the-spot' reporting.

But the pro that she was, Manisha didn't let her frustration reflect in her face as she prepared to do her first PTC. Nonetheless, her anger at the restrictions placed on her reporting by the government came through loud and clear in her sharply critical opening.

'Good morning, viewers,' she started, a grim expression on her face. 'Though, it must be said, it is anything but a good

morning for our country. In these bylanes behind me, as I stand
here in Jamia Nagar, we have just seen a counter-terrorism
operation go completely wrong. The authorities have not
released any information yet. In fact, they are not even allowing
the media on the scene. But I have managed to piece together
the events by talking to eyewitnesses who saw the attack. And
of course, by now all of you would have seen the Facebook live
video that was flashed first by our network.'

Manisha took a breath. Maybe this was not the right time
to boast about being the first to break the news. The viewing
public tended to react badly to those media outlets that seemed
gleeful about being the first to bring bad news to them. Hastily
changing course, Manisha went into reporting mode, relying
on the bare-bones information that one of her sources in IB
had fed to her on her way to Jamia Nagar.

'The aim of the operation, my sources tell me, was to
take six members of a terrorist sleeper cell into custody. This
terror cell was believed to have provided logistical support for
the Kautilya Mall attack. The building in which they met had
been under surveillance for some time. But for reasons that
are unclear, the security forces walked into a virtual trap. The
terrorists they were tracking had suicide belts strapped on, and
they blew themselves up as the raid got underway.'

The anchor interrupted with a question. 'If the flat was
under surveillance, how did the security agencies not know that
these terrorists were armed and dangerous?'

Manisha nodded as the question came through her earpiece.
'Exactly. That is exactly the question that everyone is asking.
And if you ask me, I think this is a massive intelligence failure.
And that failure has resulted in the death of more than twenty
security personnel. We are also being told around twelve to
fifteen residents of the building have died in the explosions as

well, and that an even larger number are seriously injured. But, let me clarify, these are unconfirmed reports and we are still waiting for the authorities to hold a briefing and give us some clear information.'

'Why do you think this went so wrong,' asked the voice in her ear. 'Why were the security forces unprepared to face so much resistance?'

Manisha sighed deeply. 'Where do I start? It is clear that this government doesn't know how to handle national security. First, there was the Kautilya Mall attack, which came out of the blue. The intelligence agencies had no clue about it. Once that happened, the government caved in almost immediately and released twelve terrorists in exchange for the life of Radhika Singh, the Prime Minister's sister-in-law. We've already seen how much damage Masood Azhar, who was released for the return of the hostages in the IC 814 hijack, has done to us over the years. So, you can only imagine what atrocities this lot of terrorists will commit in the future.'

The anchor gently brought Manisha back on topic. 'Yes, it's quite clear that the government is soft on security issues. But judging by today's events, its intelligence-gathering ability is rather suspect as well.'

Manisha nodded. It wasn't just the intelligence failure that was galling, she said. It was also the haphazard planning. Why, for instance, hadn't the security forces evacuated the residents from the building before they raided it? They could have saved so many lives if they had taken that basic precautionary measure.

'Not only have we seen the loss of innocent lives in this incident, we have also seen an operation that failed on every measure,' concluded Manisha. 'Not one terrorist was captured alive, so that he could be interrogated and debriefed. And there was enough reaction time for the terrorists to blow up the flat completely. So, now it will be impossible to gather any intelligence from their phones and laptops. All in all, you could say that this day has been a disaster from the point of view of the security forces. And this will go down as one of the most serious security failures of the Asha Devi government.'

Gaurav Agnihotri, watching Manisha's diatribe from his make-up chair, as he was primped and powdered to get camera ready, was getting angrier by the minute. This was his script. This was all the stuff that he had been planning to say at the beginning of his show. But this stupid bitch had stolen his best lines from him. Now, if he went and said much the same sort of thing, it would look as if he was following her lead.

And that simply would not do.

Gaurav Agnihotri was not someone who followed anyone else's lead. Gaurav Agnihotri was not one to echo the words of others. Gaurav Agnihotri was the one who set the agenda. And today, too, that's exactly what he would do.

There was no other way out. He simply had to junk his original opening and the angle he had decided for today's debate. Manisha had beaten him to the punch; but he would not play catch-up.

Instead, he would run a hundred miles in the opposite direction. Manisha had criticized the intelligence agencies; Gaurav would defend them. Manisha had called the operation a disaster; Gaurav would question the patriotism of anyone who made such criticisms. Manisha had attacked the competence of the government and its record on security matters; Gaurav would defend Asha Devi from these charges and say that all those who questioned the government on a day like this were anti-nationals.

By the time his show ended, he would have completely changed the terms of the debate. Gaurav was quite sure of that.

And not only would this help differentiate his coverage from that of Manisha's, it could also—with a bit of luck—aid him in mending fences with the Prime Minister.

Over the past week or so, Gaurav had been re-evaluating his views on Asha Devi and how he should cover her administration. It was all well and good to punish Asha Devi for giving an interview to Manisha. But Gaurav, eternal realist that he was, knew that he couldn't remain permanent enemies with the Prime Minister of India. At some point or the other, he would have to make his peace with the powers-that-be. So, what better way to initiate a reset of that relationship than by extending support to Asha on what would be one of the toughest days of her life?

By the time Gaurav was seated behind his desk, miked and ready to go, his new opening had already been fed into the teleprompter. As the producer counted down in his ear, Gaurav turned to camera, a solemn expression on his face. 'Ladies and gentlemen,' he began, 'today is a tragic day for India. More than twenty of our brave warriors have laid down their lives in the service of Mother India—but their sacrifice will live on forever in our hearts.'

Turning to the camera that captured his close-up, Gaurav raised his voice, 'Today, I have a direct message for all those who seek to destroy India, to tear it apart. A message for all those terrorists who want to kill us. You can try your best but as long as Bharat Mata's brave sons are willing to lay down their lives for her you will never succeed.

'And I would like to tell those Lutyens media-wallahs who are criticizing our security forces and asking why they went into a situation where they were blown apart, all of you who are shouting from the rooftops about intelligence failure,' Gaurav made air-quotes gestures as he said the last two words,

'I have a message for you as well. Stop questioning our brave warriors. Stop blaming them. Stop dishonouring their sacrifice. Just stop!'

Here, Gaurav paused dramatically, as if gathering control over his emotions, and then went on. 'Ladies and gentlemen, this is not the day to ask questions of our security forces, of our intelligence agencies, or even of our government. Today is the day to stand shoulder-to-shoulder with our security men; today is the day to offer our support to our intelligence agencies; and today is the day to throw our weight behind our government.

'Today, our country is at war with forces that seek to destroy us. And I want to appeal to everyone to stand strong, to stand united as Indians behind our Prime Minister Asha Devi, as she wages a battle against these forces. That is the patriotic duty of every Indian today.'

As he turned to his first guest of the day, Gaurav chuckled silently to himself. All that little speech lacked was a 'Jai Hind' at the end. But even without that sign-off, it should be quite enough to get him the undying gratitude of the Prime Minister.

And even if that was not forthcoming, he would be quite content to settle for an exclusive interview with Asha Devi— her first since she became Prime Minister.

* * *

It was a grim group that sat down to take stock in South Block half an hour later. All the members of the Cabinet Committee on Security (CCS)—the Prime Minister, defence minister, home minister, external affairs minister and the finance minister—were in attendance as were the chiefs of NIA, IB and R&AW along with the NSA, Arunoday Sengupta, and the PS Madhavan Kutty.

But while everybody was angry and upset about the way things had gone down, only one man was visibly panicked. From the time he had seen the live feed of the raid flash on national television, IB Director Suresh Shastri had been sure that his head was on the block. His career would not survive an epic failure like this. In fact, he was convinced that before the day ended, he would have lost his job.

And sure enough, the meeting began with a direct attack on him. 'What is going on, Mr Shastri?' asked Asha. 'What kind of an operation are you running? You have a flat under surveillance for weeks and you don't even know that the terrorists inside are armed to their teeth? You have no idea that these men had suicide vests on them? How does this even happen?'

Shastri took a deep breath and began reciting the explanations he had been furiously thinking up on his way to South Block. The IB had only planted audio bugs in the apartment rather than mount video surveillance because they thought it was less likely to be detected. When the bugs were planted, his officers had done a thorough search of the flat and found nothing untoward. The suicide belts must have been smuggled in at a later date. And that must have been done by some other resident of the building because they had kept an eye on the movements of Geelani at all times. And his operatives swore that Geelani and the other members of the terror cell had never taken any bulky packages into the building.

As Shastri's little speech came to a juddering halt, it was greeted by skeptical silence. It was clear that nobody in the room was buying his version of events.

But by now Asha's initial flash of anger had subsided somewhat and she had moved into damage-control mode. The worst had already come to pass. But the blame game could wait. The priority right now was to change the narrative that was being played out in the media and wrestle back some control over how the public saw things.

'I think we've gone as far as we could possibly go on this,' she said, waving down Kutty who was still berating Shastri. 'And there will be plenty of time in the coming weeks to seek accountability from those who botched this up so badly. But today, we need to focus on changing the narrative in the media and getting our version of events out.'

Home Minister Savitri Shukla, who had been squirming throughout Shastri's interrogation, wondering when her turn would come—she was, after all, directly responsible for the functioning of the IB—heaved a sigh of relief. She needed some time to evaluate just exactly what had gone wrong in their intelligence gathering, and the Prime Minister had just given it to her.

But Defence Minister Prabha Saraf was having none of this. 'With respect, Prime Minister,' she began, in her usual strident manner, 'I disagree completely. We have to focus on how our agencies went wrong, we have to identify the officers who have let us down and punish them summarily. These kinds of lapses cannot be forgiven.'

Before Asha could respond, Finance Minister Alok Ray intervened. 'Prabha ji, nobody is suggesting that these lapses should be forgiven. All the Prime Minister is saying is that our focus today must be on reassuring the Indian people that their security has not been compromised. And we can't do that if we start naming and shaming IB officers just to make some sort of point.'

Asha caught his eye and half-smiled her thanks. This was becoming something of a pattern in all her meetings: being attacked by Prabha Saraf and being defended by Alok Ray. She caught Ray's infinitesimal nod of acknowledgement to her unspoken thanks, and in the middle of all that angst, felt a pang of happiness. The next moment she was scolding herself for having all the emotional heft of an overwrought schoolgirl.

By the time Asha drifted back into the conversation, Arunoday Sengupta had waded into the fray, saying to a bristling Saraf, 'Ma'am, the media is already doing a bang-up job of blaming us for this disaster. They don't need any help from us in this matter.'

The external affairs minister and habitual peacekeeper, Aroop Mitra, hurried in to smooth matters in his bhadralok baritone. 'Prabha ji, we should not lose focus. Reassuring the Indian public and restoring confidence in the government has to be our first priority. Everything else can wait.'

'Thank you all for your inputs,' said Asha, taking back control of the meeting, 'you can rest assured that we will be examining the events of today and finding out exactly where we went wrong and who was responsible. And I can also assure you that every officer who is responsible in any way for this debacle will be punished in an exemplary manner. But today is not the day for this.'

As the meeting went on to discuss the best way of handling the bad press that had resulted from the botched operation, Saraf maintained a mutinous silence, her unhappiness palpable to everyone.

And she wasn't alone in this discontent, as Asha would find out soon enough. The moment she stepped out of the CCS meeting, and into her own office, she found Nitesh Dholakia holding out her direct line to her.

Who, she asked with a silent raise of her brows. 'Sukanya Sarkar,' he mouthed silently. And then, covering the mouthpiece of the phone with his hand, he added, 'This is the third time she has called. I think you should take it.'

Trying to control her exasperation—as if she didn't have enough to do on a day like this—Asha took the phone. And then held it away from her ear as a furious Sukanya began shouting down the line from Kolkata.

How could she allow such a thing to happen? Did she have no control over the security agencies? Why was this operation mounted in such a heavily populated area? Was she even aware of how many people had died? Or did their deaths not count because they belonged to the minority community?

Asha, who had been listening patiently until then, lost her temper at this point. 'How does the religion of those who have died matter?' she asked Sukanya angrily. 'All that matters to me is that many innocent Indians have died. I have not stopped to count how many Hindu and how many Muslim dead bodies there are. And I am appalled that you would do so!'

'You may not care about the Muslims who have died,' shouted back Sukanya. 'But I do care about them. I care about the Muslim community unlike your party. We all know your record on these matters.'

Asha, who prided herself on her secular credentials, went ballistic. 'My record? You know what my record is? I treat everyone equally, no matter what their religion. I don't discriminate against anyone. And I don't pander to any community either.'

But she was speaking into an empty line. At some point, Sukanya Sarkar had hung up on her.

# 9

It was a week later that Asha Devi and Sukanya Sarkar finally came face to face. And in the space of those seven days, the Jamia Nagar disaster had become an even bigger story.

Ashraf Mehdi, the young student who had live-streamed the entire episode on his Facebook feed, had become a national celebrity, doing the rounds of TV news channels to give a first-hand account of being an eyewitness to the raid that had gone so wrong. The families of all those who had perished when the building was blown up by the suicide bombers were out on the streets every day demonstrating against the government and asking for justice for their dead relatives.

The media were clamouring daily for some heads to fall in the security establishment. How could things go on as usual, they asked, when there had been such a monumental failure of intelligence? Surely there had to be some accountability. Somebody in the security agencies should take responsibility and quit. And if not, the Prime Minister should assign blame and fire all those responsible for this disaster. If Asha Devi failed to do that, the TV anchors fulminated, then she had no business occupying the highest office of government.

So, Asha was even angrier a week later than she had been on the day of the raid. The constant attacks from the media, most of them holding her personally responsible for the Jamia Nagar disaster, had worn her down. Firing Suresh Shastri, the head of the IB, would have made her feel a little better. But she had been advised against it by both Arunoday Sengupta and Madhavan Kutty, the two arch rivals coming together to press that point upon her. Doing that at this juncture, they explained to her, would make it seem that the security forces had screwed up. And they couldn't afford to let that impression take hold while they tried to do some damage control.

This meeting with Sukanya Sarkar was part of that damage control exercise that her private secretary, Nitesh Dholakia, had drafted for her. Given that the Poriborton Party numbers were keeping the government afloat, it was imperative that Asha keep Sukanya in good humour – no matter how much it went against her grain.

So, swallowing the anger that had been simmering within her ever since Sukanya had hung up on her on the day of the raid, Asha had invited Sukanya over to Race Course Road for breakfast. Finally, her mother's talent for putting on a breakfast buffet for champions would come to good use, she thought.

And sure enough, as she led Sukanya through to the dining room, the sideboard was groaning under an array of dishes. This time, in keeping with the tastes of the guest of honour, Amma had included some Bengali dishes as well. So along with the idlis and vadas, the puri bhajis and poha, there was some Calcutta-style singara and nimki, along with some aloo dum served with a side of fluffy luchis.

But Sukanya didn't give the spread even a cursory look. 'I will have one boiled egg and one toast,' she announced to one of the bearers in attendance, as she settled down on the dining table. 'No butter,' she shouted fiercely at his retreating back, 'no butter.'

The bearer nodded nervously as he scurried to the door. But Sukanya had one more request. 'Also, you get me some tea with little bit milk and one spoon sugar. Just one spoon, okay?' The man scuttled off, looking more petrified than Asha had ever seen him.

Asha helped herself to two idlis and some green chutney as they sat and waited for Sukanya's order to be delivered. Once her abstemious breakfast had been served, Asha nodded dismissal to the waiting staff and the two women got down to business.

But even before Asha could give voice to the many resentments boiling up within her, Sukanya disarmed her completely. 'Look, I am sorry I lost my temper with you that day,' she said brusquely, 'but you must understand, I was under a lot of pressure.'

As was I, thought Asha to herself. But voicing that thought seemed churlish given that the great Sukanya Sarkar—the woman who had a reputation of never backing away from a fight—was actually apologizing for her behaviour. Nor did it seem right to counter this apology with a laundry list of complaints—though God knows hers ran into several long pages.

So, Asha did the only thing she could. She responded graciously. 'That's okay Sukanya di. I can understand. It's been a difficult time for all of us . . .'

Sukanya didn't allow her to complete her thought. 'Yes, yes, this is what I am saying also. It is difficult time. But now we need to come together and do better.'

'Of course,' responded Asha. 'I am open to any ideas you may have.'

And ideas Sukanya had aplenty. First off, she wanted IB chief Suresh Shastri's head on a platter. Next, she wanted Asha to set up a Supreme Court of India-monitored Special

Investigation Team (SIT) to delve into the Jamia Nagar operation and assign responsibility for its failure down the line. And finally, she wanted Asha to set up an Inter-Services team to investigate the Kautilya Mall terror attack; that was the only way, declared Sukanya, to get any answers to all the questions they had.

Asha nodded along even though she didn't agree with all of this. She would get her home minister, Savitri Shukla, to push back on this in due course. And who knows, with the passage of time, Sukanya's focus may shift to other issues as well, obviating the need for another head-on confrontation.

But, as Asha was to soon discover, Sukanya was already ready to move on other matters. And one among them wasn't good news for Asha.

Canny politician that she was, Sukanya Sarkar had saved the worst for the last. As she drank up the one cup of tea that she allowed herself every day, she announced that she wanted West Bengal to be declared a Special Category State. In response to Asha's incredulous stare, she reeled off a number of reasons why this made sense.

Bengal was a border state, she argued, and one which had always had security issues. Over the last year, the infiltration problem had got even worse, and the state was finding it hard to cope with its current resources. In addition, there was considerable agrarian distress after the cyclone that had hit the coastal areas a few months back. The state needed extra help from the Center if it was to recover and get back to normal. Industry needed extra sops as well if it was to be wooed back to Bengal; and the return of industry was imperative to create new jobs.

The only way to accomplish all this, argued Sukanya, was to proclaim Bengal a Special Category State. And she hoped that Asha would make the announcement in the next few weeks.

Asha was dumbfounded. She had been worried about meeting Sukanya's demands, but even she hadn't seen this coming. How could she possibly give Special Category status to Bengal when states that were far less prosperous did not have it? And if she did give it, what answer would she give to those states that had been petitioning for this status for decades—and had more of a legitimate claim to the title and all the support that came with it?

But the moment she said all of this aloud, Sukanya came back at her with a barrage of figures and statistics to prove that Bengal was much worse off than any other state in the Indian union. As she flagged under this onslaught of numbers, none of which made any sense to her, Asha felt more inadequate than she had ever before.

If only she had asked Alok Ray to be here at this meeting, she thought ruefully. He would have known exactly how to respond to this. She could almost hear him drawling in his droll way, 'Madam Chief Minister, there are three kinds of lies: lies, damned lies and statistics.'

She only realized that she was smiling when Sukanya stopped mid-flow to ask crossly, 'What is so funny? Are you laughing at me?'

Asha rushed to assure the CM that she would never dare do such a thing. But she could barely begin to admit to herself just why she had been smiling. The truth was that the very thought of Alok Ray had been enough to bring a smile to her face. And that wasn't something Asha was at all happy about.

\* \* \*

As this meeting ended, another was beginning a few blocks away. Satyajit Kumar had finally got an appointment with the

Dalit Morcha supremo, Didi Damyanti, though the invitation didn't extend to breakfast. A cup of coffee or masala chai was as much as Damyanti was ready to offer him.

As he was escorted into the Lutyens bungalow that Damyanti called home when in Delhi, Kumar reminded himself to keep calm, to not lose his cool no matter how bad the provocation. If his party was to revive, he needed this alliance with the Dalit Morcha to fight the state elections in Bihar. Together, the two parties would have the numbers to take on Asha Devi's LJP in a two-to-one battle. But if there was a three-cornered fight, then the LJP would be home and dry with no problems at all.

At the end of the day, it was all down to electoral arithmetic. And he needed Didi Damyanti's support to ensure that the numbers made sense for him and his Samajik Prajatantra Party. If he didn't succeed in winning her over, then it was game over. The election was already lost to him, even before a single vote was cast.

In an attempt to soften up the Dalit Morcha supremo, Kumar had arrived with an enormous bouquet of red roses—he had been informed that these were her favourite flowers. And along with that he had brought some homemade goat cheese, made from the produce of the goats he milked every morning. Even if he said so himself, it stood up to any goat cheese one could buy in Khan Market.

Damyanti accepted the flowers gratefully but looked askance at the packet of goat cheese. '*Yeh kya hai*, Satyajit Bhai?' she asked, prodding it doubtfully. '*Lagta hai aap ka samaan kharab ho gaya hai. Ajeeb smell aa rahi hai.*' (What is this? It looks like this stuff has gone off. It has a strange smell.)

Kumar hastened to assure her that the cheese was just right for eating. But as he went into rhapsodies about the quality of the milk his goats produced, Damyanti's eyes began glazing over. Everyone said that Satyajit Kumar was a bore on the subject of his goats. And clearly, the reports hadn't exaggerated.

She rang a bell to summon her secretary and asked him to take the cheese away. She couldn't think straight with that strange smell overpowering her senses. Satyajit couldn't help but feel a little put out by how perfunctorily his gift had been treated. But he told himself to get over it. He was here for a cause bigger than his goats.

As if to compensate for her brusqueness, Damyanti started off with a little light gossip. 'So, how is Jayesh Sharma these days?' she asked, 'I hear that his wife left him and took the children with her.'

Kumar understood that this was a rhetorical question. Damyanti knew that the former SPP chief's marriage had collapsed when his wife, Malti, found out that he had (against her explicit wishes) leaked the naked pictures of Asha Devi. This was just her way of getting some fresh grist for her rumour mill.

Well, if that's what it took to placate her, then Kumar was happy to play along. So, he obligingly related stories he had picked up on Delhi's cocktail circuit over the past couple of months. The Sharmas were most certainly history, and the implosion of his marriage had left Jayesh in a cloud of depression. Some said that he had taken off for England so that he could recover at the Priory. Others said that he had gone to some retreat in Vermont to lick his wounds. There was one theory that he was meditating at a Vipasana center in Bhutan. But everyone was agreed that his time in the Lutyens charmed circle was over.

'I should hope so,' exclaimed Damyanti. 'How could Girdharilal Sharma's son behave like a low-class thug? Leaking naked pictures of a lady? How low can you go?'

Kumar, who was certain that Damyanti would not have hesitated to do the same if she was in Jayesh's position, shook his head gravely and said, 'Well, I was certainly very disappointed in him—as was our entire party. You know, we removed him as President straight away.'

'Well, that worked out well for you,' chortled the Dalit Morcha leader. 'If he hadn't done that you wouldn't be party leader today.'

Satyajit smiled and nodded. 'And we wouldn't be having this meeting today,' he said. 'But forget about Jayesh Sharma. He is yesterday's man. Today we have many more important things to discuss.'

Damyanti smiled. She knew exactly why Kumar was here: to negotiate a seat-share deal for the Bihar elections that were just months away. And she knew that it was in the best interests of the Dalit Morcha as well to come to some sort of arrangement. But she saw no reason why she should not make him work for it.

And that's exactly what she did over the next hour.

By the time the meeting ended, an hour and some later, Satyajit Kumar felt like he had been put through the wringer. But it had been totally worth it, he thought, as he clambered into the back seat of his car. He had an alliance that would work, and so long as he pandered to Damyanti, it would hold. The Dalit Morcha had got the better end of the deal no doubt. It would fight 135 of the 243 Assembly seats, while his Samajik Prajatantra Party got to contest on 108.

But both caste equations and electoral arithmetic would be on his side, even if he did have to become the junior partner. And if they won Bihar, as seemed certain with this alliance, then that would be the SPP's first step on the road to recovery.

It would be the first electoral reversal after the General Election for the LJP and Asha Devi. And with a bit of luck, it would be the first of many.

* * *

Asha had chosen to meet Sukanya Sarkar at home for two reasons. One, because she thought the domestic setting would disarm Sukanya and soften her for the discussions that followed. And two, because it was easier to keep a meeting under wraps in RCR than it was in the more public setting of the Prime Minister's office in South Block. There weren't as many prying eyes at Race Course Road, and the media's eyes weren't trained on the entrance to the complex round the clock either.

So, it came as a bit of a shock to the Prime Minister when barely ten minutes after Sukanya had driven out of the gates of RCR, their meeting had become the stuff of 'Breaking News'.

Asha was about to leave for South Block after her usual pit stop at her mother's room, when her eyes fell on the TV that was always on in Amma's bedroom. The screen was flashing a photograph of Asha and Sukanya hugging at the swearing-in ceremony, with a jagged line drawn between the two women. 'Is it all over between Asha Devi and Sukanya Sarkar?' the caption read.

Asha picked up the remote and did a quick check of the other news channels. 'Crisis talks at Race Course Road'. 'Asha Devi and Sukanya at loggerheads'. 'Trouble breaks out between the PM and her main ally'. And finally, 'Can this government survive?'

The hashtags soon followed: #AshaVsSukanya #Crisispoint #SukanyaTopplesSarkar. And then, the one that really got Asha riled: #CatFightAtRCR.

Why did everything involving two women have to be seen through the prism of sexism? Why did this kind of casual misogyny still flourish in the media? Couldn't two female political leaders have differences without it turning into some kind of sexist sideshow, a WWE of political sport with her wrestling Sukanya in the mud for the entertainment of those who watched?

Asha was about to call Nitesh Dholakia to tell him to ask Sukanya to issue a clarification, when she was startled to see Sukanya herself appear on the TV screen. It was the AITNN feed and the screen split into two to show Manisha Patel in the studio on one side and Sukanya on an OB link on the other.

Asha couldn't make up her mind as to which of the two women she was most irritated with. Was it Manisha, who turned up at every crisis like the proverbial bad penny? Honestly, did the woman live in her studio? Or was it Sukanya, who clearly couldn't bear to keep a single thought to herself? Did she really have to share everything with the media?

Asha knew, of course, that Manisha and Sukanya had a special relationship. In fact, there was an iconic photograph to prove it.

It had been taken at a protest march that Sukanya had led as the young leader of her fledgling Poriborton Party. Manisha, then a rookie reporter, had been assigned to cover the event. The protest had soon turned violent and Sukanya had been hit on the head by a police lathi. Manisha, who had been watching, had rushed to her side and taken the PP leader's head in her lap, even as Sukanya's white sari turned bright red with her blood. That image had featured in newspapers across the country, a testament to the brutal nature of the government Sukanya was opposing.

And ever since then, Manisha and Sukanya had been friends. If Sukanya needed anything leaked, she messaged Manisha. If she had an important announcement to make, she appeared on Manisha's show. And now that she wanted to send a message to Asha, she had called Manisha yet again.

With an exasperated sigh, Asha settled down on the sofa to listen. She caught the fag end of Manisha's question. '. . . Was the Prime Minister receptive to your suggestions?' Dear God, had Sukanya revealed the entire contents of their meeting to the whole world already?

But much to Asha's surprise, Sukanya responded with a maturity that she hadn't thought the PP leader had in her. 'Well, Manisha, that was private conversation between Asha ji and me. That should remain between the two of us,' she began. But just as Asha was about to slump with relief, Sukanya went on, 'All I can tell you is that I shared my concerns with her and we had a fruitful discussion.'

'Shared my concerns.' Sukanya might as well have carried a placard proclaiming that she was at outs with Asha. Everyone knew what 'shared my concerns' meant in this context. Sukanya would only be 'concerned' if she wasn't happy with the way things were being handled by Asha.

So it wasn't surprising that Manisha pushed the PP leader further. 'When you talk about "concerns", what exactly do you have in mind? Could you please elaborate for the sake of our viewers?'

Sukanya smiled thinly. 'I don't really want to elaborate right now. I want to keep it between Asha Devi and myself. These are matters about national security, you know. One cannot discuss in public.'

Wonderful, thought Asha bitterly. Now Sukanya had as good as confirmed that their differences were about the Jamia Nagar raid and the events that followed.

'But surely,' persisted Manisha, 'the public has a right to know about matters that impact their lives directly? Isn't that what you have always believed in, Sukanya di? The public's right to know? And that there should be transparency in public life?'

'Yes, yes, I know all that,' Sukanya said impatiently. 'But you know the Prime Minister is still young. She is very new to the job. So, you have to give her the benefit of the doubt. She needs our support at this difficult time.'

Now that was a double-edged sword if ever there was one. The Prime Minister needed our support—because she was too young and inexperienced to do her job.

Manisha eagerly jumped on this, as Asha fully expected her to. 'Are you saying that Asha Devi is not up to the job? That she is too inexperienced to deal with a situation like this? Do you think she is out of her depth?'

'Of course not. I am saying nothing of the sort,' shouted Sukanya. 'You please don't put words in my mouth. I didn't say anything of the sort. You may be saying so. I am not.'

Asha had to concede that this was a masterful performance. Without divulging the details of their conversation, without saying one bad word about her, Sukanya had managed to convey to the nation that she didn't think Asha was up to the job of dealing with national security concerns. Without saying anything very much, Sukanya had managed to say it all. As political theatre, there was much to admire here.

But then, this was par for the course for Sukanya. And frankly, Asha should not expect any better of her. So, irrational though it was, Asha's anger was aimed more at Manisha than at Sukanya.

Asha had given Manisha the story of a lifetime by choosing to speak to her exclusively after her naked pictures were leaked.

That had given such an immense boost to Manisha's TRPs that the bump lasted to this day. After languishing behind Gaurav Agnihotri for months in the ratings, Manisha was finally giving her bête noire a run for his money. And it was all thanks to Asha.

You would have thought that that would buy Asha some years, or at least months, of loyalty. And you would have thought wrong, said Asha to herself. There was no such thing as loyalty in the cut-throat world of TV news. There was only the race to stay ahead. And like everyone else, Manisha would take her 'exclusive breaks' wherever she found them.

Well, in that case, thought Asha, two could play this game. If Manisha had no problems taking stories from other people that targeted Asha, then Asha no longer had any obligations towards her.

She knew that Nitesh Dholakia had already offered her first interview post becoming Prime Minister, to Manisha Patel. And until now, Asha had been quite happy with that arrangement. But after seeing Manisha stick the knife into her on Sukanya's behalf, Asha was determined not to go through with this arrangement.

Such was her anger that she couldn't even wait to get to South Block to cancel. Picking up her mobile, Asha dialed Nitesh's number. He could barely get a greeting out before Asha interrupted, 'My interview with Manisha Patel, I want you to cancel it.'

'But why, Prime Minister?' came the bewildered response. 'We have already set aside a time next week, and the crew has come and done a recce as well. How can we cancel now?'

'I don't care how you do it. I just want it cancelled. Right now.'

'Ma'am, can we please discuss this when you get to office?' Nitesh pleaded. 'It will go down very badly if we cancel at this late stage. And we should not needlessly antagonize the media.'

'I think that ship has sailed, Nitesh,' Asha said sharply. 'The media is, and will remain, antagonistic to me as long as I am Prime Minister. And Manisha is no different.'

'But Prime Minister, we have promised her the interview. It is not advisable to cancel now,' said Nitesh, a desperate edge to his voice. 'And in any case, we have to do one interview with the TV media. And she is still the best candidate . . .'

'No, she's not. She's not any better or worse than any other anchor. And in any case, I don't want it to look like she has some sort of monopoly as far as interviews with me are concerned.'

And that's when it came to Asha in a flash. She would pay Manisha back in the same coin by giving the interview to Gaurav Agnihotri. Let's see how Manisha liked it then.

Nitesh Dholakia was horrified by the suggestion. He begged, he pleaded, he implored, he argued. Going up against Gaurav was a bad idea. The man was a loose cannon. God alone knows what he would ask her. He would get aggressive. He would be unpleasant. Asha would be making a big mistake if she went with Gaurav instead of Manisha.

But all these warnings fell on deaf ears. Madam Prime Minister had made up her mind. And that, she was insistent, was that.

# 10

Today marked two weeks of captivity for Sagar Prajapati. And he had to concede that it hadn't been as bad as he had feared. The conditions of his extradition had ensured that he was housed in a clean, well-ventilated room with an attached bathroom and toilet. He had the room to himself, the only other faces he saw were the guards who came by at regular intervals to give him water and food. He had access to one newspaper and was allowed to borrow books from the prison library, so he was doing something he hadn't done since he was a young boy—he was reading for pleasure.

His only outings were to the prison yard, where he was allowed to exercise for an hour every morning and evening, and to the interrogation room where he was quizzed every afternoon on the L'Oiseau deal and his uncle, Madan Mohan Prajapati's part in it. Mindful of his encounter with his uncle's henchman in the airport—when he had been implicitly threatened to keep quiet or risk having his throat slit—Sagar Prajapati refused to implicate the former defence minister in anything. With his high-powered lawyer by his side, Sagar tried his best to 'no comment' his way through his daily interrogation.

His nightmares of being beaten up by rough-looking police officers had come to naught. The interrogation was carried out by two senior officers of the CBI and they maintained a civil note with him despite his refusal to offer anything other than minimal information. Sagar guessed that this had something to do with the video camera that was set up in the interrogation room, which recorded every interaction.

After two weeks, Sagar was beginning to relax into the routine of prison life. He was woken up every morning at 6 a.m. with a cup of chai and two pieces of buttered toast. After scoffing that down, Sagar would start on the floor exercises his trainer had taught him. It wouldn't do to get soft and out of shape at a time like this. Then, it was time to jog in the yard for about an hour, so that he got his cardio in. The yard was the only place where he came into contact with the other prisoners in Tihar, though they tended to keep a respectful distance from him.

His interrogation usually began after lunch and lasted through the afternoon, and into the early hours of the evening, after which he got to blow off steam with another run in the yard. And then it was time for dinner, followed by lights out.

In some ways, Sagar thought to himself, it was a bit like checking into some sort of strict health farm or fitness boot camp. You had to wake up early and go to bed at a reasonable hour. You could not smoke or drink alcohol. The meals were frugal and mostly fat-free. And there was all the time in the world to walk, jog or work out. If they could fit in a massage or two, he could well convince himself that he was back on a detox break at Chiva Som in Hua Hin or at Ananda in the Himalayas.

But even without that, he felt healthier and fitter than he had in years. Those stubborn last five pounds that had refused to move from his midriff were finally gone, and he felt better for being the lightest he had been in years.

The one blight on his existence—except, of course, the fact that he was in prison—was that he still had no idea where his uncle was or what he wanted Sagar to do next. Madan Mohan Prajapati had gone underground and nobody—not the Indian government, nor his family—seemed to have any clue where he had disappeared.

Every day Sagar lived in hope that this would be the day when one of his uncle's 'associates' would drop by to see him with information or instructions. And every day that hope was dashed.

Today, as Sagar set out for his evening jog in the yard, that hope was mingled with a bit of dread. Today, for the first time in two weeks, he had finally given evidence against his uncle in his interrogation. Not that he'd had much choice. The officers had confronted him with some bank papers from Madan Mohan's Cayman Islands numbered account. The details of the money transfers matched exactly with the last few defence deals that his uncle had negotiated. And confronted with this evidence, Sagar hadn't seen any point in prevaricating any further.

They had his uncle dead to rights anyway. What difference did it make what he said?

As it turned out, it made all the difference.

As Sagar was starting his second perambulation of the yard, one of his guards fell in line with him, jogging at the same gentle pace that Sagar had set. Sagar found this a bit odd, given that his guards usually left him alone to get on with his exercise, but he didn't think too much about it. Maybe the guy just wanted to get some cardio in before he went off duty.

The two of them jogged along in silence, the only sound their slightly heavy breathing as they both worked up a sweat. But as they approached the far end of the yard a shadowy figure suddenly emerged from behind the chain-link gate. Sagar was startled enough to come to a juddering halt. But he couldn't retreat because the guard who had been jogging with him was now right behind him, propelling him forward with a rough hand in the small of his back.

As Sagar staggered forward the moonlight glinted off an object that the man in front of him held in his right hand. But even before Sagar could work out that he was looking at a knife, it had been plunged expertly between his ribs and thrust upward through his heart.

Sagar Prajapati was dead before he hit the ground.

\* \* \*

It didn't take long for the news to break, despite the security blanket the authorities threw around the Tihar Jail complex the moment Sagar's lifeless body was recovered. In fact, it took all of seven minutes. That's when Surojit Ganguly, a newspaper reporter on the CBI beat, posted a tweet: 'Unconfirmed reports coming in that Sagar Prajapati has died in Tihar Jail. A violent death, according to my sources. More details to follow shortly.'

Predictably, this set off a Twitter storm. And before you could say 'L'Oiseau', the hashtag #SagarPrajapatiDead was trending on Twitter, with every journo weighing in with his or her theories. Some said he had committed suicide. Others speculated that he had been killed. And then there were those who insisted that he had had some sort of health emergency but had passed away before medical help could reach him.

Manisha Patil quickly ended her evening edit meeting and began working the phones to find out more from her sources in Tihar. But everyone was being exceptionally tight-lipped today.

Only one of the three people she phoned even bothered to take her call. And he pretended to be home, sick, and hence, completely in the dark about how events had gone down in Tihar. Manisha hung up in disgust and decided to work her IB sources instead. Maybe she would have more luck there.

Gaurav Agnihotri was already doing that. His cousin, Abhay Budhiraja, was head of the CBI cyber cell and had promised to make some calls and get back to him as soon as possible. So, while he waited, Gaurav went into the studio to do what he did best—feed the beast of the 24/7 outrage machine that passed for TV news in India.

Today, though, he steered clear of attacking the Prime Minister directly. Nitesh Dholakia had already reached out to Gaurav and indicated that Asha Devi would give her first interview as Prime Minister to him. And Gaurav didn't want to risk that scoop disappearing because of a few throwaway remarks about the PM.

So, instead, Gaurav Agnihotri went for a target lower down the food chain: Home Minister Savitri Shukla. The administration of Tihar Jail came under the purview of her ministry so, as far as Gaurav was concerned, the buck stopped with her. While his producers scrambled to set up a link with the NTN OB van stationed outside Tihar, Gaurav began selling his new hashtag to a goggling nation: #SackSavitri. By the time he had done his opening monologue to the camera, the hashtag was trending on Twitter, just below the one that said #SagarPrajapatiDead.

In half an hour, the OB vans of every news channel were stationed outside the gates of Tihar Jail, broadcasting live even though the reporters on the ground had no clue what was happening inside. It was an hour before the authorities set up an improvised lectern from which the Jail Superintendent could brief the media.

The facts, as he recounted them, were sparse. The body of Sagar Prajapati had been discovered in the exercise yard by one of the guards on duty. The guards had been stationed at the entrance of the yard as Sagar did his daily exercise and they had not noticed anything out of the ordinary. When Sagar's mandatory hour of exercise was over and he hadn't returned to the gate, they had gone into the yard to get him.

That's when they saw him lying in a pool of his own blood, a knife wedged firmly into his chest. The doctor on duty was summoned but Sagar Prajapati was beyond any medical intervention by this point. In fact, according to the doctor who examined the wound, his death had been instantaneous, with the knife slicing right into his heart.

The moment the Jail Superintendent stopped reading from the paper held in hands that trembled visibly, the assembled press corps burst into loud, incomprehensible shouts, each one vying to be heard over the other. But their questions were all essentially the same: how could this have happened? Sagar Prajapati was the primary witness in the L'Oiseau case. He was also potentially the key to finding out where Madan Mohan was hiding. How could the authorities be so careless with his security within the prison? Why wasn't Sagar shadowed by a posse of guards at all times so that no harm could come to him?

So many good questions; but there were no good answers to any of them.

* * *

The frustration of the press corps was shared by the Prime Minister. Asha Devi had been in a meeting with the visiting Bangladeshi Prime Minister when the news of Sagar's death was first relayed to the PMO. Nitesh Dholakia decided to let the meeting go on instead of interrupting it to brief the Prime Minister. Bad news like this could wait for a bit. The PM needed a clear head to conduct this meeting and he was going to ensure that she had that.

Even so, it was only about twenty minutes after Sagar breathed his last that Asha was told of his demise. Her first reaction was disbelief, bordering on denial. And then came an incandescent surge of anger. How could this possibly have happened? How could they have let Sagar remain unprotected in custody to the extent that he was murdered? The only man who could have led them to the killer of her father had now been killed himself. And it had been done on her watch.

Not for the first time since she had been sworn in as Prime Minister, Asha felt overwhelmed by the enormity of her job. How could she keep so many balls in the air at the same time, she thought despairingly, especially when she seemed to be surrounded by incompetent fools who could not—or would not—do their own damn jobs?

As she looked back at her short tenure as Prime Minister—it had been barely three months even though sometimes it felt like a lifetime—all Asha could see was a string of failures. She had failed to take a strong stand on the Kautilya Mall attack. Instead, she had rolled over instantly and released some very dangerous men just so that she could have her sister-in-law back home safely. The one chance that they had had to capture the support cell of those who had carried out the Kautilya attack by raiding their hideout in Jamia Nagar had gone hideously wrong. The terrorists had blown themselves up, taking with them all the information they held, and killed several security men and civilians in the process.

And now, there was another disaster on her hands: the custodial death of Sagar Prajapati. It didn't really matter if he had been killed by a fellow inmate or a corrupt guard, any one of whom could have been paid off to assassinate him. What mattered was that Sagar was dead. And with him gone, the investigation into both her father's murder and the L'Oiseau deal would come to a dead end.

Asha knew that this wouldn't just get her bad publicity at home. This would also damage her government's reputation in the international arena. She had managed to extradite Sagar Prajapati by giving explicit assurances to both the government of France and the International Court of Justice that he would be keep kept safe and secure and given a fair trial.

Well, that had worked out well!

Asha switched off the mute button on the TV screen in her office and did a quick scan of all the news channels to see how the news was being covered. Her mouth twisted into a sneer as she caught the rising decibel levels and stratospheric outrage levels on every channel. The way they were singling her out for blame personally it was almost as if she had slipped into Tihar Jail in disguise and dug a knife into Sagar's ribs herself.

Surely, it was self-evident that this was the last thing she would have wanted. If anyone had a stake in keeping Sagar alive it was Asha. And it was equally clear that there was one man who wanted him dead: his uncle, Madan Mohan Prajapati. Asha had no doubt that he was behind this mysterious knifing of his nephew. Wherever in the world Madan Mohan was hiding, he still had the resources to pull strings back home in India.

And if he could pull off the murder of his own nephew, it was only a matter of time before he targeted the two other men who could provide evidence against him in the Birendra Pratap assassination case.

Asha picked up the phone to call the IB chief. The first thing they had to do was to put additional security around Gopi Goyal and Akshay Trivedi. The two arms dealers, who had been instrumental in getting the Korean-made poison pen that ended her father's life, had been in custody for months now and had provided enough evidence against Madan Mohan to hang him. It was imperative to secure them at the earliest so that they didn't meet the same fate as Sagar Prajapati.

She had just hung up on Suresh Shastri when the RAX line (a secure line set up between ministerial offices and residences) began ringing. Asha was tempted to let it go unanswered. She needed a minute to get herself together before she summoned a meeting of the Cabinet Committee on Security (CCS). But as the phone rang on incessantly, she reluctantly made her way to her desk and picked it up.

And immediately wished that she hadn't. It was Karan Pratap on the line, practically frothing at the mouth. How could Sagar Prajapati be dead? What kind of operation was Asha running? She should have given strict instructions that Sagar had to be shadowed by security at all times. Why hadn't she done that? Didn't anyone around her have the sense to brief her on stuff like this?

Speechless with anger and seething with a mounting sense of grievance, Asha let this tirade run on for nearly a minute before she interrupted her half-brother. 'Do you think I don't know this, Bhaiyya?' she finally interrupted, her voice trembling with suppressed rage. 'And do you really think that this is the time to call me up and shout at me? What purpose does this serve except to make me feel bad about myself?'

Asha stopped. Even to her own ears, she sounded less like a Prime Minister and more like a sulky teenager who was upset that her big brother was shouting at her for some minor infraction.

Ignoring her brother's conciliatory noises as he tried to pull back from his extreme position, Asha ended the call abruptly.

'I am afraid I have to go now. I'll speak to you later. I actually have work to do.'

The moment she hung up, she felt sorry about the churlish remark with which she had ended the conversation. Karan Pratap had been through a lot. He had lost his prime ministership to his half-sister. He had seen his wife taken hostage by terrorists. And he was now dealing with a traumatized Radhika who was clearly suffering from post-traumatic stress but refused to seek any help with it. And just like Asha, he must have been incensed to see Sagar Prajapati—the best hope of a breakthrough in their father's assassination case; the man who was possibly their best lead to where Madan Mohan was hiding out—murdered while in custody.

She really should have cut him some slack. Instead, like some snarky teenager she had made a crack about how she had work to do, thereby indicating that she was the one running the country now, while he sat at home, unemployed, and for all practical purposes, unemployable.

Honestly, though, how did he think she would react when he picked up the phone to yell at her like some demented father figure? The last thing she needed on a day like this was being undermined by members of her own family—especially when she had sacrificed so much for them.

But clearly, Karan's gratitude towards Asha for risking her prime ministership by getting his wife released hadn't lasted very long. He was back to being the dominant Big Brother who thought he could dictate to his sister. Maybe he had missed the memo that she was now Madam Prime Minister.

And that power now resided in her rather than him.

* * *

The CCS meeting left Asha more depressed than ever. The briefing by IB director, Suresh Shastri, had made it clear that the authorities were clueless about the attack on Sagar Prajapati. Whoever had planned the killing had left nothing to chance. The CCTV cameras that covered the prison yard had been disabled before the attack went down. And the guards swore blind that the yard had been completely empty when Sagar went for his evening run. CCTV footage of the other areas of the prison had found no outsiders lurking.

So, from the looks of it, this was another mystery that seemed destined to remain unsolved. Home Minister Savitri Shukla had proposed that a commission of enquiry be constituted to delve into Sagar Prajapati's death. Everyone had agreed that this was a good idea even though they all knew that this was just another way of postponing facing up to the inevitable truth that they would never know who had killed Sagar.

But equally, there was no doubt among them as to who was behind this murder. It was clear that the only person who could have ordered this hit was Madan Mohan Prajapati. And the fact that he had succeeded in doing so proved that, wherever in the world he was, he was still powerful and connected enough to pull off a murder inside a well-guarded prison. And that didn't bode well for the investigation into Birendra's Pratap's assassination.

On that depressing note, everyone said their 'Namastes' and made to leave. But while everyone else shuffled towards the door, Alok Ray lingered behind. Seeing the indecision on his face, Asha could tell that he was wrestling with himself if he should say something to her or just move on like the rest. Well, if he had any suggestions to make, she would be only too happy to listen.

So, she gestured that he should stay behind and have a word with her. Prabha Saraf, who had caught this byplay from her vantage point near the door, shot her a quizzical look. Asha strove to keep a neutral expression but she could feel a tell-tale blush spreading across her face. She just hoped that Saraf hadn't noticed that—and that she wouldn't spread rumours about Asha's relationship with Alok. The last thing she wanted was more gossip about her private life. And she could certainly do without innuendo-laden blind items about how she was getting too friendly with one of her ministers.

But as Asha and Alok sat back down in their seats around the conference table, the finance minister was all business.

'I am not sure if it is my place to give you advice like this,' he began tentatively. 'But I just had a thought about how we could expedite the search for Madan Mohan. It's not exactly conventional, but I think it could work.'

Asha rushed to reassure him that, at this stage, frustrated beyond measure by the lack of success in tracing the prime suspect in her father's assassination case, she was open to any suggestion, no matter how unconventional.

Alok began by telling Asha about the time one of the heads of a major hedge fund based in New York had gone missing after stealing hundreds of millions of dollars from the fund. Those who ran the fund hadn't wanted to make the story public so they had not gone to the police.

Instead, they had engaged a private investigative agency called Dark Matters, which was staffed by former intelligence operatives from across the world (most of them ex-Mossad, ex-MI6 and ex-CIA), and tasked it with tracing the fugitive down. It had cost them a lot of money but a month later they had managed to trace their target and bring him back to New York to face justice.

'You think that I should engage this agency to work on behalf of the Indian government to trace Madan Mohan?' asked Asha, with a skeptical raise of her brow. 'We already have the intelligence agencies of every country across the world working with us on this. If they haven't managed to trace Madan Mohan, what is the guarantee that this, er, Dark Matters, will manage to do so.'

'No, no, you misunderstand. I don't mean that the government should engage the agency. I think you should hire them in a private capacity to work off the books for you,' said Alok.

'In a private capacity? Why can't we hire them officially if they are so good?' asked Asha.

'Well, let's just say that they don't exactly play by the rule book,' responded Ray with a wry smile. 'And some of the methods they use are, well, pretty off-the-wall. So, just in case these methods come to light at some point, it's a good idea for the Indian government to have deniability.'

'Off-the-wall? What does that mean in real terms?' asked Asha, raising her eyebrows in interrogation.

'Well, to be perfectly frank, Asha, it is best that you don't know. What you don't know, you can't be expected to answer for.'

'I'm sorry, Alok, you're going to have to give me something more than that if I am going to hire these people. I don't want to end up working with cut-throats and murderers of every stripe.'

Alok looked horrified. 'Oh God no, these are perfectly respectable people. They just have contacts in the criminal underground across continents. And as such they are best placed to find out the movements of someone like Madan Mohan who is probably using this criminal maze to stay under the radar.'

'Do you really think this would work?' asked Asha. 'That this agency I have never heard of will succeed where the entire world intelligence community has failed?'

'Will this work for certain? I really can't say. But given that we've had no luck so far, what's the harm in trying?'

'Okay,' said Asha. 'But how would I go about engaging them? How would I pay them? Won't that become a matter of public record as well?'

'Don't worry about that,' said Alok, brushing aside her concerns. 'I'll take care of all that. You don't need to do anything at all.'

'No, no, I can't let you do that,' said a horrified Asha. 'I know how expensive such investigations can get . . .'

'You know, Asha, I have more money than I know what to do with. And I would really like to do this for you. Please let me.'

Asha could feel her eyes welling. After the day she had had, when the entire media seemed to have turned against her, when her own brother had been so unsupportive, it felt good to have someone reach out to help her.

So, ignoring her misgivings, she nodded yes.

# 11

Asha Devi settled into her front-row seat in the Lok Sabha, trying hard to shake off the dread that beat like a pulse within her. She draped her beige pashmina shawl more tightly around her shoulders. Winter had finally arrived in Delhi halfway through December. And Parliament with its vaulted ceilings and thick stone walls was always a few degrees colder than the outside.

The weather was not the only thing sending a chill up her spine. There was also the fact that she would soon be going head-to-head with Satyajit Kumar, the SPP chief. As leader of the Opposition, Kumar had filed a motion to discuss the events that led up to the Jamia Nagar operation and the consequences that followed its failure. And as Prime Minister, she had to be present and ready to answer the questions he raised.

Seated directly opposite her, across the well of the House, Satyajit Kumar looked immaculate in a kurta so white that it bled into blue, his only concession to the arrival of winter a doshala carelessly thrown over one shoulder. As he riffled through the papers placed before him, his air of calm assurance was almost palpable. That wasn't surprising in itself—Kumar was a seasoned parliamentarian and a veteran of debates like these—but Asha felt a spurt of irritation nonetheless as she took in his posture of studied confidence.

What right did he have to look so at ease when she felt so rattled even before a single word had been spoken?

Kumar was now clambering on to his feet, laying down his papers with a flourish as if to establish that he didn't need any props to make his case. Turning to the Speaker of the House, he bowed slightly and began speaking in that special baritone he reserved for occasions like this.

'Madam Speaker, thank you for this opportunity to raise my concerns in this August House,' he began ponderously. 'It is with a heavy heart that I stand here today. It gives me no pleasure to say this but this government has failed. It has failed our country utterly and completely. The Prime Minister has proved herself unfit for the post she occupies—a post she holds only because of the family she was born into . . .'

The very mention of the word 'family' triggered the LJP members of the House, programmed as they were to defend the Pratap Singh dynasty to their last breath. Kumar's next words were lost in the din they created, shouting abuse at the leader of the Opposition and raising slogans in favour of Asha. It took the Speaker a good minute to restore order so that Kumar could resume his speech.

If the ruling party members thought that this would put Kumar off his game, they were completely wrong. Past master at dealing with hecklers, Kumar remained entirely unruffled. Picking up smoothly from where he had left off, Kumar began enumerating the many ways in which Asha Devi's government had failed on the national security front. First, the government hadn't had the slightest clue that a terror attack on Kautilya Mall was imminent, which pointed to a huge intelligence failure. Then, when the attack did take place, Asha Devi had released twelve dreaded terrorists in a matter of hours just so that she could get her sister-in-law back safe and sound.

The Treasury benches erupted in outrage again, berating Kumar in at least three different languages. This time around, though, the Opposition benches gave back as good as they got. Cries of '*Asha Devi Hai Hai*' and '*Yeh sarkar nikammi hai*' began reverberating through the chamber, even as the Speaker ineffectually bleated, '*Shaant ho jayiye. Baith jayiye,*' over and over again.

Kumar smiled slightly as the cross-shouting became louder and louder, and then with a small wave of his hand, quelled the hecklers on his side. It wouldn't do for matters to get so heated that the Speaker was forced to adjourn the House. He had the whole country watching his performance and he needed to make this moment count. He wouldn't get a better opportunity than this to make an impression on the people watching at home.

So, ignoring the stray shouts from the other side, Kumar resumed his speech. 'Madam Speaker, let us accept—for argument's sake—that the Prime Minister had no choice but to give in to the demands of the terrorists. Even then it was incumbent on the government to trace the masterminds behind the attack and bring them to justice.

'Instead, what did we see? We saw a botched operation that resulted in the deaths of more than twenty security men. We saw the terrorists being allowed to blow themselves up, taking all the information they had with them. We saw high civilian casualties because the area around the operation wasn't sanitized beforehand. We saw the loss of precious lives because this government couldn't get its act together. We saw a complete absence of governance. We saw utter chaos.'

Asha could feel her temper rising to a slow boil. It took all the self-control she possessed to keep a neutral expression on her face. But even so, she could feel a vein throbbing in her forehead. And she was sure that it would be visible in the close-up that was beamed out to the country by the Doordarshan camera focused on her face.

Meanwhile, Kumar was going from hyperbole to hysteria. His voice pitched a few octaves above his usual range, he was now virtually shouting. 'Is the life of the Prime Minister's bhabhi worth more than the lives of ordinary citizens of India? Why should we release terrorists so that Bhabhi ji can be safe when we can't even evacuate a building so that our citizens are safe?'

Pandemonium raged again. A member of the LJP stood up to make a point of order. According to the House rules, members of Parliament could not name anyone on the floor of the House who was not present there.

Before the Speaker could say a word, Kumar was back on his feet. 'Point of order? What nonsense are you talking? Whose name have I taken? Bhabhi is not a name!'

'Nonsense? How dare you say I am speaking nonsense?' the LJP member responded heatedly. 'Madam Speaker, this is unparliamentary language. I demand that it be expunged from the record.'

In the time it took the Speaker to resolve the issue, the House had calmed down somewhat. And that's when Satyajit Kumar delivered his coup de grace.

'Madam Speaker,' he began, speaking more gently than he had before, 'in India we believe in family. So, it is understandable that Asha ji wanted to save her sister-in-law. But when you are Prime Minister of the country, you have to remember that every citizen of India is your family member too. Asha Devi has failed to understand that. And she has failed to look after our citizens like she would look after a member of the Pratap Singh khandaan.'

The SPP members immediately began thumping their desks in approval. Kumar held up his hand for silence. He wasn't done yet. 'Until now, Madam Speaker, we in India have lived by the slogan "*Beti Bachao, Beti Padhao*". But sadly, the events of the past few months have forced me to coin a new slogan for India: "*Desh Bachao, Iss Beti Ko Hatao*".'

As he said these words, Kumar dramatically raised his hand and pointed his finger at Asha. She looked back at him as coolly as she could manage, while the LJP members of Parliament ranged behind her went berserk. When the noise and shouting did not cease even after a good five minutes, the Speaker adjourned the House until later in the afternoon.

That's when it would be Asha's turn to speak.

* * *

Everyone from the TV anchors fulminating in studios to the viewers watching at home was agreed on one point: the morning had been an unqualified triumph for Satyajit Kumar. The Leader of the Opposition had eviscerated the Prime Minister. And he had done so with all the aplomb of a trained assassin who can murder someone's reputation without even breaking a sweat.

And in the process, he had gifted the media with a killer slogan as well: '*Desh Bachao. Iss Beti Ko Hatao*'. Save the nation. Get rid of this daughter.

With those six words, Satyajit Kumar had sent out a message to a country that was rapidly becoming fed up with dynasty. He had tapped into the feelings of those feeling cheated about being ruled by a young woman whose only qualification for the job was that she had won the genetic lottery. Though, as Kumar had put it rather pithily while speaking to cameras outside Parliament, in Asha Devi's case the words DNA stood for Don't Know Anything.

None of the media people crowded around him had pointed out the obvious: 'know' began with a 'k' rather than an 'n'. It was just too good a line to find fault with.

Manisha was not in the mood for jokes, though. She had found out only yesterday that the Prime Minister was giving the exclusive that had been promised to her to Gaurav Agnihotri instead. So, her mood today could best be described as murderous. 'Well, that was brutal,' she said, as she turned to her studio guests to begin the debate. 'I thought that Satyajit Kumar would give Asha Devi a bad time. But even I hadn't thought that he would be quite so effective in destroying her completely.'

Pivoting left to look at the LJP spokesperson, Dhruv Sahai, Manisha asked, 'That was a pretty devastating summary of the many ways in which Asha Devi has failed this country. How on earth can your Prime Minister recover from this?'

'What do you mean by "your" Prime Minister?' asked Sahai belligerently. 'Asha Devi is not just my Prime Minister. She is the Prime Minister of the country. She is "your" Prime Minister too . . .' The man had clearly decided that offense was the best defense.

'Yes, yes, all right,' Manisha cut in impatiently, not prepared to play this game. 'I agree. She is my Prime Minister too. She is everyone's Prime Minister. Now could you please answer the question?'

Mollified by her rapid climbdown, Sahai softened his tone. 'Manisha ji, how can you pass judgement on the Prime Minister even before she has had a chance to defend herself? All you have seen so far is the Leader of the Opposition making up absurd allegations against Asha ji. He is spreading Fake News, and instead of challenging him on it, you are falling for it hook line and sinker!'

The SPP spokesperson, Lokesh Bharadwaj, who had been shaking his head all through, butted in. 'Fake News?' he asked incredulously. 'How is any of this Fake News? The whole country watched aghast as the Prime Minister released so many dreaded terrorists in exchange for her sister-in-law's life. We saw for ourselves how the Jamia Nagar disaster unfolded . . .'

'Please stop spreading untruths,' countered Sahai. 'The Prime Minister did not release terrorists just because her sister-in-law was held hostage. You seem to forget that there were 200-odd other women inside the mall at the same time. Are you seriously suggesting that Asha ji should have risked the lives of all these people? If she had done that you would be sitting here criticizing her for that. It really is a case of damned if you do, damned if you don't.'

Bharadwaj wasn't having any of that. 'Oh, I am sorry. I didn't realize that we had to be cheerleaders for a Prime Minister who has shown zero leadership skills from the day she took charge. Look at the Jamia Nagar operation she mounted! What a complete disaster . . .'

'She mounted the operation? Did Asha ji put on a flak jacket and go into the building?'

'Obviously not! But the fact is that she is Prime Minister now. And the buck stops with her . . .'

The usual suspects had been rounded up in the NTN studio as well. But unlike Manisha, Gaurav was hamstrung by the fact that he had an interview with the PM scheduled in a week's time. The last thing he wanted was to risk it being cancelled, like Manisha's had been. So, he had to be more circumspect when conducting the discussion in his studio.

'Well, ladies and gentlemen,' he began, pushing up his spectacles on his nose, 'it looks like the country finally has an Opposition worth its name. Satyajit Kumar has shown us what true opposition looks like. And he has done so without following in the footsteps of his predecessor who had to resort to leaking naked photos of his adversary to do so . . .'

As expected, the SPP spokesman immediately jumped into the fray. 'Gaurav ji, please do not make these wild accusations. You cannot slander our leader in this way . . .'

'Your leader?' sneered Gaurav, 'You didn't waste any time in getting rid of Jayesh Sharma the moment he proved to be a liability. How is he your leader now?'

The SPP spokesman subsided meekly as he remembered, belatedly, that he had a new boss now. And that he should rightly be singing the new boss's praises. 'You're right. Jayesh ji is not our leader now. We have Satyajit ji in charge now, and as even you have conceded, he has done a brilliant job in Parliament today.'

Gaurav turned to the LJP spokesman to take the discussion forward. 'This was not a good day at the office for Asha Devi. How does your party recover from a day like this?'

The LJP spokesman grabbed this softball gratefully with both hands. 'Bad days and good days are just a matter of perspective. I can assure you that Asha ji does not see this as a bad day. For her, this day provides her with an opportunity to lay her case before the country. She will present all the facts as they are later today. And the people watching can make up their own minds as to who is in the right—the Leader of the Opposition or Madam Prime Minister.'

Gaurav decided it was time to bring a neutral party into the debate. Turning to one of his regular panelists, Shaila Kaul, the political editor of a national daily, he asked, 'You have been watching the debate. What did you make of it?'

Shaila Kaul, having gauged Gaurav's mood, decided to tread softly. 'Well, Gaurav, we have only seen half the movie yet. We should not be rushing to post reviews in the interval. Fairness demands that we listen to Asha Devi's side of the story as well.'

Arindam Datta Ray, ex-editor of a newspaper, wasn't prepared to be quite so charitable. 'I usually agree with Shaila,' he said, with a smile towards his co-panelist, 'but today we will have to agree to disagree. Satyajit Kumar just gave us a master class in how to destroy one's opponent. And I really don't see how Asha Devi can recover from this, given that the facts are on Kumar's side. She has been a complete failure as Prime Minister . . .'

Gaurav cut him off before he could say anything more damaging. Turning to the SPP spokesman, he said, 'I know that everyone is going crazy over the slogan that Satyajit Kumar gave us today. *Desh Bachao, Iss Beti Ko Hatao.* But is this really the right message to give to a country when female infanticide and foeticide is so prevalent? Whatever your differences with Asha Devi, whatever your view of dynasty politics, is this the right message to send out to a nation that still doesn't give daughters their rightful due?'

The SPP spokesman had a trapped look on his face. He hadn't expected Gaurav Agnihotri to go down this path. And he had no ready answer for this question. So, he resorted to blustering instead. 'Gaurav ji, the one thing you cannot fault my party on is its treatment of women. Do you know that we gave as many as 34 per cent of seats to women candidates in the last election? We look after our betis very well, we don't need lectures on how to treat our daughters.'

'So, you have respect for every beti in this country, except for the beti of Birendra Pratap Singh?' sneered Gaurav. 'That makes zero sense!'

'No, it makes perfect sense. We stand by the daughters of India who are struggling to find jobs, to put food on the table, to live a life of dignity, or just to be safe when they walk the streets. We do not stand by a daughter who has done nothing in her life except trade on her family's wealth and privilege. We do not stand by a daughter who has a job only by virtue of who her father was. You may stand by dynastic succession in politics; we do not. And I think the country agrees with us rather than you.'

With an uncharacteristic flash of restraint, Gaurav ignored this direct attack on him, and turned to the LJP spokesman instead. 'What do you have to say to the charge that Asha Devi's only qualification to her job is her DNA?'

'That is complete nonsense,' retorted the LJP spokesman. 'Never before in the history of this country has a Prime Minister been tested so rigorously in the first three months of her tenure. And Asha ji has more than proved her mettle. Why is it that nobody remembers the decisive action she took when she ordered a surgical strike against the terrorist camps run by Pakistan? That one action prevented at least another ten terrorist attacks in the future. How come you don't give her credit for that?'

Before Gaurav could respond, the voice in his ear told him that the Lok Sabha had been reconvened and the studio feed cut back to the House. And not a moment too soon. Asha Devi was on her feet and ready to speak.

* * *

The thumping of the desks began as soon as she stood up. The Prime Minister held on to the desk in front of her in an unconscious attempt to steady herself as the LJP members of

Parliament ranged behind her began chants of 'Asha, Asha, Asha,' until they were finally silenced by the Speaker.

Grateful for that small moment of respite to collect herself, Asha took a deep breath and began. 'Madam Speaker, thank you for this opportunity to address the House today,' she said. Turning to face Satyajit Kumar, seated across the Well of the House, she added, 'I would also like to thank the Leader of the Opposition. If it hadn't been for all the lies that he spewed earlier today, I would not have had a chance to put the truth before the people of India.'

Immediately members of the SPP were on their feet protesting this libel against their leader. The word 'lie', they insisted, should be expunged from the record. After a bit of back and forth, the Speaker conceded their demand and Asha resumed her speech.

Laughing ruefully, she said, 'Madam Speaker, I apologize. I misspoke when I used the term "lie". What I should have said is that the Leader of the Opposition was economical with the truth. But then, Satyajit ji only has a passing acquaintance with "truth" so that was only to be expected.'

The LJP members laughed obediently at this flash of wit and Asha felt her nerves settling down. Maybe she could do this, after all.

'One of the charges that the Leader of the Opposition leveled at me is that I let go of twelve terrorists only so that I could get my bhabhi back home safely,' began Asha. Then, turning so that she faced Kumar head-on, she added, 'I would like to ask him if he was aware of how many bhabhis, betis, behens, bahus and matas were among those taken hostage that day.'

Pausing for a moment, almost as if she expected him to respond, Asha answered her own question, 'There were 225 women inside that mall that day. There were also ten children and fifteen men. All these people had families waiting for them at home. All of them had loved ones who died a thousand deaths thinking that they may have lost them forever.'

Asha paused, and then, with a dramatic break in her voice, continued. 'Satyajit ji may not know how that feels. But I do. Because I was one among those hundreds of people who had no idea if their loved one would make it back home.

'Madam Speaker, I don't know what the Leader of the Opposition would have done if he had been in my position. Maybe he would have made different choices than I did. Maybe he would have been happy to risk the lives of all those people just to tell the world what a strong leader he was. It's what men do, isn't it? Show off their strength and power no matter what the cost to others?'

Asha aimed a complicit smile at the Speaker, almost as if to say that, as women, they knew just what men were made of. And then, ignoring the many shouts of protests from the Opposition benches, she continued, 'Well, I decided to put the interests of my people above the interests of my government. Because that's what good leaders do. That's the lesson that my father taught me: always put your people above all else. And I am proud to say that this beti learnt that lesson all too well.'

Asha stopped for a minute to allow the applause from the LJP ranks to wash over her. Then, turning to face Kumar, she continued, 'Satyajit ji, you have a daughter too. And I am sure that you love her as much as my father loved me. Do you think she would be proud of you today when she hears your attack on another beloved daughter? Do you think she will be happy to hear you use the slogan you raised against me?

'*Iss beti ko hatao?*' asked Asha, pointing to herself. 'Is that what it has come to? Attacking me because of whose daughter

I am? Insulting my martyred father by saying that my DNA stands for Don't Know Anything?

'Well, at least I know one thing. I know that the word 'know' begins with a "k" and not an "n". You, sadly, don't even know that.'

The LJP members burst into loud laughter at this, while Kumar smiled weakly, trying to show that he wasn't stung by this attack. But as Asha began speaking again, looking around the House to make her points, she realized that something was off. It took her a minute to work out what it was.

But when she did, she could think of nothing else. While the Opposition benches lost no opportunity to heckle her, using their newly minted slogan '*Desh Bachao, Iss Beti Ko Hatao*' and her party members applauded every line she spoke, the middle of the House—where the members of the Poriborton Party sat—was conspicuously silent. Yes, they weren't joining in the slogans against her, but they were not cheering her on either. Instead, they watched the proceedings in rapt silence, not bothering to thump their desks in approval when their allies in the LJP did so.

No, she wasn't imagining this, thought Asha as she concluded her speech. The PP members were sitting on their hands deliberately. And they could only be doing so on the instructions of their Supreme Leader, Sukanya Sarkar.

Her ally had decided to abandon her to her own devices—at least in Parliament. Would it only be a matter of time before she did that outside of the House as well?

Asha realized that she didn't know the answer to that question. And that left her more rattled than the entire Lok Sabha debate had.

# 12

Asha was in a rare upbeat mood as she drove out of Race Course Road. She had just been briefed by the NSA, Arunoday Sengupta, on the investigation into the Kautilya Mall terror attack. And much to her relief, there had finally been another breakthrough.

As is usually the case, this had come about entirely unexpectedly. Last week, the Army had—on the basis of an anonymous tip-off—raided a house in the Pulwama district in the Valley. By the time the army men arrived, though, the militants were long gone. But a search of the premises had provided a plethora of information. Among the many papers that were seized were detailed schematic maps of Kautilya Mall, surveillance photos of the exteriors and interiors of the structure, and many close-ups of Radhika Pratap Singh, the Prime Minister's sister-in-law and primary target of the hostage-takers.

Clearly, the men who had carried out the attack had planned it in that very house. Forensic experts had been called in and the house was dusted for fingerprints and examined thoroughly for DNA evidence. The results of these tests had then been put through the combined database of the security agencies—and for once they had struck lucky.

The fingerprints and DNA results were traced back to four militants with suspected links to Jihad-e-Azaadi (JEA), the group that had claimed responsibility for the attack. The houses of these men had then been raided by the investigative agencies, and more evidence had been uncovered in these raids. On the basis of that, the security agencies had been able to identify and arrest another twelve people who had been involved in the planning of the Kautilya Mall attack. They were now being interrogated in one of the black sites that the army had set up all across Kashmir.

Sengupta was hopeful that in a few days—after what he euphemistically referred to as 'sustained interrogation' and Asha understood to mean 'torture'—these men would crack and reveal all the information that they had about the JEA and its workings. Then, it was only a matter of time before the masterminds behind the operation were identified and put behind bars.

At last, there would be a resolution to the Kautilya attack. The nation would have some closure. And the Prime Minister would redeem her reputation.

So, it was with the unfamiliar feeling of optimism that Asha headed out to her first meeting in the Prime Minister's office in South Block, even though she knew that it would bring her no pleasure. This was her first face-to-face meeting with her Poriborton Party ally, since Sukanya Sarkar had made her case for getting special category status for Bengal. Asha had hemmed and hawed on that occasion and asked for some time to consider the issue.

Well, her time was now up. A month had passed and Sukanya was now ready to push her case once more—and, Asha was sure, more vigorously than ever.

But Asha wasn't entirely unprepared for this onslaught either. Remembering how helpless she had felt at the last meeting when Sukanya had drowned her in facts and figures that made zero sense to her, she had her own numbers man helping her out today. She had asked her finance minister, Alok Ray, to sit in on the meeting. Given that she didn't want any bureaucratic involvement at this stage (for fear of the story leaking) Ray seemed like the best man to invite to the meeting. It didn't exactly hurt either that, as a fellow Bengali, he had a special rapport with Sukanya, which Asha was only too glad to exploit.

Asha wasn't ready to admit—even to herself—that there was another reason why there was a spring in her step as she bounded up the stairs to her first-floor office in South Block. And it wasn't just that Ray was coming with a progress report of the Dark Matters investigation into Madan Mohan. It was also that after weeks she would finally get to spend some alone time with Alok; though she didn't want to examine too closely why exactly this made her so happy. She could tell herself it was because she was hopeful of a breakthrough in the investigation into her father's killer—but she knew deep down that that wasn't the entire story.

As it turned out, Alok did have some encouraging news to report. Dark Matters had thrown their net far and wide in the dark corners of the international criminal underground and had come up with four leads, two of them credible and two less so.

The first came from their informers in Chile, who had reported that a mysterious figure had just bought a hilltop villa in the central Andes. This villa, which had lain vacant for many years, was now surrounded by top-notch security, manned by what looked like former military men, armed to the teeth. The Dark Matters team was trying to trace the money that had been used to buy the villa, but the transaction had been routed through so many numbered accounts that they had yet to track down the source. And even though they had deployed drones to aerially survey the property, they still hadn't got a good look at its shadowy owner.

The other tip-off had come from Brazil, where a similar mysterious entity had taken over an estate in Manaus, in the Amazon rainforest area. Dark Matters was trying to get one of their operatives hired as close security to the estate owner, and they were hopeful that they would manage to do so in a matter of weeks. Once their man was in place, they would be able to tell in days if the man living there was Madan Mohan or another shady character.

The other two leads were not quite as promising. Both involved European nations that had extradition treaties with India, Ray explained, so it was extremely unlikely that Madan Mohan would risk being caught within those borders. The sightings that had been reported to Dark Matters in these countries, he believed, were most likely to be cases of mistaken identities. But as a measure of abundant caution, the company was investigating these as well.

'Do you think this is actually going to go somewhere?' asked a skeptical Asha. 'Or are we just on a wild goose chase that is costing you countless millions?'

'Honestly, Asha, don't worry about the money,' said Alok, a hint of exasperation creeping into his voice. 'That should be the least of our concerns.'

Asha, who had never stopped feeling guilty about having someone else bankroll the investigation into her father's killer, was about to demur when a sharp knock sounded on the door. Nitesh Dholakia stuck his neck in to announce that Sukanya Sarkar was in the building and would be in Asha's office in seconds.

So, Asha put all her qualms aside—she could always raise them with Alok another day—and walked to the top of the staircase so that she could usher Sukanya in herself. It was a small gesture but if it mollified the PP leader even a little bit before their contentious meeting got underway, it was worth it.

* * *

Even as Asha was extending a warm, if insincere, welcome to Sukanya at South Block, another duo of politicians was getting ready to announce their alliance to the world. A few miles away from South Block, the Lutyens bungalow of Didi Damyanti, the leader of the Dalit Morcha, was the venue of a hastily organized press conference.

Sitting beside Damyanti on the raised dais in the lawn was a somewhat glum Satyajit Kumar. He had fought hard to have the press conference staged in his own Lutyens bungalow. The rustic shed in his yard with his goats mewling and milling around would have formed the perfect picturesque backdrop to the event. It would not only have bolstered his credentials as a son of the soil, but the images would also have appealed to his rural constituents in Bihar. But that wasn't to be. Kumar had lost to Damyanti's insistence on playing hostess—and more importantly, senior partner in this alliance.

Kumar, the ultimate realist, was well aware that this was not the only loss he would suffer at the hands of his new partner and her gigantic ego. And he also knew that he had no option but to take these body blows and soldier on. He needed this alliance much more than Damyanti did—and she knew it as well, and was going to milk it for all it was worth.

The moment the word 'milk' popped up in his head, so did the images of his beloved goats. It really wasn't fair that they had been deprived of such a perfect photo opportunity. What brilliant footage it would have made, as he headed off to milk his goats, just like any old humble farmer, once he was done with the press conference. He was sure that TV news would have led with that story, and that the pictures would have made it to the front pages of every newspaper.

Instead, here he was, stuck on this silly little stage, sitting beside Damyanti on the lawns of her bungalow, his very presence in her house advertising the fact that the SPP was very much the junior partner in this alliance.

But the moment the reporters finally settled down on their chairs and the TV cameras began rolling, Kumar stuck on the smile that he carried in the front pocket of his kurta in case of emergency. It was just as well that he was unaware that it was unctuous at best and smarmy at worst. But for better or for worse, it was plastered on his face as Damyanti began reading out a statement announcing that the Dalit Morcha and the SPP would fight the Bihar assembly elections together.

As she read out the details of their pre-poll alliance, there was a surprised buzz among the assembled press corps as the numbers made it evident that the SPP, the national party, was playing second fiddle to the Dalit Morcha, a regional outfit. The Dalit Morcha would be contesting 135 seats to the SPP's count of 108. The raised eyebrows all around made it clear that the media thought that the SPP had been played by Damyanti. And that Satyajit Kumar had made a grievous strategic error by agreeing to an arrangement in which Damyanti was the dominant partner.

Kumar could read their expressions as well as the next person (in this case, Didi Damyanti herself) but he pretended to be oblivious as he smiled and smiled, and then smiled some more. Finally, Damyanti stopped for breath and the questions began.

Predictably enough, the first question was lobbed at Kumar. His party, the SPP, was a national party, the primary

Opposition in the Lok Sabha. The Dalit Morcha, on the other hand, was a regional outfit, with a presence only in a few states. So, why had he agreed to an arrangement in which the Morcha contested more seats than his party?

Kumar had his answer ready. 'Politics,' he announced grandly, 'is not about numbers alone. It is about doing what is best for the nation. And the number one priority for the nation is to get rid of this government.'

He paused theatrically before pulling out his now well-worn slogan. '*Desh Bachao, Iss Beti Ko Hatao*. That is what Damyanti ji and I are going to do. That is the big picture. And it doesn't matter who has more seats and who has less. What matters is that we will have many more seats than the LJP when the results are in. And this will be the first of several defeats we heap on Asha Devi.'

The next question was addressed to Damyanti. Did she agree with Kumar's slogan? As a woman leader, and a beti to her own father, did she not find it offensive and sexist?

Damyanti laughed uproariously. 'Are you serious?' she gasped finally, when she had caught her breath. 'Are you seriously comparing me to Asha Devi? Yes, we may both be daughters of our fathers. But that's where the comparison ends. Everything that I have achieved, everything that I am today, is because of my own hard work. The only thing I got from my father was the values I live by. I didn't become Prime Minister of this country simply because I was someone's daughter!'

By the time she finished this little diatribe, Damyanti's voice had risen several octaves. In an attempt to calm things down, Kumar interjected in a jocular fashion. '*Arre bhai, aap logon ko maloom hona chahiye ke hum log kaamdar hain, naamdar nahin.*' (You chaps should know that we rely on our work not on our family name.)

One of the reporters had had enough by now. Scrambling to his feet, he asked Kumar, '*Agar aap log kaamdar hain, toh phir Jayesh Sharma aap ke leader kaise baney? Who bhi toh naamdar thhey, na?*' (If you believe in merit, how did a dynast like Jayesh Sharma become your leader?)

Kumar waved away the question dismissively. '*Arre bhaiyya,*' he said, slipping into Rustic Big Brother mode, '*woh toh kal ki baat thi. Aaj ka daur alag hain. Ab hum aur Damyanti ji mil ke vanshvaad ka vinaash karengey.*' (That's yesterday's story. In today's world, Damyanti ji and I will destroy dynasty).

Saying that, Kumar got up to his feet and gestured to Damyanti that she should follow suit. Then he held out his right hand to her in a dramatic gesture. The moment she took it into her left hand, he raised their linked arms in a tableau reminiscent of a referee declaring victory for a wrestler. The two leaders held this pose for a couple of minutes as the photographers captured it for posterity—and for tomorrow's newspapers. And then, both Damyanti and Kumar headed indoors for their first strategy meeting.

* * *

As Sukanya Sarkar said her goodbyes and prepared to leave, Asha Devi felt her jaw relax. She could finally wipe that false, ingratiating smile off her face. It had been with a supreme effort of will that Asha had kept it in place, refusing to rise to the many baits that Sukanya dangled before her.

It had been a bit of a strain, but all things considered, Asha wasn't entirely dissatisfied with the way the meeting had gone. In retrospect, getting Alok to attend had been a masterstroke. Every time things had got a little hairy, he had cracked out his Bengali. He and Sukanya had nattered away with Asha being none the wiser about what they were discussing. But as long as Sukanya was smiling, she didn't mind being left out of the conversation.

Initially, Sukanya had been unwilling to budge an inch on her demand to get Special Category status for her state. But, as Alok plied her with figures that proved even to Sukanya's satisfaction that more than ten other states had worse developmental statistics than Bengal, the PP leader had slowly softened. It took a good fifteen minutes of persuasion, large parts of it conducted in Bengali, before she agreed to concede the point.

Not entirely, of course, and not forever. She was Sukanya Sarkar, after all. But she was prepared to be mollified with Rs 1,000 crore grant towards emergency relief for the coastal areas affected by floods in her state. And Asha had to promise that they would revisit the subject of Special Category status once again in six months' time. Asha agreed with alacrity, and the meeting ended with some pleasantries to paper over the unpleasant moments that had gone before.

The second the door shut behind Sukanya, Asha heaved a rather theatrical sigh of relief and turned to Alok gratefully. 'Thank you so much for being here. I don't think I could have managed to placate her quite so completely on my own,' she said, holding out her right hand impulsively.

Alok reached out and clasped it between both of his. 'Happy to be of service,' he grinned, mock-bowing to her.

Suddenly, all that Asha was aware of was the feel of his palms, as they held her hand in their warm but dry embrace, for just a tad too long. She freed her hand with a gentle tug, aware that her tell-tale blush was telegraphing her embarrassment almost as if she had voiced it.

But Alok had the grace not to notice, as she gestured to him to sit down again.

Regaining her composure, Asha said lightly, 'She really does seem to genuinely like you. And you have no idea how rare that is. Sukanya Sarkar is one of the world's Great Haters.'

'I think you do her an injustice, Asha,' replied Alok, suddenly turning serious. 'I have seen this sort of thing time and time again. Women who are trying to make it in a man's world build this hard husk around their inner selves as a sort of defence mechanism. They try to project an image of being tough and unapproachable—of being a "hater", as you put it. But beneath this veneer there is often a softness lurking. And if you can get through to that, well, then you get a glimpse of the real woman. And you realize that she is not a hater at all.'

Asha was struck dumb. Not just by the fact that he seemed to have such great insight into the personality of Sukanya Sarkar. Or even that he had the empathy to understand how women had to overcompensate as they moved through what was a man's world. What really struck her was that Alok could just as well have been describing her.

Ever since she had entered politics in her own right, and more so after her photo scandal, Asha too had retreated behind a barrier of brittle reserve. And as Alok described how Sukanya had changed as she navigated a universe ruled by men, Asha couldn't help but feel that he had managed to look deep into her own psyche and see how she handled the world. And that left her feeling curiously exposed, even a little vulnerable.

She shook off the feeling with a nervous laugh. 'I know what you're thinking,' she said. 'You are thinking that this could describe me as well.'

'No,' responded Alok, far too quickly for it to be true. Then, he paused, and smiled, his eyes crinkling up at the corners. 'Okay, there may be an element of that. But you are still in the early stages. There is still hope for you.'

Asha bridled indignantly at that, and then gave in to the infectious laughter lurking in his eyes. The two of them were still giggling when there was a knock on the door and Nitesh Dholakia put his head through it, an apologetic expression on his face.

'Sorry to interrupt, Prime Minister, but there's something you should see,' he said, gesturing to the TV which was, for once, switched off.

Asha sobered up instantly and waved him in. Dholakia turned the TV on and switched to the AITNN feed, which was showing the joint press conference of Didi Damyanti and Satyajit Kumar. As they tuned in, one of the reporters was asking Damyanti how she, as a daughter to her own father, felt about Satyajit Kumar's slogan, *'Desh Bachao, Iss Beti Ko Hatao'*.

Despite herself, Asha sat up a little straighter in her chair. She wanted to hear Damyanti's answer to this question more than anyone else. How could a female political leader, a woman who had worked so hard to rise up in Indian politics, which was still very much a man's world, possibly approve of a sexist, misogynist slogan like the one Kumar had coined? Surely, Damyanti had to say that she disagreed with it, that there was no room for such sexism and misogyny in Indian politics.

Of course, Damyanti said nothing of the sort. Instead, she burst into laughter and then sneered about how there was no comparison between her and Asha at all. She was a beti who had made it on her own steam; Asha Devi was a beti who had inherited her position from her father.

Seeing her expression darken, Alok picked up the remote from the table and muted the sound on the TV. 'You don't need to pay any attention to this sort of thing, you know,' he said gently.

Asha shook her head. 'No, I do need to pay attention. I need to know what I am up against.' She turned the sound back on. It was more of the same really. *Vanshvaad ka vinash.* *Naamdar* vs *Kaamdar*. And then, Damyanti and Satyajit stood up, raised their linked arms for the benefit of the cameras and the feed cut back to the studio.

Manisha Patel was in the anchor's chair, scrolling through her phone, clearly caught unawares by the camera. Just the sight of her face was enough for a sudden surge of intense irritation to irradiate Asha's body. Was the bloody woman homeless? Did she actually live in a little room above the studio? How else could you explain the fact that whenever a story broke, there she was: Manisha Patel, sitting pretty behind her desk, swishing her highlighted hair from side to side as she ran down the events for the benefit of viewers across the country?

Asha paused her inner monologue to pay attention to what Manisha was saying. There were no surprises there. Like the rest of the media, she was convinced that this alliance between Damyanti and Satyajit would spell disaster for Asha. The way the electoral arithmetic worked in Bihar, once the Dalit Morcha and the SPP joined ranks, there was no path to victory for the LJP.

Seeing the look on Asha's face as she listened to the panel discussion that followed, Nitesh hurriedly changed channels and tuned into NTN. But Gaurav Agnihotri didn't provide much succor to Asha either today.

It was clear to Asha that the news cycle would now be dominated with stories about how the Prime Minister had been set up for a fall by the combined forces of Didi Damyanti and Satyajit Kumar. The entire media would be talking of nothing else but how Asha had been defeated roundly even before a single vote was cast. And the subtext would undoubtedly be that the new PM was too green and inexperienced to stitch together alliances of her own, and had been taken by surprise by the speed with which Kumar had got Damyanti on his side.

The news channels were already treating her like a loser. And these kinds of prophecies were usually self-fulfilling. Call someone a loser long enough and often enough on prime-time news, and sooner rather than later, the country would begin to believe that that person was, in fact, a loser.

Asha could not afford to let that narrative take hold. She had to do something to change it. And she had to do it fast. And just like that, her father's face hovered before her as she remembered the lines he had repeated so often to her. 'If you don't like what you're hearing on the news, Asha, give them something else to talk about. That is the secret of success in politics. Never forget that.'

Well, Asha had never forgotten. And now was the time to put that lesson to good use. She didn't like what she was hearing. So, it was time to give them something else to talk about. And she knew exactly how to do that.

Switching off the TV, she turned to Nitesh Dholakia. 'You know that interview we have scheduled with Gaurav Agnihotri . . .'

'Yes, Madam Prime Minister,' Nitesh interrupted, 'it has been scheduled for the day after tomorrow.'

'Well, I want to do it today,' said Asha briskly. 'Call Gaurav and tell him he needs to be here by 8 p.m. today. We will do the interview today. And we will do it live.'

Nitesh Dholakia turned pale. 'But ma'am, we have not prepped for this completely. You haven't been briefed on so many issues . . .'

'Did you not hear what I said, Nitesh?' asked Asha, an icy tone creeping in. 'I want to do the interview this evening. Please set it up.'

'But ma'am, the channel may not be ready . . .'

'Well, if they are not ready, you will just have to find another channel that is. I am doing this interview today. I don't really care which one of these media vultures does it.'

Nitesh shot a mute look of appeal to Alok Ray. But the finance minister just shrugged infinitesimally to indicate that he had no power—or perhaps no inclination—to change Asha's mind either.

So, Nitesh Dholakia shuffled off to carry out Asha's wishes, his demeanor very much resembling that of a man heading for the gallows. And gauging that Asha's anger was not going to dissipate any time soon, Alok Ray said his goodbyes and followed suit.

# 13

Gaurav Agnihotri was never happy leaving the security of his studio and heading out for a 'location' shoot. So, no matter how rich the industrialist, how famous the film star, or how powerful the politician, he always insisted that they come and sit at his desk in the studio if they wanted to be interviewed.

But when a call came from Madam Prime Minister's office, summoning him and his camera crew to the PMO for a shoot at a few hours' notice, Gaurav had no choice but to obey. It was either that—or forfeit the scoop of the year to the competition. If he didn't scramble to take this interview there would be plenty of others willing to shove him aside and take his spot.

And Manisha Patel would probably be leading the pack.

So, here he was, driving into South Block an hour in advance to make sure that the lighting and set up was perfect by the time Asha Devi arrived. The interview would begin at 8 p.m. sharp and would go out live through a link, and Gaurav knew that he could afford no errors. There was no do-over button as far as 'live' shows went. You only got one shot at it—and you had to make it count.

As he sat on his assigned chair with the hair and make-up people fussing around him, Gaurav felt a little glow of satisfaction. Manisha Patel would die a thousand deaths when she tuned into NTN tonight. After that first interview she had done with Asha in the aftermath of the naked pictures scandal, Manisha had come to believe that she had some sort of special bond with Asha, and that the Prime Minister would chose her over everyone else when it came to speaking to the media. Well, Manisha would soon find out how wrong she was.

Actually, thought Gaurav, there was a lesson for him there too. He could not afford to push Asha too hard. It was clear that the Prime Minister felt beholden to no one; that she believed she didn't owe anyone any favours. A woman like that could just as easily drop him as she had dropped Manisha. At the end of the day, Asha was her father's daughter: ruthless, merciless, and devoted only to herself. He would do well to remember that.

The only thing you could say in her favour was that she was rather easier on the eye, he thought, as Asha bustled into the room, at the head of a large entourage, led by Nitesh Dholakia.

As he rose quickly to his feet, Gaurav noticed that the Prime Minister was looking especially fierce. Unlike the pastel chiffons she usually favoured, Asha was resplendent in rustling silk today. Her sari was a blazing red with a navy border, accessorized with an outsized red bindi on her forehead, and strong red lipstick. It was almost as if she was channeling the Goddess Durga, with her sparkling, slightly slanted eyes accentuated with lashings of mascara, and her lustrous hair let loose in riotous curls half-way down to her waist.

This was a very different woman from the one who had addressed the nation after the surgical strike on terrorist camps across the border. On that occasion, Asha had been dressed down in a somber black sari with no discernable make-up, her hair pinned back in a demure bun, looking severe, almost grim. In contrast, the woman who appeared before him today virtually glowed with power and pride.

After a perfunctory greeting, Asha sat down on her chair, and allowed one of the women on the crew to mike her up, countering Gaurav's attempts to make small talk with monosyllabic answers that didn't encourage further conversation.

Flailing a bit, Gaurav fell back on his standard patter in these circumstances. 'Shall we quickly go through the questions, Madam Prime Minister?' he began.

Asha was quick to cut him off. 'Thank you but it's not necessary. Let's just keep it spontaneous, shall we? It always works much better that way.'

Despite himself, Gaurav was impressed. He hadn't met many politicians who were so cool about doing an interview on live TV; so relaxed that they didn't even want to know about the line of questioning. The only one he could think of who possessed a similar sangfroid was the Leader of the Opposition, Satyajit Kumar, himself.

The make-up lady bustled up to Asha with a powder puff at the ready. '*Thoda* shine *hai*,' she whispered to the Prime Minister. But Asha Devi was having none of that. Waving her away, she said to Gaurav, 'I'm ready to start if you are.'

Gaurav gestured to the producer that they were good to go. And the countdown began, 'Five, four, three, two, one, go . . .'

\* \* \*

Satyajit Kumar was so exhausted by the time he got back home that he refused to join the rest of the family for dinner and asked that a tray be sent to his room instead. His daughter was visiting, and in the normal course, he would have loved to spend the evening catching up with her. But tonight, she had brought her two young children along, and he really wasn't up to dealing with their roughhousing and constant demands for attention from Nana ji.

It had been a long day and as he changed out of his dhoti kurta into the loose pyjama-suit he wore at home, Kumar felt every one of his 66 years. The joint press conference to announce the alliance with the Dalit Morcha had gone off well enough, but the effort to pretend that he didn't mind playing second fiddle to Didi Damyanti had been a tremendous strain. But that was nothing compared to what had followed.

After the presser, he had joined Damyanti and senior members of both their parties for a strategy meeting to work out the details of their partnership. But as they discussed everything from ticket distribution to election strategy, and he came up against an obstreperous Damyanti again and again, Kumar began to get a bad feeling about his decision. That uneasiness only increased when the SPP's demands for dates for joint appearances by Kumar and Damyanti came up against the proverbial brick wall. As the discussions became more and more fractious, it rapidly became clear to Kumar that Damyanti had no intention of fighting this election as a team.

Their resources, she had announced grandly half-way through the proceedings, would be better utilized if their campaigns worked in distinct areas. The Dalit Morcha was strong in the northern and eastern parts of the state, so the SPP should not waste any resources there. In turn, the Dalit Morcha would steer clear of south and west Bihar where the SPP had its strongholds. As for holding joint rallies, or even putting on a joint road show, that made no sense at all. They should campaign individually; not only would they cover more ground, they could also better appeal to their own power bases.

By the time the meeting ended, Satyajit had begun to wonder if he had made a grievous error by brokering this alliance—and if Damyanti had any intention of transferring her vote to his party candidates, while she happily gobbled up SPP support on the ground. He knew that if his candidates lost while the Dalit Morcha candidates romped home, that would make his position weaker in any post-poll scenario. And that would be the unkindest cut given how much he had sacrificed to play to Damyanti's egotism and essential pettiness.

When a knock on his door signaled that dinner was here, Kumar decided to give up on his ruminations. It would do him good to flush his mind out and return to the problem afresh tomorrow. So, as he sat back in bed, desultorily dipping into the dinner laid out on the tray propped on his knees, he fumbled for the remote and switched on the television to catch up on the 8 p.m. news bulletin. It always cheered him up to watch himself on TV and his press conference was bound to be the lead story today.

It just so happened that the first news channel he came upon was NTN. And he nearly choked on his chicken soup as he saw that—far from featuring snippets of his press conference—the channel was broadcasting a live interview with the Prime Minister.

His irritation with Didi Damyanti now transformed into an unreasoning rage towards Asha Devi. This was supposed to be his day—or, at the very least, his hour. This was meant to be the time when his pithy rejoinders at the press conference would lead the news and kick off debates across TV news channels.

And that's exactly how things would have played out if it hadn't been for this nuisance of a woman. Madam Prime Minister had stolen his headlines yet again by the simple expedient of giving an interview. And sure enough, after this telecast was over, all the other channels would be tripping over themselves to conduct debates and discussion programmes based on what the PM said. So much for his hopes for dominating this news cycle!

But despite his exasperation, Kumar could not bear to turn to another channel that might be focusing on his press conference. Instead, he watched, transfixed, as Asha—glowing as if she was lit from within—changed the narrative yet again and ensured that tomorrow's newspapers headlines would be all about her.

In less than 12 hours, she had turned the saga of his alliance into stale news—and had, once again, transformed herself into the only story that mattered. And before he knew it, from amidst the annoyance, a smidgen of admiration came sneaking out to catch him unawares.

Asha Devi may be a rank novice in politics compared to him but she was proving herself to be a worthy opponent.

And there was nothing Satyajit Kumar loved more than a good fight.

\* \* \*

The NTN screen had been split into two on Gaurav Agnihotri's explicit instructions. He wanted one half of the split-screen to carry a close-up of Asha Devi as she answered his questions and the other half to carry a close-up of his own face so that every 'reaction shot' could be broadcast to the millions watching.

Mindful of the fact that he only had half an hour to get the most out of the Prime Minister, Gaurav eschewed his usual bombastic long opening and plunged straight into interview mode.

'Good evening, Prime Minister,' he began, 'though this can't be a very good evening for you. Your two rivals, the SPP and the Dalit Morcha, have announced a pre-poll alliance for the Bihar election. And your party's loss seems pretty much guaranteed.'

Asha smiled broadly, almost as if she was genuinely amused by the question. 'Good evening to you too. And don't worry, Gaurav ji, it is a good evening for me as well. You see, unlike you, I know that electoral politics is not a question of arithmetic. It is a question of chemistry. When it comes to elections, two and two don't make four. They often add up to minus two . . .'

'Minus two? How is that even possible?' Gaurav interrupted.

'It's quite simple, really. All these calculations you media people keep doing, taking the vote blocks of two parties and adding them up? They make zero sense. People who have always voted for Party A won't turn over their vote to Party B just because two political leaders sitting in Delhi have decided to enter into an alliance. The people of this country don't like their votes being taken for granted. And the SPP and the Dalit Morcha will find this out the hard way.'

'You may well be right about that,' Gaurav conceded. 'But why would they vote for the LJP? What does your party have to offer them? The LJP has been in power in Bihar for the last five years and the state's economy is in tatters. The law and order situation has been deteriorating year after year. Why would anyone give your party another five years?'

Asha had been shaking her head throughout this tirade. 'I'm sorry Gaurav ji, but that is complete nonsense. You are entitled to your opinion but not to your own facts . . .'

As Asha began reeling off facts and figures to prove that Bihar's prospects had improved considerably over the last five years, Gaurav began to panic a bit. He didn't want to keep interrupting the PM but he only had 24 minutes left and far more ground to cover.

'Well, Madam Prime Minister,' he cut in as Asha paused to take a breath, 'let's leave Bihar aside for the moment and concentrate on the state of the country. There is an atmosphere of fear and insecurity all over India ever since the Kautilya terror attack happened. And people believe that you let down the country by releasing so many dreaded terrorists in exchange for your sister-in-law . . .'

'In exchange for my sister-in-law?' echoed Asha in outraged tones. 'In exchange for my sister-in-law?' she repeated, speaking even louder. 'That is an outrageous allegation. There were more than 200 women in the mall whose lives I saved that day. Yes, one of them happened to be my sister-in-law. But that's not why I made the decision I did. And believe me, there is not a single politician in India who would have made a different decision had he or she been in my position.'

'I think, Prime Minister,' said Gaurav, 'what people are most upset about is that there has been no progress in the investigation into the attack since then. We had the botched raid in Jamia Nagar and since then, nothing . . .'

'That's where you are wrong,' Asha interrupted. 'There has been major progress in the investigation since then. In fact, that is one reason I decided to talk to you—and to the nation—this evening.'

Asha paused at this moment to look straight into camera, not even willing to give Gaurav the dignity of eye contact any longer. It was clear that she was done with speaking to Gaurav Agnihotri. She was now talking directly to the people of India.

And for once, she had good news for them. There had been an important breakthrough in the investigation into the Kautilya attack. The Army had been conducting raids on suspected militant hideouts based on intelligence the IB and NIA had gathered over the last few weeks. The raid on one such location had led them to the masterminds behind the Kautilya Mall attack. Forensic and DNA evidence had proved, beyond a shadow of a doubt, that the top leadership of the JEA was behind the attack. Most of the men thus identified had already been taken into custody and were being interrogated.

As Asha spoke on, Gaurav tried hard to control the elation that was threatening to overwhelm him. He hadn't just scored an exclusive interview with the Prime Minister. He had also been handed the newsbreak to beat all newsbreaks. He was sure that the PM's revelations would be the lead story on all TV channels. And the newspapers would have no choice but to feature his interview on the front pages.

It was with an intense effort of will that Gaurav brought himself back to earth from cloud nine and composed his next question. 'You say that you have the masterminds of the Kautilya attack in custody. Fair enough. But we all know that these terrorist attacks are actually masterminded by the ISI across the border. You may take a few JEA operatives in custody, but how exactly will you prevent Pakistan from launching another such attack?'

'You know as well as I do, Gaurav ji, that I cannot discuss matters pertaining to our national security on television. These decisions are taken behind closed doors—and that's where they will remain. But surely, like the rest of the world, you must have seen how we carried out a surgical strike a few weeks ago and took out terror camps in the POK area. And you can rest assured that we will not allow them to reopen for business ever again.'

Gaurav stole a quick look at the sheet containing his list of questions. He only had a few minutes left so he could only really pose one more. He came to a quick decision. It had to be the one about Sagar Prajapati and Madan Mohan.

'Madam Prime Minister,' he began solemnly, 'I know that this is a sensitive matter for you given that it concerns your father. But I have to ask, because the entire nation wants to know, what is the progress on the investigation into his assassination? And how badly have those investigations been hurt by the custodial death of Madan Mohan Prajapati's nephew, Sagar Prajapati?'

Asha's jaw tightened slightly as she listened to the question. But it was with a completely neutral expression that she replied. 'As you know, Sagar Prajapati was in custody because of his involvement in the L'Oiseau arms scandal. He was not involved in the assassination of my father in any way . . .'

'Yes, I know that,' Gaurav interrupted, 'but surely he would have had some information as to Madan Mohan Prajapati's whereabouts? The uncle and nephew were as thick as thieves, quite literally in their case . . .'

'I'm sorry, but I can't really discuss ongoing cases,' Asha cut in. 'But yes, it is a matter of concern that a crucial prisoner like Sagar, who had much information to impart, was killed in the manner that he was. But I can assure you that we are investigating the matter thoroughly; there will be no cover-up on my watch.'

Gaurav looked up from his notes and inadvertently made eye contact with Nitesh Dholakia, who was standing directly in his line of vision, gesturing frantically that his time was up. He nodded in acknowledgement and turned to camera to wrap up.

As the cameras cut out, Asha was quick to remove the lapel microphone from her sari blouse and hand it to a production assistant. As she stood up to leave, Gaurav sprang up from his chair, still miked, and held out his hand. Asha reluctantly took hold of it as he made his effusive thanks.

But if he had any illusions that the Prime Minister would stay back to make a little chit-chat with him, that he could use this post-interview time to bond with her, he was in for a disappointment. Dropping his hand as if it had scalded her, Asha chose instead to make a quick tour of the room, thanking every member of the crew.

As he watched her work the room, Gaurav suddenly understood the charm of Asha Devi. When she wanted to mesmerize you, she had no problem doing exactly that. That much was clear. But what was even clearer was that she had no intention of wasting her charms on Gaurav Agnihotri. He had just been a conduit to get her message out. He had served his purpose and Asha was now done with him.

Gaurav should have felt insulted. But he was so delighted by the scoop he had been handed, that he found it hard to even take offence.

* * *

The one person who was not taken by surprise when Gaurav's exclusive with Asha Devi aired was Manisha Patel. Her sources in PMO had tipped her off that Asha Devi had decided to prepone the interview with the intention of stealing Damyanti and Satyajit Kumar's headlines. And that Gaurav's 'exclusive' would be on at 8 p.m. that night.

Even through the haze of anger that overwhelmed her every time she thought about how Asha had thrown her over for Gaurav, Manisha couldn't help but marvel at the chutzpah displayed by the Prime Minister. No matter what life threw at her, the woman just picked herself off the floor and soldiered on. Whatever else you felt about her, you had to give Asha Devi full marks for resilience.

As she sat in her tiny, untidy office, watching the interview unfold, trying not to let her jealousy of Gaurav obscure her judgement, Manisha's admiration for the Prime Minister grew with every soundbite. Asha batted away every question with skilled elegance, and she never lost sight of why she had granted the interview in the first place: to change the narrative. Brushing aside Bihar and the small matter of the SPP–Dalit Morcha alliance, Asha built up quickly to her revelations about the Kautilya attack investigation.

And with that, she had succeeded in giving the media enough fodder to keep it chewing contentedly for weeks to come. Manisha had no doubt that from now on the Damyanti–Satyajit alliance would be treated as stale news while everyone concentrated on the news points that had emerged from the PM's interview.

But Manisha would not be among that number. Even before Gaurav had signed off, Manisha had come to that decision. She was only going to mention the Prime Minister's revelations at the top of the hour as part of the headlines. And after that, she was going to run with the show she had planned this morning, discussing if Satyajit Kumar had been played by Didi Damyanti. There would be pushback from the channel for sure, but she was determined to do this. She saw no reason why she should amplify Gaurav's newsbreak for him; the rest of media would be doing a super job of that anyway.

She had five clear minutes before she headed to the studio to do the 9 p.m. show. On a sudden impulse, Manisha picked up her mobile and dialed Sukanya. She was fully prepared to leave a message for the Poriborton Party leader, asking her what she had thought about Asha's interview. But, much to her surprise, Sukanya actually took her call. '*Kemon achho, Sukanya di,*' asked Manisha, slipping into Bengali, 'Did you just see Asha Devi's interview?'

That was all it took for Sukanya Sarkar to have a little explosion on the phone. She shouted so loudly that Manisha actually had to hold the phone away from her ear as she tried to make sense of the chief minister's fulminations. Clearly, Asha had not briefed Sukanya about the breakthrough in the Kautilya terror attack investigation before going on national television to break the news to every Indian. Sukanya was outraged at not being kept in the loop, and she made no bones about her upset.

Manisha was torn between letting Sukanya rage on in the hope that she would let slip something that she could use in her reportage, and getting her to hang up so that she could make it to the studio on time. She could see her executive producer behind the glass door, looking anxious and pointing repeatedly at her watch. Manisha mouthed a heartfelt 'sorry' to the hapless woman, even as she made soothing noises to Sukanya on the phone.

When the chief minister finally stopped for breath, Manisha said quickly, 'Sukanya di, I have to be in the studio in the next 60 seconds, can we talk on the phone after my show?'

'No,' said Sukanya, 'I don't want to talk on the phone. You come to Kolkata tomorrow. I will talk to you then. And let me tell you, my interview will be much better than Asha Devi's.'

Manisha, who knew from first-hand experience how good the Poriboton Party leader was at creating controversy, had no doubt about that. There was an extra spring in her step as she made the short hop to her studio.

Gaurav may have won this skirmish. But the war was far from over.

# 14

Asha Devi settled into her seat with an audible sigh of relief. Thankfully, for once, there was no one around to hear her—or speak to her, for that matter. The Prime Minister's cabin on Air India One was about as private as it was possible for her to get these days.

As the plane accelerated and took off, Asha looked down on the foggy capital that she was leaving behind. Visibility was so low that it was impossible to glean even the outlines of buildings. It was as if Delhi was dissolving before her eyes as the plane gained altitude. And after the week she had had, that came as something of a relief. It would be a pleasure to leave all of this behind and spend a few days in snow-clad Davos, being wined and dined by the international community that had, once again, begun projecting India as the Next Big Thing.

Asha needed that salve on the wounds inflicted upon her by her coalition partner, Sukanya Sarkar. Memories of the interview that Sarkar had given to Manisha Patel last week surfaced afresh, hard as she tried to push them away. And Asha's mood darkened as Sukanya's veiled barbs came back to haunt her as the seat belt sign was switched off. By now, she had stewed over them so long, she knew the 'greatest hits' by heart.

'The Prime Minister is so young, we have to make allowances for her'; 'Asha Devi is new to the job, we must give her enough time to settle in'; 'Yes, yes, there are issues, there are always issues; but I am sure the PM will learn from her mistakes.'

Behind these seemingly well-meaning statements lurked the truth that Asha could no longer afford to ignore. Sukanya Sarkar may be a coalition partner but she was no ally. The only loyalty she possessed was to herself. And given her track record in politics, it was only a matter of time before she turned on Asha as well.

If she needed any confirmation of what she felt in her guts, Asha only had to read the newspaper analysis pieces or watch prime-time TV news. Everyone was acting as if Sukanya had already called time on her coalition with Asha. 'Fresh fractures surface in Asha–Sukanya relationship', 'Sukanya Sarkar is not happy with Asha Devi—and she doesn't care who knows it', were some of the less lurid headlines that had followed that interview. And if you listened to some of the more sensational TV channels, you might well believe that the LJP–PP coalition was going to collapse in a matter of days.

Asha didn't take such a pessimistic view of the situation. She was sure that Sukanya would not pull the plug any time soon. But while she was safe in the short term, in the medium term anything was possible— and that included Sukanya exiting the government in high dudgeon exasperated by some slight or insult, real or imagined.

If that happened—or more realistically, when that happened—where could Asha turn to for the numbers to shore up her minority government? Her only other option, the Dalit Morcha's Didi Damyanti, had already signed up to partner the SPP in the Bihar election. So, that door was closed to her.

If Sukanya decided to pull the plug in one of her more impetuous moments, Asha's government would be a goner. There was no doubt about that. And then, the country would be plunged into fresh turmoil as the assorted parties in a hung Parliament tried to cobble together some sort of majority.

If that did happen, the chances of the LJP and Asha coming back to power were next to nil. And if she were ousted as the Prime Minister, what would happen to the investigation into her father's assassination case? Would the next government pursue it with the same zeal? Or would it be put on the proverbial backburner? And would Madan Mohan Prajapati ever be brought to justice?

Asha's chain of thought was interrupted by a knock on the door of her cabin. It was Nitesh Dholakia with a pile of files in his arms. She may have left Delhi, but Delhi wasn't ready to leave her just yet.

Asha sighed again—this time only inwardly—and prepared to settle down to do some work. Maybe if she finished all this stuff on the plane, she would get to enjoy some downtime in Davos. God knows that she needed that, after the scorching pace of the past few months.

* * *

Back in first class, Alok Ray had put his noise-cancelling headphones on and was feigning sleep. Anything to escape being bored to death by External Affairs Minister Aroop Mitra, who seemed to have a special fondness for bending his ear with interminably tedious stories referencing their shared Bengali heritage. There was a limit to how many times you could listen to the same conspiracy theories about the death of Netaji Subhash Chandra Bose before your eyes glazed over.

When he heard soft snores emanating from Mitra's seat, Alok mustered up the courage to open his eyes and begin reading the book he had packed for the flight. But for some reason, no matter how hard he tried to concentrate, the words kept swimming in front of his eyes and his attention kept wandering to the cabin in which Asha was ensconced in solitary splendor.

After struggling with himself for a few weeks, Alok had finally come to terms with his feelings towards her. It had started off as a protective urge towards a young woman who seemed both fragile and vulnerable behind the stiff exterior she presented to the world. It had turned into admiration for a leader who often seemed palpably out of her depth but never let that deter her from powering on. It was a burgeoning affection that had propelled him to offer help with the investigation into her father's death by hiring Dark Matters.

And now, he had to admit to himself, it was love he felt every time he looked at her.

Alok hadn't seen this coming. After an acrimonious divorce had left him feeling like he'd gone ten rounds in a wrestling ring, he'd told himself that he was done with love. Sex was fine, he didn't intend to give up on that. But love was for losers. And he had been sure he would find enough women who were happy with just that—a loose, no-strings relationship that was based on lust rather than love.

He had even had a few candidates lined up, thanks to introductions affected by his old friends when Asha had arrived in his life, throwing all those calculations to the wind. He had tried hard to resist, even though his heart had melted every time their eyes met across the room. He had tried not to notice how her eyes crinkled when she smiled at him, her dimples creating deep crescents in her cheeks. He had done his best to ignore the quickening of his pulse every time she held his hand to bid him hello or goodbye.

Most of all, he had tried to put out of his mind the images of her naked body, which he had seen along with the rest of the world, when her private pictures were leaked. It seemed like an intrusion of the worst kind, to strip her bare without her consent, without even her knowledge so to speak. And yet, there was no denying his baser instincts. Even though he told his conscious mind to desist, his subconscious-self had no such inhibitions.

In an attempt to clamp down on his feelings, Alok had gone on a handful of dates with beautiful, pliant, eager-to-please women who had made it clear that they would not be averse to sharing his bed at the end of the evening. But every single time he had tried to summon up some sexual energy in these situations, the only thing he could see was Asha's smiling face as she looked up at him through those absurdly long eyelashes. And just like that, every other woman suddenly looked plain and insipid by comparison.

Alok prided himself on being a realist. He knew that there was zero chance that he would ever get together with Asha. For one thing, she had shown no romantic interest in him. She was grateful for his help, both in Cabinet and when it came to investigating Madan Mohan, and seemed to have some sort of easy affection for him. They had also bonded over their common experience of losing a parent to an untimely death. But she had never offered him anything more than friendship. And he couldn't presume that that would ever change.

At a rational level, Alok was okay with that. Not only was she more than a decade younger than him, there was also the fact that Asha was his boss. And having been tempered by American corporate culture, Alok was programmed to keep his love life and professional life in watertight compartments. So, he was prepared to keep his feelings to himself, telling himself time and again that they were completely inappropriate. It was just that every time he looked at Asha, he could feel his insides twist with the depth of his love for her.

So lost was he in his reverie that Alok almost jumped out of his seat when Nitesh Dholakia tapped him gently on the shoulder and gestured that he should step into the Prime Minister's cabin. Asha needed a word in private.

Even though Alok knew that this was only because Asha wanted to be briefed on the Dark Matters investigation, his pulse still quickened at the prospect of being alone with her. But his emotions were not visible on the bland visage he presented as he entered the Prime Minister's cabin.

He was startled to see that Asha had changed out of the sari in which she had boarded the plane and was now wearing a pair of black leggings with a short white T-shirt. His surprise must have reflected on his face because Asha laughed easily as she rose from her seat behind her desk to sit down on the adjoining sofa. 'Do I look an absolute fright?' she asked. 'I'm sorry, but this is my go-to outfit for long flights. I promise I will change before we disembark. Mustn't frighten the children!'

'Not at all. You look great!' responded Alok quickly. And then, scared that he had come too close to making a comment on his boss's appearance, quickly added, 'That's the best way to deal with long flights. I wish I had brought along a change as well.'

And then, tearing his eyes away from the distracting sight of Asha's thighs, clad in skintight lycra, he settled down to bring her up to speed on the Dark Matters investigation.

They had ruled out one of the sites shortlisted as a possible Madan Mohan refuge. The ownership of the hilltop villa in Chile, nestled amidst the peaks of the central Andes, had been traced to a Nigerian industrialist on the run from the authorities in his country. Now their efforts were concentrated on the estate in Manaus, in the middle of the Amazon rainforest, where a mysterious entity had taken over the property recently.

The Dark Matters team had managed to get one of its operatives hired as part of the security team, but the man in question had yet to lay eyes on his principal, who stayed behind closed doors at all times, served only by a small group of trusted people. But chatter among the rest of the staff indicated that the owner of the property was an Indian billionaire. So, the probability that this was Madan Mohan Prajapati himself was strong.

'When will we know for certain?' asked Asha, trying to temper her innate optimism.

'I think we will get a visual confirmation in a week at the latest. And in that time, we will try and trace the payment trail to see if it tracks back to Madan Mohan . . .'

'Will that be evidence enough to get him extradited, you think?' asked Asha.

Alok paused. Then, he shook his head. 'I don't think the extradition route will work in this case. The systems in these South American countries are notoriously corrupt. The moment you put in a request, someone will tip him off. And even before you can get your legal team ready, Madan Mohan will vanish, never to be found again.'

'So, what do you suggest we do?' asked Asha.

'Leave it to Dark Matters,' said Alok. 'They have the expertise in such matters. They will find a way of flying him to a friendly country in Europe or even the Middle-East. And we can bring him in from there.'

As she took this in, Asha felt herself getting a bit teary. After so many months, it looked as if the end was in sight.

Madan Mohan Prajapati had finally been hunted down. Even though there was no real confirmation as yet, Asha felt in her bones that they had come to the end of the road—and that it was now only a matter of time before the man behind her father's death could be brought to justice.

As Alok suddenly broke off and stared at her intently, Asha realized that a solitary tear was making its forlorn way down her cheek. She quickly brushed it off and offered up a smile instead. 'I'm sorry,' she said, 'I didn't mean to cry . . .'

'Don't apologize, Asha,' said Alok, reaching across the length of the sofa to take her hand in his. 'This is an intensely personal issue for you. And you shouldn't have to apologize for being emotional.'

Powered by a sudden impulse, Asha leaned across and kissed Alok quickly on the cheek. 'I can't thank you enough,' she said, unsteadily. 'You have been such a good friend to me. I can't imagine what I would have done without you.'

Alok shook his head mutely, to indicate that it was nothing, momentarily struck dumb by the feelings unleashed in him by the touch of Asha's lips on his cheeks. His whole body felt as if it was on fire and it took all his self-control not to take the woman seated beside him into his arms and kiss her senseless.

But better sense arrived in the shape of Nitesh Dholakia, who burst into the room after a perfunctory knock. Alok hastily dropped Asha's hand, both of them colouring at the realization that Dholakia may have caught them in an intimate moment.

But dedicated civil servant that he was, Dholakia's attention was fully focused on the fresh batch of files he was carrying. Grateful for the respite, Alok quickly got to his feet, said his goodbyes and hurried back to the safety of his seat.

* * *

The blast of freezing air that greeted her the moment she stepped off the plane left Asha reeling.

It wasn't the cold that sent a shiver through her, though; it was the memories it evoked. Just a whiff of that fresh alpine air was enough to transport her back to the skiing holidays she had taken with her father. As she walked down the staircase to meet the party assembled to greet her, her mind flashed back to the first time Baba had taken her on the slopes, looking on with watchful pride as the instructor put her through her paces. She could not have been older than ten, but the moment when she went swishing down the slope of her own volition was as clear in her mind's eye as if it had happened yesterday.

Asha didn't have a lot of time to dwell on this as she shook hands and exchanged pleasantries with the Indian diplomats who were arrayed on the tarmac to greet her. As the wind picked up, she pulled her fur coat closer around her and thanked her stars that there were no photographers around to record her arrival. Thanks to Narendra Modi, who had started the trend, no Indian Prime Minister now travelled with a press pack on his or her plane. So, there was no one to take a picture that would set off a controversy about her use of fur.

Honestly, though, what else could you wear in cold like this? Wool and cashmere simply didn't cut it. Asha hurried down the rest of the receiving line, and headed for the limos that were waiting to transport the Indian delegation to their hotel. The moment her car drove off, she shrugged off the fur coat to luxuriate in the warmth of the car's interior, and fished her phone out of her bag.

But as the majestic views whizzing past her window caught her attention, she tucked it back inside and gave herself permission to window-gaze. There was nothing quite like Switzerland, she thought, to make you appreciate the beauty of nature. Today, the landscape was a study in white with twelve inches of snow having fallen overnight, with the bare trees that lined the route providing the only splash of colour—even if that colour was a leaden grey.

Asha's mind flashed back to her first memory of a snowy scene like this one. She had been on her first trip to Gstaad with her parents, and her childhood-self had been so excited by the sight of snow that she had run on to the hotel lawn the moment they arrived to make her first snowman. Her father had followed her outside, while her mother unpacked, and stuck a carrot on the snowman's face to give him a nose, placed two plums where his eyes should have been, and used a bright-red apple to give him a mouth. For some reason, this had struck Asha as hysterically funny, and both father and daughter had collapsed laughing, rolling around in the snow.

She and Baba had always had the same sense of humour, laughing at the silliest of things, while Amma looked on uncomprehendingly. The only person with whom she had shared the same kinds of laughs, since her father died, was Alok Ray. Not only did he have the same dry wit that her father had possessed in spades, he was also amused by silliness. Often in Cabinet meetings, she had to take care not to meet his eye when something like this occurred for fear that he would set her off.

Asha wondered what her father had really thought of Alok. Birendra Pratap had chosen him as RBI Governor on purely professional grounds, she knew, but had the two men grown to like one another? Did her father approve of Alok? Or, more accurately, would he approve of her growing closeness to him? Or would he judge her for developing personal feelings for a man who wasn't just a professional colleague but someone who reported to her?

Asha could no longer deny that what she felt for Alok went beyond a platonic friendship, though she had sworn to herself that she would not act on these emotions. But when he had broken the news that they were finally closing in on Madan Mohan Prajapati, she had momentarily lost control and had reached out impulsively to kiss him.

As kisses went, it had been a rather chaste affair. But the feelings that it had evoked in her were anything but chaste. And looking at Alok's face, she had been sure that he had felt the same rush of heat that she did.

Just as well, then, that Nitesh Dholakia had interrupted them when he did. She didn't know how things would have ended if he hadn't walked in right then. And the absolute last thing she needed was a messy personal involvement with a man who worked for her. Or, if she was being brutally honest, with any man at all.

The way her last relationship had ended had left Asha scarred for life. Even though she shrank from acknowledging it, even to herself, what Sunny Mahtani had subjected her to during that cataclysmic afternoon—when they were attending a British society wedding no less—was nothing short of rape. And that trauma was never very far from the surface no matter how hard Asha tried to bury it in the recesses of her mind.

And then had come the final blow that had nearly destroyed both her personal and professional life in the run up to the General Election: the release of the nude pictures that she had happily posed for while in a relationship with Sunny. Even though the release of the pictures had been traced back to then SPP leader, Jayesh Sharma, Asha knew with certainty—even in the absence of any proof—that the pictures had been provided by Sunny himself.

Months later, Asha was still trying to wrap her mind around the fact that the man who had professed to love her could turn on her in this vicious manner. And if Sunny, who had promised to cherish and protect her all his life, could do this to her, what was the guarantee that the next man she fell in love with would be any better?

Alok Ray may well be a decent and kind man. Frankly, on the basis of how he had behaved with her, she had no reason to doubt that. But even so, Asha was determined not to act on the attraction that she felt for him. Her life had nearly imploded the last time she indulged her passions; there was no way she was making that mistake again.

And yet, as the Indian delegation was greeted by the general manager of the hotel in the lobby, and she found herself in close proximity with Alok again, Asha felt that familiar tug in her heart. In another life, she may well have given in to it. But as Madam Prime Minister, here to represent her country at an international conference, there was no way she could act on, let alone acknowledge, these desires.

Knowing that if she looked at him, she would be lost, Asha restricted herself to nodding a curt dismissal to the rest of her delegation, and headed straight up to her suite. But even though she hadn't laid eyes on him, she was acutely aware of the hurt expression lurking on Alok's face.

Well, she told herself sternly, as she readied a bubble bath to soak in, he would get over it. Better to hurt him a little now than wallow in a world of pain herself later on.

If life had taught her anything in the last year, it was to put herself first. And Asha wasn't going to forget that lesson in a hurry.

# 15

By the time Asha had bathed and dressed for her first meeting of the day, she had her emotions under control. So, she was able to greet Alok with a cool smile when he entered the conference room attached to the presidential suite in which she was housed, gesturing him to take the seat at her right hand. He nodded back affably, and then turned his attention to the stack of briefing notes that had been placed before him.

There was no time for private chatter anyway. The rest of the Indian delegation followed him in and there was some milling around before everyone found their places in accordance with the pecking order that all bureaucrats carried around in their head. In a couple of minutes, they were joined by the American trade delegation that had been petitioning to meet the Indian Prime Minister for weeks now.

As the head of the American party began making his pitch to the Prime Minister, Asha didn't even bother to listen closely. She and Alok had already decided that he was going to do all the talking in this meeting. This was not her area of expertise, and she was only too willing to defer to the finance minister, for whom the world of finance, tariffs, taxes and trade-offs was a natural habitat.

As the discussion grew more and more technical, Asha found herself struggling to keep up. After about ten minutes, she decided to give up and instead admire the skill that Alok brought to the negotiating table. Ray was by turns charming, persuasive, tough, implacable, and even intractable at times. And it was solely down to his skill that the meeting ended with the American side making far more substantial concessions than she had thought possible.

Asha would have liked to congratulate Alok on his performance. But there was scarce chance for that as one meeting spilled into another. The good thing about how quickly the day went was that Asha soon lost her initial awkwardness around Alok. By the time the last meeting was over, she was back on the same easy terms with him. And the relief she felt at this was reflected in his eyes as well, even though neither of them—both acutely aware of the many ears that surrounded them—actually said a word to each other.

Then it was time for Dholakia to usher the Indian delegation out of the suite, and Asha sank down on the living room sofa to savour a rare moment of solitude. But a quick look at her watch sent her scrambling to the bedroom. She had just 15 minutes to change and get ready for the dinner party she was scheduled to attend that night.

Hosted by Behram Adamji, an old-style Indian billionaire, this was the soiree that always kicked off the Davos Economic Summit as far as the Indian business and political elite were concerned. Every single Indian industrialist of any consequence would be in that room tonight. So, this was the perfect opportunity for her to make friends and influence people—and lay the grounds for them to donate generously to the party. The Bihar Assembly election was around the corner and LJP funds were running low after the huge spends the party had had to incur in the General Election. She needed all those men—and the odd woman—in the room to refill those coffers, so she had to be at her charming best that evening.

Asha quickly brushed her teeth and washed her face before settling down in front of the three-way mirror to do her make-up. Her face looked pale and pinched to her, so she applied blush with a rather more liberal stroke than she was used to. Her hands reached out, almost automatically, for the pale pink lipstick she usually wore. But no, she thought, that would look wrong with that dramatic stroke of blush. Tonight, she needed a bright shade, to complete the power-dressing mode she had embarked on.

Her saris had been steamed by her personal staff and hung up in her closet. Asha ran her hands over all of them. In the end, it came down to two—the red-cream-and-yellow Patola that her mother had lent her or the black-white-and-maroon ikat that had been a present from her father. In the end, Asha decided to go with the ikat; it was the spirit of her father she wanted to channel that evening.

She gave herself a final critical look in the mirror. The sari looked magnificent, making her pale arms and neck stand out in relief. Her smoky eyes loomed dramatically in her face, competing for attention with her blood-red lips. Suddenly, the chignon in which she had spent the day seemed boring and staid. Asha dismantled it swiftly and brushed her hair out, letting it fall in soft waves down her back.

There was something missing in the picture in the mirror, she thought. Ah yes, the bindi. She riffled through her make-up case until she came upon a packet of dark maroon ones. As she stuck one on her forehead, the doorbell went. Nitesh Dholakia was back, ready to escort her down to the dinner party.

It was show time. And with her game face on, Asha felt more than ready for it.

* * *

A few streets across, in much more humble accommodation, Manisha Patel was getting dressed for the same party, with much less success. For one thing, she had never thought that she would score an invite so she hadn't packed any outfits that made the cut. But just hours earlier, she had interviewed Behram Adamji for her nightly special report from Davos, and he had been so pleased with the way it went that he had extended an invitation to her on the spot. She had accepted with alacrity, even though part of her was already riffling despairingly through her wardrobe.

Now, as she dismally viewed the contents of her closet— one black puffa jacket, one camel overcoat, three white shirts, one pair of black trousers, and her one trusty dress in poppy red with black polka dots—she felt something close to despair. She had finally been invited to the ball; only to discover that she had nothing to wear.

Suddenly, her mind flashed back to those Hollywood movies in which the hero swept the heroine—who also had nothing to wear—down to the hotel gift shop to buy her the perfect dress. Manisha smiled cynically to herself. There was no hero in her life who could make that possible. And her own middle-class soul rebelled at the thought of spending thousands of euros on a dress, no matter how beautiful and becoming.

There was nothing else for it. Her trusty polka-dot number would have to do. She would tart it up with opaque black tights and her black pashmina. And anyway, she scolded herself, she shouldn't agonize about her outfit. The odds were that no one would notice what she wore anyway. She was bound to pale into insignificance against all the Indian socialites who would be out in full force, decked out in the best that Sabyasachi, Manish Malhotra, Abu-Sandeep and Tarun Tahiliani could produce.

But even so, Manisha took extra care blow-drying her hair, so that it fell fetchingly around her face. She put on a second lashing of mascara for good measure. And as she pulled on her high-heeled black boots, she rehearsed what she would say to Asha Devi, if she was lucky enough to get within speaking distance of her.

Relations between the two of them had deteriorated dramatically since Asha Devi became Prime Minister. The rapport that had flowered between them after Manisha did a sympathetic interview of Asha after her naked photos leaked had withered and died with the critical reportage Manisha had produced in the aftermath of the terror strike at Kautilya Mall. And post the Jamia disaster, when Manisha had torn into the government every night on prime-time TV, relations had hit rock bottom, with the PM refusing to even take her phone calls. Manisha had also been thrown off the list of select editors and anchors who were allowed an off-the-record briefing with Asha every week.

The final blow had come when Asha had given her first interview as Prime Minister—long promised to Manisha—to Gaurav Agnihotri. Manisha had been incensed to begin with, and had plotted revenge for many days before good sense finally dawned. There was no winning a war against the Prime Minister of the country. At the end of the day, power vested with the PM, who could cut off access whenever she wanted. And if Manisha wanted her access to be restored, she would have to grovel and make things right with Asha Devi once again.

Manisha was convinced that if she got close to Asha tonight and made her contrition clear, she would be able to rekindle the fondness that had prevailed between them in better times. The question was: would she be allowed to get within a few feet of the PM?

Manisha had never been to Adamji's Davos bash before, so she didn't know how it worked. But she had been to enough A-list parties like this one to know that there was no guarantee of getting within sniffing distance of the main players. There was always a VVIP room within the VIP room and then there was an area set aside with a velvet rope that was meant exclusively for the VVVIPs who couldn't be expected to mingle with the less rich and far less famous.

If Adamji's party followed this pattern then there was little to no chance that she would get to see Asha, leave alone meet her.

But at the very least, she would get to glad-hand the major industrialists of the country and spend time building contacts in the business world. If she ever decided to start her own channel—and she most definitely did—then she needed one or more of these moneybags to back her. So, this would be the ideal opportunity to lobby them.

Even if that didn't work out, she told herself, she could just let down her hair and enjoy the party. Adamji had a reputation as the host with the most, so the champagne would be excellent and the food to die for.

And sometimes that was quite enough to make an evening bearable.

* * *

The room hushed into silence and all heads turned to look at Asha Devi as she entered the Grand Ballroom of the hotel.

By now, Asha was used to being something of a conversation-stopper, so the smile on her face did not falter. But she did feel a flutter of trepidation as her eyes searched, in vain, for an unfamiliar face. Everybody who was anybody in India was gathered in this glittering room in Davos. And every single face wore an ingratiating smile, as their eyes settled on her, the Prime Minister of India.

It was in that moment that it dawned on Asha that she had got it all wrong. She didn't need to work the room and she certainly did not need to turn on the charm. These people in this room, they would do anything to please her; and giving money to her party was the very least of it. No matter how rich and famous and influential they might be, the real power in this room resided in her person. And she did not need to ask, let alone beg or cajole; she could command, and whatever she wanted would be given to her.

Behram Adamji had come rushing up to greet the Prime Minister. Asha, who had known him since she was a child, greeted him with an affectionate kiss on the cheek. Adamji flushed pink as this mark of favour was bestowed upon him in a room full of his peers and rivals. He then took Asha by the arm to escort her around the room and introduce her to his guests, gesturing to Nitesh Dholakia to fall back. Dholakia, who was used to the rich and the powerful showing him his place, was content to do just that. Asha Devi was more than capable of taking care of herself in a situation like this, and he could do with a respite—and a glass of champagne—as well.

Alok Ray, watching this pantomime from one corner of the room, where he had been pinned down by two industrialists who wanted their bad loans written off, was a little put out by the proprietorial manner with which Adamji was showing off his prize guest. He sneaked the odd look at Asha, and when it looked as if she was happy to play along, he relaxed slightly and turned his attention back to his interlocutors.

Asha, for once, was actually enjoying herself. Everyone she met was full of compliments about how well she was handling her new job. Some expressed admiration for the air strike on Pakistan. Others expressed gratitude for the stimulus package she had announced a week ago. And everyone mentioned how good she was looking, given that she had got off a long flight and gone straight to work.

Her defences were, therefore, completely down, as she made her way to the next knot of people waiting to greet her. And suddenly there he was, the man who had nearly destroyed her world. Sunny Mahtani, wearing that same smile that had once made her melt and now only made her see red.

Adamji faltered to a stop, his face turning pale as he recognized Sunny. He had deliberately left the Mahtanis off his guest list this year, just so that this kind of situation did not occur. And yet, here he stood, the scion of the Mahtani family, the man who had been engaged to Asha, and the man whom the Prime Minister privately blamed for the leak of her naked pictures.

How on earth had he managed to sneak past security without the barcode that every guest was supposed to scan at the door? But of course, he thought a moment later, Sunny had the run of this hotel, which was owned by one of his best friends. He had probably been escorted through the kitchen entrance by his own security. No hotel staffer would have had the nerve to try and stop his entry.

Adamji turned to look at Asha, and realized she looked as sick as he felt. Her face had turned so white that the strokes of blusher on her face gave her a faintly comical look. Her mouth was frozen in a rictus grin, but there was no mistaking the stricken look in her eyes.

The only person who seemed perfectly at ease with the situation was Sunny himself. He smiled into Asha's eyes as he extended a hand to her. 'How are you Madam Prime Minister?' he asked. 'It's nice to see you again.'

It was an innocuous enough greeting. Only Asha, attuned for years to his tone, could detect the sarcasm lurking behind the words.

In the end, it was that implicit sneer that stiffened her spine. Sunny could mock her as much as he liked, but she was the Prime Minister of India—and she had become that despite his best efforts to blow her world apart after she left him.

She was no longer the woman he could force himself on; she was now a force in her own right.

With a supreme effort of will, Asha summoned up a smile for her former fiancé. But she ignored the hand held out to clasp her own. Instead, she folded her hands into a formal 'namaste' and bowed slightly. She felt a brief flash of satisfaction as she saw Sunny flush at the snub and lower his hand quickly. But that satisfaction faded as she realized that the entire room had fallen silent and was watching this silent pantomime, as if it were being played out for their express amusement.

No doubt, this was a story that these people would dine out on for years to come. 'Do you remember that time in Davos when Asha Devi finally came face to face with Sunny Mahtani?' 'How on earth did he even get into the party?' 'I will never forget the expression on his face when she refused to shake his hand.' And it wouldn't be long before these accounts were embellished further, by those with more active imaginations than others.

What on earth had Adamji been thinking? The whole world was aware of her history with Sunny. How could he have possibly thought that it was okay to invite her former fiancé to a party she was chief guest at?

But one look at the quivering mess at her elbow told her that Adamji had done no such thing. Sunny's appearance had come as a shock to him as well. And he was looking so shattered that it was clear that she could not depend on him to be rescued.

Asha looked wildly around the room. Where the hell was Nitesh Dholakia? There was no getting rid of him when he wasn't wanted. But now that he was needed, he was nowhere to be seen.

Instead, her grateful eyes fell upon Alok Ray, who was cutting across the room rapidly to reach her. Almost involuntarily, she reached out her hand to him. He took it in his and said in tones that were so normal as to be oddly reassuring, 'Prime Minister, if you have a minute, there are some people I would like you to meet.' Asha nodded mutely and allowed herself to be guided away from Sunny Mahtani.

Manisha, watching this entire drama unfold from one corner of the room, had clocked the concern that darkened Alok's face as he saw Asha come face to face with Sunny. She had seen the look of abject relief that appeared on Asha's face when Alok charged forward to rescue her. And when Asha impulsively held out her hand to Alok and he took it into his own, something clicked in Manisha's brain.

Ah, so that was how matters lay, she thought to herself. Asha Devi and Alok Ray were an item. Even though she only had a handclasp to go on, she would bet her last rupee on it.

Despite how wrong things had gone between her and Asha, Manisha felt a pang of satisfaction at this realization. After all that Asha had been through, she deserved a bit of happiness. And if she found it in the arms of her finance minister, well, who could grudge her that? Or even judge her for it?

Yet Manisha knew that if their liaison ever came to light, it would trigger yet another scandal revolving around Asha Devi's sex life. And that was something that the Prime Minister could ill afford.

Given her past experience, Asha would be well aware of the dangers she was risking but did Alok Ray know what he was getting into? In this era of political correctness, the world would not look kindly on a man who entered into a relationship with a woman more than a decade younger than him—especially if she was his boss.

But when it came to matters of the heart, which one of us could ever behave totally rationally? So, why expect Asha and Alok to be any different?

Manisha rapidly scanned the throng of people in the room to see where Asha was. Maybe this was the best moment to speak to her; Sunny's appearance may end up reminding Asha of how Manisha had helped rehabilitate her with an interview after her naked pictures leaked.

But both Asha Devi and Alok Ray were nowhere to be seen. While she had been speculating about their relationship, they had slipped away from the party, which was now buzzing with excitement, as people discussed the scene they had just witnessed.

This would feed the gossip mills for months to come, thought Manisha cynically. But little did these people know that they had missed the real story. And that, yet again, it was Manisha Patel who had scored the scoop.

\* \* \*

They rode up the elevator in complete silence. When the door opened on Asha's floor, Alok stepped out alongside her.

'No,' she said abruptly, 'there's no need for that. I will be just fine.'

Ignoring her completely, Alok accompanied her down the corridor, while her SPG detail followed a respectful distance behind.

'Seriously, Alok, you don't have to babysit me,' Asha whispered agitatedly, 'I am perfectly capable of looking after myself.'

'Yes, I am well aware of that. But, if you don't mind, I could do with a bit of looking after,' he said. 'I have had a bit of shock, you see.'

Asha looked up at him, startled. 'Shock? What shock could you possibly have had?'

'Well, to be honest, it came as something of a shock that you could have gone out with a smarmy bounder like him.'

And just like that, a smile flowered on Asha's face. 'Bounder? Honestly Alok, sometimes it seems as if you have just stepped out of a P.G. Wodehouse novel. Bounder? Who even uses words like that anymore?'

Alok grinned by way of reply, bowing low, as if accepting a rare compliment.

They were at the door of her suite by then, and by unspoken agreement, Alok entered right behind her, while the SPG took their customary positions outside. The moment the door was closed behind them, Asha threw off her heels and collapsed on to the sofa. Alok headed straight for the bar, where he poured a few inches of Scotch into a glass and added three ice cubes. He brought the drink over to Asha, and she gulped it down in one go, making a moue of distaste as it went down.

'Whiskey? You gave me whiskey? Don't you know that I am strictly a vodka girl?'

'Now, how would I know that?' asked Alok, setting off again for the bar. 'I know so very little about you.'

Silence reigned in the room as he set about assembling vodka, a few slices of lemon, some tonic water and lots of ice in two tall glasses. Then he carried the drinks across, handed one to Asha and took a deep gulp from the other. The silence lengthened between them, as they sat side by side on the couch, sipping their drinks. It fell to Asha to break it.

'That's not true,' she said quietly, 'you are one of the few people who actually does know me pretty well. You may not know my favourite drink, but you know much more important stuff.'

'You feel like telling me a little more?' asked Alok. Asha nodded.

'Why did you react so badly to seeing Sunny? Do you still have feelings for him?'

After a moment of incredulity, Asha began laughing, though it was laughter tinged with an edge of hysteria. 'Feelings for him?' she finally spluttered. 'Are you serious? The man tried to destroy my life. You bet I have feelings for him. I fucking hate him!'

And then, much to Asha's horror, she felt the tears coming as the memories of her time with Sunny flashed back to her. As she began crying silently, Alok slid closer and pulled her into his arms. She collapsed against him, muffling her sobs against his chest, as he ran one hand soothingly down her back.

Once the tears had abated, Asha relayed the salient facts of her relationship with Sunny to Alok, over another vodka tonic. The only time she faltered was when it came to relating how things had ended.

They had been at an English stately home, attending a society wedding at which Asha was the bridesmaid. She had had too much champagne to drink at the reception that followed and had retreated to her room to sleep it off. She had woken up to find Sunny on top of her. When she told him she was too tired to have sex, he had lost his temper and slapped her across the face. And then, even as she struggled to get away, he had forced himself on her.

Once he was done, he had simply rolled off her and gone to the bathroom, as if nothing out of the ordinary had occurred. Asha had pulled her torn bridesmaid outfit tightly around her and had run to take refuge with a friend, who had taken her back home to London.

As she related this story, Alok's hold over her tightened so much that it actually hurt. Asha made a small protesting sound, and his arms relaxed immediately.

'I am so sorry you had to go through that,' Alok whispered into her hair. 'If I had known, I would have knocked the senses out of that guy.'

'Well, in that case, I am glad you didn't,' said Asha. 'You know, you are the first person I have ever told this to. I didn't even tell my friend who brought me back to London, though she must have guessed what happened.'

'Why didn't you go to the police, Asha? You should have had the guy arrested.'

Asha freed herself and moved back to stare Alok in the face. 'Are you serious? Are you fucking serious? Did you really expect me to put myself to the indignity of a trial, to answer questions in open court, and then, in all probability, see him walk free? I would rather die!'

Alok was instantly contrite. 'I'm sorry, I wasn't thinking. Of course, you did the best thing for yourself. You cut yourself off him . . .'

'Fat lot of good it did me. He leaked all my pictures anyway, and now anyone with access to the internet can watch my naked body any time they like,' said Asha bitterly.

Alok had the grace to look a bit abashed. He was guilty of looking at those pictures too, just like the rest of the world. And as he looked down at Asha, her chin quivering as she tried to get her emotions under control, he suddenly realized just how much she had lost with the leak of her pictures. It wasn't just her dignity and privacy that had been destroyed, it was also her agency over her own body.

Stirred by an emotion that fell halfway between pity and a deep, abiding sorrow, Alok pulled Asha back into his arms to console her. But instead of resting her head on his shoulder, she raised it to look deep into his eyes, her lips inches from his own.

No, Alok told himself, it wouldn't do to kiss her, no matter how much he wanted to. This was a young, vulnerable woman, in the throes of a crisis. There was no way he was taking advantage of her at a moment like this.

But those thoughts were blown away as Asha used both her hands to pull his head down, and kissed him on the mouth, her tongue flickering against his closed lips. His mouth opened of its own volition and his tongue reached out to touch hers. And then, as their tongues probed each other, his hands took on a life of their own and reached for her breasts, caressing her erect nipples through her sari blouse.

Asha suddenly wrenched herself away from him. Alok was about to apologize and draw back, when she whispered, 'Not here, someone may come in. Let's go into the bedroom.'

He followed her inside the bedroom. She locked the door behind them. And then, the two of them fell upon each other, kissing and caressing one another as if their lives depended on it.

By the time they tumbled into the four-poster bed that dominated the room, they had managed to tear each other's clothes right off.

Finally, they were naked on the cool grey sheets, Asha's breasts full and engorged with desire, Alok's well-muscled body glistening with sweat, both their faces flushed and their breath ragged with desire.

As Alok entered her, Asha cried out, almost as if in pain. He made as if to withdraw, thinking he was hurting her. But her arms held him in place, as she whispered into his ears, 'Don't stop. Please don't stop.'

And he didn't.

# 16

It was a bone-weary Asha Devi who clambered back on to her private jet at the end of a long and tiring day on the campaign trail. There was just a fortnight to go before polling began in Bihar and she needed to cover as much ground as she could every single day. Today, she had addressed as many as eleven different rallies, being ferried around from town to village in a chopper. And after a week of this routine, her voice was beginning to give up on her.

The moment the seat belt sign went off, she asked the stewardess to get her some hot water infused with ginger, lemon and honey, and settled back to read the files that Dholakia had packed for her perusal. But her attention kept wandering off the densely-printed pages as vignettes of her day kept popping up in her mind.

The memories were far from comforting. On the contrary, they imbued a deep disquiet in her. A past master of election campaigns, Asha had a gut feeling about how things were going.

And she had to admit that despite all her efforts, the LJP was in big trouble.

On the face of it, her party's ground game was as strong as ever, and every rally she addressed had been packed; what her father used to call 'jostling room only'. And yet, there was something off about the energy of the crowd. They remained unmoved by her best lines, the applause, when it finally came, was grudging and lukewarm, and on a few occasions, she had seen the people at the back begin filing out while she was still speaking.

Asha, who had become used to a rapturous reception only a few months ago during the General Election, didn't know what to make of this. She was the same person she had been then. She was making the same kind of speeches. But the response to them was now completely different.

What made the situation worse was that she didn't know what she could do to change it. She was the star campaigner of her party. Her half-brothers, Karan and Arjun, were doing their bit by going on road shows and even campaigning door-to-door, but they had met with an even more tepid response.

The truth (amply borne out by the LJP's internal polling) was that the Pratap Singh siblings' love affair with the Indian electorate seemed to be over. And there seemed to be no way to rekindle the passions that had once been theirs to command. At least, there was no way that she could clearly see.

Asha had spent a lot of time thinking about why this should be so. And she had come to the reluctant conclusion that Satyajit Kumar's slogan '*Desh Bachao, Iss Beti Ko Hatao*' had had an unexpected resonance with the Indian people. Such had been his success in portraying her as a daughter of privilege, a pampered dynast who had been handed the country on a silver platter, that it was that image that popped up in people's minds whenever they saw her.

What made things worse was that Asha was aware that there was some truth to this charge. A realist to the core, she knew that the allegations of her being a *naamdar* had the ring of truth to them. If she hadn't been the daughter of Birendra

Pratap Singh, there was no way she would have had such an easy entry into politics. If she hadn't had her father's legacy behind her, there wasn't a hope in hell that she would have become the leader of her party. Or Prime Minister of the country, for the matter.

But it was one thing for Asha to acknowledge the truth of this in the privacy of her mind. It was quite another for the Leader of the Opposition to hammer away at this, hoping to chisel support away from her. She couldn't allow that to happen if she was to survive in politics. And yet, she didn't know how to prevent it.

Asha's phone buzzed and pulled her away from this futile internal monologue. Her face lit up the moment she saw Alok's name come up with an iMessage icon next to it. She clicked the message open and smiled as she saw a Bitmoji load. It featured a towel-clad Alok clutching a single red rose between his lips. Before she could type out a reply, another Bitmoji popped up. This one had a written message too: 'Love you to bits.'

Suddenly, the miasma of gloom that had descended upon Asha lifted and an involuntary giggle broke through. Over the last month, as their relationship deepened, she had discovered that behind the urbane, sophisticated front he presented to the world, Alok was actually a sucker for sentiment. And no matter how much Asha teased him about what she called his 'cheesy' side, he remained entirely unrepentant and unembarrassed.

After poking fun at him for a week or so, Asha had succumbed as well. As the adage went: if you can't beat them, join them. So now, she gave as good as she got. Taking another sip of her drink, she opened the Bitmoji app to find a suitable riposte to her boyfriend.

Boyfriend.

How strange that word sounded, even in her head. But that was the right word to describe Alok Ray, even though their relationship hadn't exactly unfolded along conventional patterns. Given that she was the Prime Minister of India and he was her finance minister, there was no way they could go on dates like any other normal couple without setting off the rumour mills—which neither of them wanted to.

So, over the last month, Asha and Alok had been snatching some private moments whenever they could. He would drop by her office in South Block after all her appointments were over, and the two of them would make out on the sofa like a couple of oversexed teenagers. On occasion, Asha would invite him over to 3 Race Course Road for dinner, so that they could have a meal together even if they had to share the table with her mother.

Amma, who seemed to have guessed that something was brewing between them, behaved like the epitome of discretion. The moment dessert was cleared away and the servants had retired for the night, she would excuse herself and go to bed. And soon after, so would Asha and Alok.

Asha knew that it was only a matter of time before her entire family became aware of her relationship with Alok. The world of Race Course Road was a small, rather incestuous one, and the staff members at Numbers 3, 5 and 7 were notorious gossips. Soon enough, there would be talk about how Alok and Asha met for dinner as often as twice a week and were then left alone by her mother after the servants had gone to their quarters. After that, everyone's imagination would take over. And for once, their fantasies would be very close to reality.

Radhika would probably be the first person to become cognizant of these rumours. She had always had an easy way with staff, and they found it comforting to confide in her. And once she knew about Alok and Asha, it was only a matter of time before Karan and Arjun were brought into the loop.

Asha was reasonably confident that Amma, who had developed a near-instant rapport with Alok, would give her blessings to her new relationship. But she wasn't sure how the rest of the family would react. Would her half-brothers judge her for getting intimate with a man who effectively worked for her? Would Radhika, who had nursed her back to sanity after her breakdown after her naked photos leaked, approve of her entering into another romantic relationship so soon?

But, as her plane came in to land in Delhi, Asha realized that she didn't really care what anyone made of her getting together with Alok. She had finally found happiness, when she had least expected it—and she wasn't going to let the world ruin it for her.

\* \* \*

It would have cheered Asha up immensely to know that Satyajit Kumar also had enormous misgivings about the Bihar election campaign, though they were a little different to hers. Kumar had no doubt that the alliance he had set up with the Dalit Morcha would win the Assembly election. The way the electoral arithmetic worked, with the SPP and the DM combining, the LJP didn't stand a chance in the first-past-the-post system that prevailed in India.

So, Kumar wasn't worried about losing the election. His fears were very different. All the polling that he had commissioned over the past few weeks, as the campaign heated up, suggested that while the SPP votes were getting transferred to the Dalit Morcha, the Dalit Morcha votes were not transferring to SPP candidates on the ground. In effect, this meant that the DM

candidates were better placed than the SPP candidates to win
their respective seats.

The last such report that Kumar had received had
suggested that of the 108 seats that the SPP was fighting on,
they were favoured to win in only 59. The Dalit Morcha, on
the other hand, was much better placed. Their candidates
were likely to romp home in as many as 106 seats of the 135
seats they were contesting.

That meant that when the votes were finally counted,
the alliance would have an easy majority of 165 in a house
of 243. But the Dalit Morcha MLAs would far outnumber
the victorious SPP candidates. That in turn would ensure that
Damyanti was in a much more powerful position than Kumar
when it came to the task of government formation. And he
had no doubt that this would make the Dalit Morcha leader—
who was unreasonable at the best of times—a nightmare to
deal with.

But that was the scenario that Damyanti was aiming for.
Which is why she had refused to campaign in the constituencies
where SPP candidates were in the fray, and turned down every
request to do joint rallies with Kumar. She knew perfectly well
that all it would take for Dalit Morcha supporters to vote for the
SPP candidates was one word from her. But she was refusing to
say that one word—no matter how often and how hard Kumar
and his party begged for it.

So, while Kumar had been canvassing for votes across the
state and encouraging his voters to vote for the alliance candidate
in their constituency regardless of whether he was from the SPP
or the DM, Damyanti had restricted her campaign to those
areas where her party candidates were standing for election.
And with a couple of weeks left to polling day, she was unlikely
to soften her stand.

Her strategy was paying off for the Dalit Morcha. Going by the projected numbers, Damyanti would be the leader of the largest group of MLAs with Kumar being relegated to the role of the junior—make that very junior—partner. So, when it came to government formation, not only would the chief minister be from the DM but all the plum portfolios would go to that party as well, while the SPP consoled itself with whatever dregs were flung in its direction.

Kumar kept trying to tell himself that the alliance had been worth it, nonetheless. This was the first election that Asha Devi was fighting as Prime Minister. And when her party was routed at the polls, despite the fact that she had flung herself into the campaign with full vim and vigour, it would be seen as a personal defeat for Asha herself.

And once a Prime Minister was seen as a loser, that impression tended to persist for the rest of his or her term in office.

This election wasn't just about electing a government for Bihar. It was, ultimately, about destabilizing the government of India. And if, in order to achieve that, Satyajit Kumar had to endure some humiliation at the hands of Didi Damyanti, well then, that was a price well worth paying for the dividends that were bound to come.

That, at least, was what Kumar told himself every night before going to bed, and every morning when he woke up to a fresh day of campaigning.

But hard as he tried to convince himself, even he was finding it increasingly hard to believe his own pep talk.

* * *

The first thing Asha did after deplaning in Delhi and getting into her car was to pick up the phone and call Alok. This had become something of a ritual with them. The moment either of them landed after a flight, the first thing they would do is phone the other to exchange sweet nothings.

This time, though, Alok plunged straight into business mode.

'You know, Asha, I have been thinking about the Bihar election. Don't you think we are making a mistake by not using Sukanya Sarkar as a campaigner in the border areas with Bengal? Those places have a huge Bengali population, and her intervention may have a huge impact on the election result there.'

Asha controlled her impatience at having the obvious pointed out to her. Taking as reasonable a tone as she could manage, she said, 'Yes, Alok, the party has already reached out to her several times. But we still haven't had any response from her. Clearly, she doesn't want to do it . . .'

'Have you spoken to her yourself?' interrupted Alok. 'I am sure that if you were to make a personal request, she would not be able to turn it down.'

'What makes you think so?' asked a sceptical Asha. 'She has no problem saying no to me. In fact, I have lost count of the number of times she has said it.'

'Well, what do you have to lose, anyway?' persisted Alok, clearly unwilling to let go of this idea. 'The worst-case scenario is that she refuses. How would that make you any worse off?'

Asha bit back the retort that rose in her throat. What did she have to lose? Well, her pride, for starters. She had already been humiliated in public by Sukanya in numerous interviews in which she held forth on how raw and inexperienced a leader Asha was. The last thing she wanted to do was to hand the Poriborton Party leader an opportunity to do so in private as well.

And Asha had no doubt that this is exactly what would happen if she called up Sukanya to make a personal request for her to campaign on behalf of the LJP in Bihar. First, the chief minister would faux-commiserate with her about how the LJP was performing in the state. Then, she would give gratuitous advice on how Asha could improve her party's chances. And then, after she had had her fill of patronizing the Prime Minister, she would turn down her request anyway.

If Sukanya had had any intention of campaigning in Bihar, she would have done it by now. The fact that she had not done so was ample proof that she was going to sit this one out. She knew that the LJP was going to lose. And she wasn't going to risk her reputation by campaigning for the losing side.

But Alok, who had a slightly exaggerated sense of how much Sukanya liked him, was not convinced by Asha's arguments. So, it was with a certain amount of pique that Asha told him to go ahead and speak to Sukanya himself if he was so sure of convincing her to enter the fray. And, for the first time since they had begun seeing one another, Asha hung up on Alok without her customary, 'I love you.'

Undeterred by this, Alok immediately picked up the phone and called Sukanya. His first hurdle was actually getting through to her. Each time he dialed her mobile number, Sukanya's secretary picked up and assured him that 'Madam' was busy on another call and would call him back. It took him six tries and a good hour before he managed to get the PP leader on the line.

Once she came on, there was a marked absence of the effusive Bengali greetings he had become used to. Instead, Sukanya stuck to English, almost as if using a language other than their mother tongue served as a distancing device.

'Yes, Alok,' she began tersely, 'how can I help you?'

Alok immediately embarked on the speech he had been rehearsing ever since he hung up on Asha; a speech that was specifically designed to appeal to Sukanya's vanity. But he could barely get a sentence out before he was rudely interrupted.

'If this is about campaigning for the LJP in Bihar, let me stop you right there. I don't have the time to do all this nonsense. In any case, the party is going to lose. Why should I waste my time campaigning for them? I have to think of my reputation also, na?'

Alok was taken aback by the aggressive tone. This was the first time that Sukanya had employed it with him, and it was a jarring experience for someone who had been used to being treated like a favoured nephew.

But overcoming his initial shock, Alok decided to press on. Now that he had embarked down this path, he didn't see any profit in backing off immediately. In for a penny, in for a pound, he told himself, as he switched into persuasion mode. But no matter how much he tried to tell Sukanya that she alone could change the course of this election, that she could easily reverse the results of as many as 20 seats if she wanted, that they were dependent on her to change the tide, she remained unmoved.

It was a very chagrined Alok Ray who finally hung up on her. It took him a few minutes to collect himself and process the comprehensive snub that had been delivered to him. And then, feeling shamefaced, he called up Asha to admit that she had, in fact, been right all along.

Asha had had the true measure of the Poriborton Party leader, while he—pumped up with his own consequence—had entirely failed to read her.

\* \* \*

A fortnight later, both Asha Devi and Satyajit Kumar were proved right. By 10 a.m. on counting day, the picture was clear. The SPP-DM combine had won comprehensively, with 176 seats, while the LJP garnered a measly 55 (with 12 going to smaller parties and Independents).

Asha's humiliation was complete. But so was Satyajit Kumar's. Of the 176 seats that the alliance had won, as many as 110 had gone to the Dalit Morcha, with just a paltry 66 being added to the kitty by the SPP.

The alliance may have won the right to form the new government in Bihar. But there was no doubt that this victory belonged to one person alone. And that person was the leader of the Dalit Morcha, Didi Damyanti. Satyajit Kumar, SPP party chief, was very much an also-ran.

As Asha surfed the news channels on result day, trying to keep track of how the story was unfolding, she took a certain perverse comfort in that. She may have lost but the man who had coined the slogan that had hurt her chances the most— *Desh Bachao, Iss Beti Ko Hatao*—had also been rejected by the electorate.

Did these numbers represent a glimmer of hope for her, Asha wondered. Did this mean that the Indian electorate was not receptive to such sneering slogans—the kind that politicians like Kumar took such delight in coining? Did Kumar's bad performance owe something to the fact that most people had reacted with revulsion to a man who had come up with such a sexist, misogynist slogan?

No, she told herself a moment later. She was probably reading too much into this. The media pundits probably had it right this time. Kumar had been played for an idiot by Damyanti, who had quickly mopped up all the support he had to offer and then failed to keep up her end of the bargain. And

without the Dalit Morcha vote bank being added to his kitty, it
was inevitable that Kumar should underperform at this election.

As Asha came upon NTN as she channel-surfed, Gaurav
Agnihotri was making the same point. 'Satyajit Kumar, I am
afraid to say, has made a fool of himself,' he said, addressing
some hapless SPP spokesman who had been dispatched to the
studio that day. 'He gave away far too many seats when it came to
striking an alliance with Didi Damyanti. And now he has failed to
win even most of the seats that the SPP was contesting from . . .'

The SPP spokesman was driven to protest. 'I am sorry,
sir, but that is simply not true. Our party contested 108 seats
and we have won 66 of them. That is a more than 50 per cent
strike rate . . .'

'Is that anything to boast about?' sneered Gaurav. 'You won
just over half the seats you contested. And that is despite having
the support of the Dalit Morcha, so there were no three-way
contests in the state. You should have won at least 80 per cent
of the seats you contested, not just over 50 per cent. Honestly,
if you ask me, Kumar should be ashamed of his performance as
party leader. He has completely destroyed the SPP in the state
of Bihar. From now on, you guys will just be the junior partner
to the Dalit Morcha . . .'

Asha had begun smiling halfway through this diatribe. It
was fun to see Gaurav go hammer and tongs, just so long as
his attacks were directed at someone else. And, truth be told, it
felt good to watch Satyajit Kumar get a pasting in the press—
especially on a day when his alliance had actually won.

As the SPP spokesman began spluttering in reply, Asha
switched channels and tuned into AITNN to see how Manisha
Patel was covering the election results.

She was entirely unsurprised to find that Manisha was
laying into Asha yet again. 'Nobody expected the LJP to win

this election,' she was saying to one of her panelists, 'but did you think that the party would perform quite so badly? Especially given that Asha Devi spent so much time campaigning in the state? Clearly, her presence made no difference. Or do you think it actually worked to the detriment of the party?'

Asha was incensed. Did the woman never give up? Didn't she ever tire of this constant negativity? And what did she mean by laying the entire blame on Asha? Everyone knew that anti-incumbency—along with simple electoral arithmetic— had played a major role in the defeat of the LJP. Some of the responsibility must rest on the local leadership of the LJP. As Prime Minister, she was not without fault, but surely there was enough blame to go around?

The panelist this question had been addressed to made much the same point. 'To be fair to the Prime Minister, this election was lost from the moment that Satyajit Kumar and Didi Damyanti announced their alliance. The moment that happened, it was game over for Asha Devi. In fact, I think it is highly creditable that the LJP managed to secure as many as 55 seats, that's only 11 seats less than the SPP. So, how is that a bad performance?'

The SPP spokesperson was not willing to let that pass. 'How is that a bad performance?' he echoed. 'I'll tell you how. This is the first time the LJP has gone to the polls under the leadership of Asha Devi. Please remember, the General Election victory was won by her brother, Karan Pratap. So, the first time she has led her party, it has come third in a field of three . . .'

'Field of three? How on earth is that a "field of three"?' retorted the LJP spokesman angrily. 'The SPP and the Dalit Morcha fought this election as a single bloc. They had a pre-poll alliance and seat adjustments that ensured that there was a one-to-one contest in each constituency. How can you possibly call it a field of three?'

Manisha hurriedly conceded the point so that she could move the discussion along. But Asha had seen quite enough by then. Switching off the TV, she picked up the phone to speak to her party general secretary.

This was not the time to sit around moping about her loss. If her father had taught her anything, it was that in defeat lay endless possibilities. And this was probably the best time to effect a change in the LJP leadership in Bihar. She would have to ask the now former chief minister to resign as state party chief—if he was foolish enough not to volunteer to do so himself—and reconstitute the local unit. This was as good a time as any to get her own loyalists in position in the state.

Asha Devi may have lost this battle, but she had to get ready to fight the next skirmish in the ongoing war that was Indian politics.

# 17

The breakthrough came, as is so often the case, completely by accident. Or, more accurately, because of an accident.

Weeks of sustained interrogation of the Jihad-e-Azaadi members who were in Army custody had only yielded the locations of middle-level operatives of the terrorist organization. And even after these people had been rounded up and tortured to within an inch of their lives, the security agencies were no closer to tracking down the two main leaders of the JEA.

It was as if Salim Soz and Wajahat Abdullah had vanished off the face of the earth or—more likely—had slipped across the porous border and gone to ground in POK (Pakistan Occupied Kashmir).

If that was true, then it was game over for the investigation into the Kautilya attack. There would be no way of tracking these men down to their hideouts across the border and rendering them back to India to face justice.

But just as the investigators were beginning to suspect that this might be the case, they were proved conclusively wrong. And it all happened because of a minor road accident.

It had snowed around eight inches the night before, so the roads were slippery and slushy when the NIA officer in charge set off for the black site where all interrogations of the Kautilya attack suspects were being conducted. His driver, a local, knew the route like the back of his hand, and once he had negotiated the turns and twists of the road and come to a relatively open stretch, he allowed himself to go into autopilot mode.

Big mistake. For as he gained speed, he was brought up short by a flock of mountain goats being guided across the road by a couple of wizened men, bundled up in pherans with their faces well-muffled against the cold.

The driver braked sharply but it was too late. The jeep careened into a couple of goats, which had a domino effect on three others down the line. Piteous bleats rent the air as the jeep finally came to a standstill, and the driver braced himself to deal with the indignation of the goat owners.

But much to his astonishment, the two goatherds, instead of berating him for injuring their animals and demanding compensation, abandoned their herd and ran off full tilt towards the treeline a few hundred yards away.

The first person to react was the young army lieutenant who had been assigned to babysit the NIA hotshot during his sojourn in the Valley. Watching the events unfold from his vantage point in the front seat, his training instincts took over.

Whenever someone makes a run for it, give chase. So, that's exactly what he did, pulling out his service revolver before he left the sanctuary of the jeep.

'Stop,' he shouted at the retreating backs, 'Stop, or I will shoot.'

The men slowed down slightly, but it was only to draw their weapons from beneath their pherans. But before they could turn around and take aim, the lieutenant fired two shots, one of which hit one of the men in the lower back. The other goatherd was brought down by a jawan who had been travelling in the back of the jeep, with an expert shot in the knee. The two injured men were quickly disarmed by the two army men, handcuffed, and bundled into the jeep to make the journey to the black site.

Their interrogation commenced almost immediately and continued for the rest of the day. Where had they come from? Who had given them these weapons? Where were they headed? Which organization did they belong to? Whom did they report to?

The questions piled on, but answers were not forthcoming, no matter how 'sustained' the 'interrogation'.

It took until 5.10 p.m. for the first of them to break. And when he did, all hell broke loose as well.

These were no humble goatherds who had been co-opted as foot soldiers of the Jihad-e-Azaadi. They were trusted members of the JEA and had been assigned the task of leading Salim Soz and Wajahat Abdullah across the Line of Control (LOC). They had been on their way to join two others of the escort party when they were taken into custody. Their destination, it turned out, was a small village in the Kupwara sector, where the two JEA leaders had been smuggled into the house of one of their supporters.

But Soz and Abdullah weren't going to be there for long. In fact, they were scheduled to cross the LOC early the next morning, going across the river Neelum—which served as a natural bifurcation between the two countries—to seek sanctuary in POK.

Time was of the essence if the JEA leaders were to be captured before they disappeared across the border. An operation needed to be mounted in a matter of hours, which meant sending commandos into a hostile terrain at short notice, and in inimical weather conditions. It was an enterprise fraught with risk, and there was every possibility that the casualty rate would be high. And yet, there was no other option but to attack before the primary targets disappeared for good.

After hasty consultations, the decision was made to call in the Special Forces commandos from the 4th Para Regiment of the Indian Army. A handpicked team of thirty would be flown in by helicopter and airdropped as close as it was possible to get without alerting the terrorists by the sound of the chopper. They would then make their way on foot to the area in which Soz and Abdullah were holed up.

The visibility was bad, so it would be slow going. But even so, it was believed that the commandos would be in place to storm the house three hours from now.

In normal circumstances, operations like these were the meat-and-potatoes of the Special Forces. A few rounds of firing were enough to reveal the positions of the terrorists inside, as they fired back at the soldiers. Once the terrorists had given their locations away, the snipers, positioned strategically on the rooftops of neighbouring buildings, could take the targets out.

If that didn't work, it was time to bring in the heavy artillery or even lob a few hand grenades. If the terrorists survived that as well, then the house in which they had taken refuge would be blown up, with the terrorists inside it.

But those tactics wouldn't work today. The objective of this mission was to take Soz and Abdullah alive so that they could stand trial for the Kautilya attack. And that made this operation far trickier than most.

\* \* \*

Back in Delhi, Asha Devi was being briefed about a rendition of an entirely different type. Alok had called and asked for an emergency meeting to discuss 'developments' in the Dark

Matters case. They had decided on Race Course Road as the venue because it was a more private set-up than the one that prevailed in the Prime Minister's Office in South Block.

A few weeks ago, Asha had given instructions to the SPG that Alok Ray was to be allowed to drive in directly to Number 3, without having to suffer the indignity—like other lesser mortals—of having to disembark from his vehicle and board a 'ferry car' to his destination. So, Alok skipped past all the usual security protocols and drove straight to Asha's residence, fairly bursting with the news he had for her.

He bounded out of the car and went through the door the SPG guard opened for him. But was brought up short by the presence of Asha's mother, who was clearly on her way out. Sadhana Devi looked startled to see him. This was the first time he had arrived at RCR unannounced and in the early evening. Until now he had only ever come over at night when he had been invited to join them for dinner.

The moment she laid eyes on him, Sadhana Devi blushed beetroot red. It took Alok an instant to realize why. Amma clearly thought that she had stumbled on some secret rendezvous that Alok and Asha had set up, taking advantage of the fact that she was planning to be out for the evening. And by delaying her departure by 10 minutes, she had surprised them with her presence.

The moment this dawned on him, Alok flushed bright red too. Despite his forty-odd years, he felt like an errant teenager who has been caught sneaking into his girlfriend's bedroom by her mother. What made matters worse was that there was no good way to explain to Sadhana Devi that he wasn't here on an errand of passion but to brief Asha on an important matter.

The two of them would probably have stood right there, rooted in their mutual awkwardness, for minutes altogether, both too embarrassed to break the silence, if Asha hadn't come into the hallway just then. Taking in the situation at a glance, she suppressed her giggles, and put them both out of their misery.

'Amma, are you off already?' she said lightly. 'Are you sure you don't want to stay for a bit and have coffee with Alok and me?'

Turning to Alok, she added, 'You have time for a coffee, right? The briefing can wait another ten minutes?'

A relieved Alok nodded gratefully even as Amma demurred. 'No, beta,' she said, 'I am already running late for the movie.' She then held out her hand to Alok, and said, 'I hope to see you for dinner sometime.'

'Oh, yes,' he said, finally recovering himself. 'I would love that.'

The moment the door shut behind her mother, Asha began laughing uncontrollably.

'What is so funny?' asked Alok, as he took her in his arms, and rained kisses all over her face.

'The two of you, of course,' she chuckled. 'The expression on both your faces when I entered . . . it was such a sight!'

'You do know what she thought, don't you?'

'Yes, of course, I do,' said Asha, laughter still burbling in her voice. 'That you were here for a bit of action . . . and frankly sir, I don't mind if you do . . .'

Alok firmly put her away from him after one last lingering kiss. No, he said, the news he had could not wait.

Instantly sobering up, Asha settled down on the sofa and gestured for Alok to begin. And when he did, Asha began to understand his impatience.

They had finally had the breakthrough they had been striving towards for months. The Dark Matters team had conclusively identified the mysterious man in the Manaus mansion as Madan Mohan Prajapati. Now that his identity had been verified, the rendition team was fine-tuning a plan to capture him and stash him in a safe house near an airfield, from where he could be flown out.

How exactly would they do that, asked Asha. It was imperative that they took Madan Mohan alive. The last thing she wanted was for her father's killer to be felled in a firefight as they tried to capture him.

She wanted Madan Mohan Prajapati back in India, in handcuffs, and in prison for the rest of his life.

'Don't worry, Asha,' said Alok reassuringly, 'these people know what they are doing. And their instructions are clear. They have to capture him alive and bring him back to India.'

'But how will they do that without some sort of gunfight?' asked Asha. 'And once bullets are flying around, how can we be sure that one of them will not hit Madan Mohan?'

'Look, don't sweat the details,' responded Alok, a bit of impatience creeping into his tone. 'I don't want to know how they do this kind of stuff and nor should you. That gives us plausible deniability if this operation ever comes to light.'

The thought of something like this becoming public should have made Asha nervous. The leader of a country hiring a squad of hitmen to find her father's murderer wasn't a story that would go down well in the world media. If it ever leaked, Asha's reputation would likely never recover.

But as she imagined Madan Mohan's face as justice finally caught up with him, Asha found that she did not care about any putative damage to her reputation. All she cared about was getting the man behind her father's death and bringing him back to India to face the full force of the law.

'Let's assume that all goes well,' she asked Alok, 'how do we bring him back to India?'

She half expected Alok to say that this too fell into the no-need-to-know category, but this time he was more forthcoming. And that's because Madan Mohan could not be brought back to India without the connivance and support of the Indian government. And that was something only Asha Devi could pull off.

The Dark Matters team would have no problem spiriting Madan Mohan out of Brazil in a private plane. The company had paid off enough people in strategic positions over the years, so it had a ready-made operation to do this completely under the radar. The idea was to fly him to a friendly country, which would then facilitate his rendition to India.

Given the preponderance of ex-Mossad agents in the Dark Matters set up, they were naturally inclined to choose Israel as the midpoint destination. But given the strict security in that country, there was no way an unknown flight could land or take off from Israel without being shot down by its ever-vigilant air force.

That's where Asha Devi came. As Prime Minister of India, she had to make a personal call to the Israeli Prime Minister, take him into confidence, and request that he allow Israeli airspace to be used in this operation. She also had to impress upon him the need for secrecy, so that the news didn't leak before they could successfully get Madan Mohan back to India.

'When should I make the call?' asked Asha. 'Should I set it up right away? We need to give him some advance notice . . .'

'No, no, no,' interrupted Alok. 'We can't risk giving anyone advance notice. The success of the plan depends on complete secrecy.'

Dark Matters had made it clear that she should call her Israeli counterpart only after Madan Mohan's plane was over international waters, so that nobody could put a spanner in the works.

Asha was sceptical. What if the Israelis refused permission? Where would the plane land then? It made no sense, she told Alok, to cut things quite so fine.

Alok was sanguine, though. Don't forget, he told Asha, that the Israelis were looking to sell India over two billion dollars' worth of arms over the next few months. They were not going to jeopardize that contract by saying no to the Indian Prime Minister, especially on a matter that was so personal to her.

'Look Asha, it is imperative that word doesn't leak,' reiterated Alok. 'So, you have to keep this to yourself. You can't tell anybody. Not your mother. Not your brothers. No one.'

Asha was about to argue the point when they were interrupted by a knock on the door, which quickly opened to reveal Nitesh Dholakia. He looked startled to see Alok sitting across the sofa from his boss. Asha felt her colour rise as she saw a dawning comprehension in his eyes. But she restricted herself to a neutral, 'Yes, Nitesh, did you need something?'

'No, Prime Minister. Er, yes, Prime Minister,' he stuttered. Then, taking a moment to recover his equilibrium, he said, 'There's been a breakthrough in the Kautilya case. They've traced Soz and Abdullah to a village in the Kupwara district. And the Special Forces are undertaking an operation to flush them out . . .'

'I hope they have been instructed to take them alive,' interrupted Asha. 'I don't want a repeat of the Jamia operation that left everyone dead—and no hope of collecting any intelligence whatsoever.'

Dholakia rushed to reassure her that the Special Forces had been given these instructions. The commandos were scheduled to be choppered out to Kupwara shortly, where they would be airdropped at a discreet distance, to make the rest of the journey on foot.

In a few hours' time, Soz and Abdullah would be making their last stand. And if all went well, by the time a new day dawned, they would be in the custody of the Indian state.

\* \* \*

In their snow-white camouflage uniforms, the Special Forces commandos blended right into the stark white landscape stretching before them, studded with just the occasional clump of trees, now shorn of all foliage. They were still halfway to their target destination when it began snowing again, which made the going even slower and rougher.

But after about an hour and ten minutes, the soldiers were finally within firing range of the two-storied gabled house in which Soz and Abdullah were supposed to be hiding. The house stood in pitch darkness, illuminated only by the faint moonlight that reflected right off the snow. And as the Paras took refuge behind the treeline some distance away, with one party of twelve men peeling away to stand guard at the rear of the house, they could see no activity whatsoever around the house.

There were no heavily-armed men standing guard outside, no rifles peeked out from the many windows in the façade, and there were no mysterious figures on the roof.

For a minute, the commanding officer, Major Murtaza Quereshi, wondered if he had been sent on some sort of fool's errand. This house didn't even look inhabited, let alone the sanctuary of the top leaders of the JEA. Surely, if Soz and Abdullah were in residence, the grounds outside would have been well patrolled. Instead, there wasn't a soul in sight.

But just when Quereshi was about to radio in and report this, he caught a flash of light in one of the windows. One of the men inside was lighting a cigarette and in the brief moment when the flame of the match lit up, Quereshi could see the silhouette of an AK-47 by his side.

If there was one terrorist on site, then it stood to reason that there would be others. Quereshi signaled the go-order to the advance party of six, who were supposed to sneak in close to get the lay of the land, conduct reconnaissance to find out how many terrorists were in there, and report back. At his signal, the men set off stealthily, crawling on their stomachs, inching closer and closer to the property. They were about 250 yards from the front door, when the first shot rang out.

Quereshi, whose eyes had been fixed on the façade of the building, quickly identified that it had come from the same window in which the man had been lighting up. He took aim with his machine gun and began shooting, aiming straight at that window, even as the soldiers behind him set up covering fire so that their colleagues could make it back to relative safety behind the treeline. The advance party hurriedly scrambled back, firing at the house all the while.

By now, every window in the house had a rifleman or two stationed at it, and the firefight began in right earnest. Quereshi led with a fusillade of shots, peppering all the windows in turn, and his men followed his lead. He could now hear screams of pain issuing from within the house, along with the occasional shouted instruction.

Quereshi felt a moment of qualm. He had been instructed to take Soz and Abdullah alive. But with bullets being sprayed in every direction, there was no saying which of the terrorists holed up inside had died.

It could be that Soz and Abdullah were being shielded by their foot soldiers, and that these men had fulfilled their purpose of being cannon fodder, while their leaders survived. It was equally possible that Soz and Abdullah, both battle-hardened commanders, had taken the lead in fighting against the security forces. In which case, it was very likely that one or both were among those who had been killed.

There was simply no way to tell until they took over the building. And if they didn't do that soon, there was every possibility that every man inside would be dead by the time this encounter ended.

Quereshi made up his mind in that instant. They had to storm the building and take the men who were still alive into custody. Signalling to his men to follow, he set off towards the house in a crouched run, dodging bullets and firing blindly as he went. He could feel his party following close on his heels, and in less than thirty seconds they were at the front of the house. He did a quick count. There were eighteen men with him. With twelve of them having gone off to guard the back, that made thirty. That meant they hadn't taken a hit yet.

But the trickiest part of the operation was yet to come.

He signaled that he was going in, asking his second in command to provide cover. The two of them burst into the hallway, which had several rooms leading off in different directions. There were two dead bodies lying on the floor. Quereshi kicked them aside, and instructed the rest of his party to enter. They came in two abreast and then fanned off to check all the rooms on the ground floor, while Quereshi and four others climbed up the rickety wooden staircase to clear the first floor.

They made it to the half-landing, before there was a burst of firing from above that took out two commandos, who fell backwards down the stairs. Quereshi took aim at the shadowy figures above him and had the satisfaction of seeing both of them go down.

Quereshi and his men hastily climbed the next flight of stairs and halted at the top. There was an eerie silence all around them.

Had they managed to kill every one of the terrorists who were hiding here? Or were there still a few lying in wait, who would reveal themselves as they tried to take a shot at them. By now, eight more of his men had made it up to the first floor as well, and Quereshi signaled that they should split up and go through each of the rooms.

Quereshi took the first room to the right himself, with one commando providing him cover. Pushing the door open with the butt of his gun, he stayed in the shadows, preparing to take cover in case the terrorists inside were still alive and offering resistance. When nothing happened, he ventured into the room, his gun moving in slow arcs, ready to take aim at any target that presented itself.

The room was pitch black, with the curtains drawn against the pale moonlit sky. It took Quereshi's eyes a moment to accustom themselves to the darkness. By the time he discerned the shape of a man in one dark corner, and turned his gun on to him, the terrorist was on his feet and heading straight for the intruders.

The moment he saw the suicide vest on the man, and the detonator in his hand, all thoughts of trying to take him alive vanished. Quereshi fired several rounds from his machine gun, hoping to kill the terrorist before he could press the trigger. But it was too late. The entire room exploded outwards, blowing the bodies of everyone present to smithereens.

Quereshi died without ever knowing that he had taken both Salim Soz and Wajahat Abdullah with him. And with them, all hope of any resolution of the investigation into the Kautilya attack.

# 18

Bad news travels fast. But its speed tends to slow down a bit when the recipient is none other than the Prime Minister of the country.

So, it wasn't surprising that it took half an hour after the Kupwara operation was over for the National Security Advisor to arrive at Race Course Road to brief Asha Devi. Arunoday Sengupta was accompanied by the Principal Secretary, Madhavan Kutty. Clearly, the two men who never saw eye to eye on anything much, were decided on one thing. When it came to delivering bad news, there was safety in numbers.

Nitesh Dholakia greeted them at the door of Number 3 and in the short walk to the drawing room let drop that the Prime Minister was not alone. Asha Devi, he informed them in portentous tones, was being briefed by Finance Minister Alok Ray on a confidential matter.

Perhaps it was Dholakia's manner of conveying this information, an odd mixture of pomposity and embarrassment. Or maybe it was the relaxed body language of Asha Devi and Alok Ray that hinted at an intimacy that went beyond the professional. But as soon as Sengupta and Kutty laid eyes on Asha and Alok, they exchanged significant looks. Even though this was more reflexive than reflective, the gesture was not lost on Asha. Alok, however, remained oblivious and greeted both men with his trademark good humour.

That didn't last, though. Sengupta plunged straight into the narrative of how the Kupwara operation had gone down. With every word he said, Asha's hopes sank further. But even so, it came as a punch to the gut when Sengupta announced the Salim Soz and Wajahat Abdullah had been killed in the operation.

For one wild moment, Asha wondered if there was some sort of curse on her. Whatever she touched, crumbled to dust. Every operation she ordered, resulted in more death and destruction. And every line of enquiry, as a consequence, ended up at a dead end.

Sagar Prajapati, the prime accused in the L'Oiseau arms scandal, had been murdered in prison, despite his status as a high security prisoner. The terrorist cell in Jamia Nagar, from which they had hoped to gather reams of intelligence, had been blown up in the operation staged against it. And now, when there finally seemed to be a chance to resolve the Kautilya terror attack by capturing the top leadership of the JEA, Soz and Abdullah had put themselves beyond her reach.

Their death, Asha knew in her bones, marked the end of any meaningful investigation into the perpetrators of the Kautilya attack. The investigative agencies may keep up their probes, but everyone would know that they were just going through the motions, with no hope of being rewarded with a breakthrough.

But realistically speaking, how long could the government keep up this fiction?

At some point, Asha, as Prime Minister of the country, would have to admit that they could never ever bring those behind the Kautilya terror attack to justice. That there was no way of granting closure to the families of the SPG guards who had sacrificed their lives to save that of her sister-in-law. That the commandos who had died in the Jamia disaster had, for all intents and purposes, laid down their lives in vain. And that the deaths of the soldiers in Kupwara had amounted to nothing as well.

When she articulated these thoughts, there was no disagreement voiced. Everyone agreed that this was a setback. But they were also agreed that there was no way that they could admit as much to the Indian public. The government simply could not afford to lose face yet again.

There was no other way out. Asha Devi had to spin this into a victory. She had to act as if this outcome was exactly what she and her government had wanted all along. The Kupwara operation had to be sold as an attempt of the Indian state to wreak revenge on those who had attacked it.

'And why not, Madam Prime Minister?' argued Sengupta, now fully convinced by the case he had only just made up. 'After all, the Israelis go after anybody who has killed their citizens and wipe them off the face of the earth. Why can't we claim that we meant to do that same? If we want to come off as strong on terror, then that is the best way to do that.'

Kutty was quick to add his voice to that. 'I agree with Arunoday,' he interjected. 'We need to come off as a strong state. And what better way to do that than to make it clear that we will eliminate all terrorists as and where we find them.'

Alok, who had been shaking his head all through this, was finally moved to words. 'I'm sorry, Prime Minister, but this kind of reasoning makes me very uncomfortable. There is such a thing as rule of law. And our policy has to be that we will bring these people to justice, not blow them to kingdom come.'

'Well, in an ideal world, of course that is what we would do,' interrupted Sengupta, rather testily. 'But we don't live in an ideal world, do we? We have to do the best we can, given the circumstances we are dealing with.'

Alok looked as if he was about to press the point, but Asha silenced him with a look.

'You make a fair point, Alok,' she said, 'but Arunoday ji is right too. We have to deal with the circumstances as they exist. And the only option open to me now is to declare that these were the results we were hoping for all along and declare victory. We've given too much bad news to the Indian public already. They need some good news now, and that's what we are going to give them.'

And half an hour later, as the Doordarshan team hurriedly set up at Number 7 RCR so that the Prime Minister could address the nation, that's exactly what Asha Devi did.

* * *

Once again, prime-time news was disrupted by a live address by the Prime Minister. The Doordarshan feed featuring Asha Devi was carried across all channels, as every news outlet crashed into its regular programming.

Both Manisha Patel and Gaurav Agnihotri had just kicked off their debate shows when they were thrown off air by Asha Devi's 'address to the nation'. Both stayed on in the studio to watch, all set to analyze her words the moment she ceased speaking.

And as they listened in, they realized that there would be a lot to discuss and debate.

It was with a pugnacious set to her jaw that the Prime Minister announced that an operation had just been carried out in the Kupwara district of Kashmir, to target the masterminds of the attack on Kautilya Mall. Intelligence reports had suggested that the two top leaders of the JEA, identified as Salim Soz and Wajahat Abdullah, were all set to cross the border into POK. So, the army had sent out its commandos to capture them before they went beyond the reach of the Indian state.

Their orders, Asha Devi announced, had been to take the terrorists dead or alive. And given that these were highly motivated terrorists who thought nothing of blowing themselves up, the Indian army had gone into the operation fully prepared to use deadly force if necessary.

'The fearless commandos of our army mounted this operation in record time,' continued the Prime Minister, 'knowing that they may lose their lives in bringing these terrorists to justice. Tragically, some of our men were killed in the course of this operation when the terrorists set off their suicide vests. But even in the face of death, they fulfilled their mission. They took down both leaders of the JEA with them.

'Tonight, it is my privilege and great honour to announce to the Indian people that the Kautilya terror attack has been avenged. Both Salim Soz and Wajahat Abdullah, the leaders of the JEA, are dead. The two men who masterminded the Kautilya attack have met their end at the hands of our security forces.

'We will be forever grateful for the sacrifice of our soldiers,' said Asha, with a catch in her voice. 'We will never forget these bravehearts who laid down their lives to avenge the lives of those who were killed by these terrorists. It is thanks to them that justice has finally been served.

'At this time, I would also like to make special mention of the commanding officer, Major Murtaza Quereshi, who led the attack on the terrorists, and was killed in action. The entire nation bows down in homage to Major Quereshi's bravery and that of the men he led.'

By the time she finishes, thought Manisha cynically as she watched, there won't be a dry eye left in households across the country. Sacrifice! Bravehearts! Justice! What a great use of trigger words to divert attention from the fact that this operation had failed in its primary objective. Surely, it had been imperative to take Soz and Abdullah alive if there was to be any chance of furthering the investigation into the Kautilya attack. Their deaths had effectively led to the investigation being shut down forever.

And how clever to throw in that the officer leading the operation had been named Murtaza Quereshi. By identifying his religion, Asha Devi had effectively shielded herself from accusations of anti-Muslim bias, and made the point that the war on terror was not, by extension, a war on Muslims. It was a war fought by both Hindus and Muslims on the nation's behalf. And the soldiers who fell in the battlefield did not belong to one religion alone.

Not that such niceties necessarily mattered, thought Manisha, when all you were trying to do was use the deaths of our men in uniform to inflame passions in the country. When you were trying to turn failure into success by clambering over their dead bodies to make a political point.

Invoking their 'sacrifice' was a sure-shot way of making all questions stop. Those who still insisted on raising queries would now be dismissed as 'anti-nationals' and 'traitors' to the nation. And that threat alone was enough to make the media fall into line when it came to matters of national security.

But Manisha was determined not to fall into that trap. She would hold the Prime Minister to account if it was the last thing she did.

Gaurav, on the other hand, had no such reservations. On the contrary, he was very happy to take the 'martyred soldiers' story and run with it. Fortuitously, today he had one of the most rabid retired army Generals on the panel and it was to him that Gaurav turned first.

'General Trikha,' he asked, putting on the voice of faux humility with which he addressed all former army men, 'you must be a happy man tonight. Your boys have scored a remarkable victory against all the odds.'

General Trikha's moustache quivered with emotion as he nodded along vigorously. 'This is a great day, Gaurav, a great, great day! I can't remember the last time I was so proud of our boys in the army. They have taken the bull by the horns and have brought him crashing down on the ground.'

'But it is a sad day too,' interjected Gaurav, pulling a solemn face. 'We have lost many brave soldiers in this operation. And we must give thanks for their sacrifice and keep them in our hearts forever.'

General Trikha's moustache obediently wilted as he pulled his mouth down in a mournful expression. 'Of course, of course. The death of any soldier is a dark day in the history of our country. And to have so many of them killed in action is a tragedy of monumental proportions.

'But,' he continued, raising his voice a couple of octaves, 'you have to remember that these are Indian army men you are talking about. They are always prepared to make the ultimate sacrifice. In fact, there is no greater honour for a soldier than to lay down his life for his motherland.'

This was too much for the journalist on the panel. Nazia Ansari, who had just been laid off by her paper and depended on her appearances on Gaurav's show to eke out a living, was usually careful to go along with Gaurav's party line on all issues. But this celebration of a soldier's death was too much for her to take.

'With due respect, General Trikha,' she interrupted, 'surely there is nothing to celebrate in the death of our soldiers? Yes, they are always prepared to lay down their lives. But there must be something wrong with an operation in which so many of them are killed in the process of taking two terrorists into custody. And what's even worse is that the terrorists are dead too, which means that we can never get to the bottom of the Kautilya terror attack.'

Gaurav was not prepared to have such treasonous poison pollute his airwaves. Shutting Nazia up with an imperious wave of his hand, he turned to face the camera. 'Ladies and gentlemen,' he thundered, 'this is the problem with this country: people like Nazia Ansari, who don't appreciate the sacrifice of our soldiers. People like Nazia Ansari, who even on a day like this, want to run down our army. It is time that we told people like Nazia Ansari that we, the people of India, will no longer stand for this!'

Ansari, who had turned pale at this direct attack on her patriotism, could not even summon up the courage to mount a defense of her position. So, as always, Gaurav Agnihotri carried the day in the studios of NTN—and in drawing rooms across the country.

In the studios of AITNN, however, Manisha's disillusionment with Asha coloured the discussion that followed. The first guest she turned to was a former R&AW operative, who had been let go in controversial circumstances, and had been a reliably anti-government voice ever since.

'Mr Raichand,' she said, 'as a former intelligence officer, what do you make of this operation? Would you call it an unqualified success, like the Prime Minister just said? Or would you say it failed its primary objective, which was to further the investigation into the Kautilya terror attack?'

Raichand came in all guns blazing. 'This is a complete disaster, Manisha,' he bellowed, 'a complete disaster. What kind of intelligence did the army rely on before mounting this operation? How did they manage to lose so many brave soldiers in the course of this operation? After all, if our aim was to kill these terrorists rather than capture them alive, we could have just blown up their hideout with a drone. There was no need to risk the lives of our men in this manner unless the aim had been to take Soz and Abdullah alive. And we failed dismally to do that.'

The LJP spokesman on the panel had been shaking his head all through this outburst. So, the moment Raichand paused to take breath, he interjected, 'Manisha ji, I am amazed. Not just by the absolute nonsense this man is spouting but by the fact that you are allowing him to say all this without challenging him at all. Is this what it has come to? That our brave men in uniform lay down their lives and we, who are sitting in the air-conditioned comfort of TV studios, scoff at their sacrifice?'

Even though she was familiar with this script by now, Manisha felt herself going on the defensive. But before she could respond to this frontal attack on her, she heard the urgent tones of her producer in her earpiece. Sukanya Sarkar's office had called in from Kolkata. The Poriborton Party leader wanted to phone in and give her reaction to the Kupwara operation. Did Manisha want to cut to her?

Did she ever? It wasn't every day that a chief minister called into the show. And when it was the Bengal chief minister, you could be sure of generating a few headlines for the next day's papers.

So, Manisha apologized to her panelists and turned her attention to Sukanya Sarkar's gravelly voice in her ear. 'Sukanya di,' she began deferentially, 'thank you for joining the show. You have been following the events of this evening. What is your first reaction?'

Sukanya's Bengali accent always became more pronounced when she was agitated. And she was so agitated today that at some points she was almost unintelligible. But even so, it was clear that Sukanya was not happy with the way things had panned out in Kupwara.

'It is very sad, very sad, what has happened today. . . (unintelligible) . . . my prayers go out to all the families who have lost loved ones today . . . (unintelligible) . . . but this is not the way . . .'

Manisha interrupted at this point, interjecting a question for the sole purpose of calming Sarkar down so that she became a tad more comprehensible. 'Have you spoken to the Prime Minister yet, Sukanya di?' she asked. 'Have you congratulated her on the success of the operation?'

If anything, Sukanya Sarkar became even shriller in her reply. 'No, I have not spoken to Asha Devi. What is there to speak about? What is done is done. The right time to speak would have been before this operation was mounted.'

Manisha was quick to take her cue. 'Am I to understand that you didn't know of this operation beforehand? That the Prime Minister did not take you into confidence?'

'No, the Prime Minister did not take me into confidence. Nor has she called to brief me after it was over. I guess she was too busy appearing on TV!' said Sukanya snidely, quite unmindful of the irony that she was on TV herself, making her own case to the country.

But Manisha was not going to draw attention to that. She was more intent on burrowing into the divide that had clearly developed between Asha Devi and Sukanya Sarkar. 'But surely

Sukanya di, you must be glad to see that the masterminds of the Kautilya attack have been eliminated?'

'Yes, they have been eliminated. That is the problem, you see. When you just go in and kill everybody, then how will you ever find out the truth?'

'But ma'am,' said Manisha, playing devil's advocate for form's sake, 'what option did the commandos have? They had to attack when they did or the JEA leaders would have slipped across the border. And if the terrorists chose to blow themselves up, then where was the question of taking them alive?'

'You explain one thing to me, Manisha,' replied Sukanya fiercely. 'Just explain one thing to me. How it is that everything this government touches blows up in our faces? First you had Jamia Nagar. Now you have Kupwara. Why is it that we can never take anyone alive so that we can interrogate them and get to the bottom of things?'

'What exactly are you suggesting?' asked Manisha. 'Are you saying that the government is deliberately closing the avenues of a proper investigation? Are you alleging a conspiracy? Or are you accusing them of incompetence?'

'I am not suggesting anything. I am asking you a question. You are an experienced journalist. You have covered terrorism. You have covered Kashmir. Have you ever seen such things before? People are just being blown up here, there and everywhere, and we can't seem to control anything? What is going on? I am asking you, as a journalist, please tell me what is going on?'

Of course, Manisha knew that this was exactly what had been happening in Kashmir for decades now. She was also well aware that Sukanya wasn't really expecting her, a mere journalist, to tell her what was going on. This bewilderment she was portraying was just a way of telegraphing to those watching that she had no idea what was going on, a way of distancing herself from the government of Asha Devi.

And this time around, Sukanya Sarkar hadn't just restricted herself to mealy-mouthed platitudes about how the Prime Minister was 'very young' and needed more time 'to learn on the job'.

This time round, she had come right out and said it. Sukanya Sarkar didn't believe Asha Devi was up to the job of Prime Minister of India. And she had no problem announcing that to the world.

And to Asha Devi herself.

* * *

Asha had yet to come off the high of making a live address to the nation. Her heart was still pounding with an adrenalin rush as she made the short car journey back home to Number 3 Race Course Road. Alok, who had been watching her speech on the TV in the study, walked to the door to greet her. Taking her in his arms, he said, 'That was fantastic. You were fantastic.'

Asha laughed and said, in her usual self-deprecatory style, 'Well, you would say that, wouldn't you? You are hardly the most unbiased of observers!'

Alok smiled and demurred as the two of them wandered back to the study, both of them curious to see how the news was going down with the media. Asha's mood lightened as she did her usual rounds of the news channels, where everyone was praising her decisive action against the terrorist masterminds.

Until she came to the feed of AITNN, that is. And there, like the wicked fairy at the christening of a baby, was Sukanya Sarkar. Or, more accurately, her voice over a phone line, conveying her displeasure with the operation, with the government, and with Asha Devi, to the world.

As she listened, Asha felt herself growing angrier and angrier. If Sukanya Sarkar was upset about being left out of the decision to mount this operation, then she should have picked up the phone and spoken to her. Though quite how, as Prime Minister, she was expected to keep the Poriborton Party leader always in the loop was beyond Asha.

Operations like this one had a momentum of their own which could not be stalled to take the opinions of every ally on board. The truth of the matter was that you simply could not decide on matters like these by committee. They had to be decided in a split second, and the only people who could do that were the ones on the ground.

Alok kept a wary eye on Asha, who he could see was seething with unexpressed anger. But it was only when Sukanya Sarkar finally went off the line did he dare to voice his thoughts. 'I know how you are feeling, Asha. But it's no point allowing her to get to you this way . . .'

He didn't get any further. Asha's anger finally exploded and she hissed at him. 'You have no idea how I am feeling, Alok. No idea at all. And don't patronize me by saying I should not allow her to get to me. I can hardly ignore her, can I, given that my government depends on her support?'

Then, seeing the shock register on Alok's face, Asha took it down a notch, though with a visible effort. 'I am sorry, Alok. I shouldn't have snapped at you. I'm really sorry. But this pressure is beginning to get to me.'

Alok allowed himself to be mollified, even though he was rather miffed. 'That's okay,' he said. 'Don't worry about it. If you can't take your frustrations out on me, then who can you take them out on?'

That teased a smile out of Asha. 'Do you really see yourself as my favourite punching bag? Believe me, I don't see you like that. And I really am sorry.'

Alok reached out and held her hand. 'Don't worry about it. Seriously. You have far more important stuff to worry about right now.'

That she certainly did. And while Asha had begun the evening believing that containing the fallout of the Kupwara operation was top priority, she now knew that she had been mistaken. Far more important than that was dealing with what she now thought of as the Sukanya Sarkar Problem.

It was crystal clear to Asha that her coalition with the Poriborton Party leader was living on borrowed time. Sukanya had already made her displeasure with Asha and her government public on more occasions than she could count. And given her mercurial disposition, there was no saying when she would fly off the handle and pull the plug on Asha's government.

It was equally clear to Asha that she could not afford to sit around and wait for Sukanya to make the next move. As her father's daughter, she knew the key to good politics was to be proactive rather than reactive.

And that meant giving up on Sukanya before Sukanya could give up on her. The tricky bit was in achieving this without sacrificing her government in the bargain.

As she sat in the study with Alok, both of them eating dinner off trays as they desultorily flipped through all the news channels, Asha could hardly concentrate on the images on the television or on the occasional comment that Alok made. Her mind was racing through scenarios in which she could ditch Sukanya without losing Race Course Road in the bargain.

Staying in alliance with the Poriborton Party leader was no longer even a short-term option, let alone a medium or long-term one. She just had to work out how to push Sukanya off the ledge before she jumped, taking Asha Devi's government with her.

# 19

The problems between Didi Damyanti and Satyajit Kumar had started even before the Bihar government was sworn in. Given his party's performance at the hustings, Kumar had been resigned to getting far fewer ministries than he had initially hoped for. But as coalition partner, he did expect that at least two heavy-duty portfolios would be assigned to his party MLAs, even though it went without saying that the chief minister would be from the Dalit Morcha ranks.

In the first round of negotiations, he had held out for the home ministry and the finance ministry, even though he knew that he would only score one of the two. But when it came to bargaining with Damyanti, it made sense to start out from a maximalist position. That was the only way to end up with the bare minimum that he would be satisfied with.

But even that bare minimum had not been granted to Satyajit Kumar. Damyanti had practically laughed in his face when he made his demands. There was no way, she declared, that the two most important portfolios would be assigned to anyone other than her Dalit Morcha loyalists. These ministries were critical to the functioning of the state government. And she was not going to risk giving them to anyone other than those she had complete faith in. And on that score alone, no member of the SPP qualified.

Satyajit had persisted for days, delaying the swearing-in of the ministers as a consequence. But Damyanti had refused to budge. In the end, Kumar had given in with bad grace and accepted less important ministries. And a good three days after the results were declared, the government had been duly sworn in, with Kumar looking visibly sullen, while Damyanti radiated good cheer.

Since then, things had gone steadily downhill. Ministers from the SPP found their routine decisions being countermanded by the Dalit Morcha supremo, who kept a close watch on their departments through her handpicked bureaucrats. All of them complained to Satyajit Kumar, who in turn called up Damyanti to remonstrate. But eight times out of ten, he could not get her on the phone. And on the rare occasions when he did manage to speak to her, she denied his charges flatly, getting incensed if he persisted, and effectively ended all further discussion by enquiring angrily if he was calling her a liar.

After a few such confrontations, Satyajit had decided that there was no point in even engaging with the Dalit Morcha leader. He would let his ministers get on as well as they could, profit as much as he could from the ministries that had money-making potential, and build up his war chest for future elections. Bihar was done and dusted for another five years. He should now move on and concentrate on the other states that were due to go to the polls.

So, a month after the new government had been sworn in, an uneasy truce prevailed between the SPP and the Dalit Morcha ministers in Bihar. And that's how matters would have chugged along for months, if not years, if it hadn't been for an incident involving health minister and SPP leader Raghubir Yadav.

Yadav was scheduled to visit a remote village called Sitagarh to inaugurate a new maternity care centre, accompanied by the usual entourage that shadows ministers on such visits: officials from his ministry, some SPP local leaders and his security detail. But as his cavalcade made the long and bumpy journey, the rains came crashing down. So heavy were the showers that the roads were soon flooded and their pace slowed down to a crawl.

By the time they finally reached Sitagarh—a couple of hours late—and pulled up before the maternity care centre, the rain had mercifully stopped. But the downpour had flooded the front lawn and pathway that the party had to traverse to get to the main door of the centre.

Yadav took one look at the expanse of water and another at his shoes: pristine white sneakers he had purchased at a designer store on his last visit to Delhi. They had been so expensive that he was scared to tell his wife how much they cost. And he certainly could not bear the thought of sitting through her recriminations if he were to ruin them by trudging through ankle-deep water.

In a split-second, Yadav made a decision that would have repercussions on the rest of his life. Swinging his feet out of the car, he signaled to his PSO (Personal Security Officer) to kneel down and unlace his shoes, and slip them off for safekeeping. Ever since he had had an operation for a hernia, Yadav had been rendered incapable of bending down and taking his own shoes off. So, members of his staff were used to being pressed into this service.

His PSO, Kamal Dev, who had performed this duty on numerous occasions in private, thought nothing of kneeling on the wet floor and wrestling the shoes off his boss' feet in full view of the cameras. Then, as Yadav made the short journey across the waterlogged lawn, Dev followed close behind, holding the shoes in his hands as if they were a rare prize that had been conferred upon him. Once Yadav got on to dry land, down went Dev again, to help his boss put on his shoes again.

Nobody in attendance—all of whom were used to ministers being treated like colonial overlords—thought that there was anything out of the ordinary in this, and the rest of the engagement proceeded as per usual.

It was only when the video ran on one of the Patna-based regional channels, that all hell broke loose. The anchor could barely conceal his glee at having scooped this little clip that was bound to create a nation-wide controversy. Here was a minister, he sneered, so high and mighty that he would not even bend down to untie his own shoelaces. He needed a minion to do that, and then carry his shoes around until he was ready to wear them again.

Just who did Yadav think he was? The Viceroy of India in the days of the British Raj?

It took only about ten minutes for the other local channels to jump on the story. And in half an hour, the national TV channels had bought the clip and were running it non-stop as well. And it was their reportage that gave an added edge to the story. Kamal Dev—notwithstanding his upper caste-sounding last name—was a Dalit.

Now the optics looked even worse. It wasn't just that the minister had made a policeman conduct a menial task for him. He had, in fact, shown a Dalit man that his proper place was at his feet.

The commentary now took on an even shriller edge. Now, it wasn't just about the arrogance of power that Yadav had displayed. The issue at stake now was Dalit pride.

How could a minister in a Dalit Morcha-led government behave like this with a Dalit? Surely Didi Damyanti wouldn't possibly stand for it? And what was the fair punishment for a crime like this one?

* * *

That was precisely the discussion that Satyajit Kumar and Didi Damyanti were mired in a mere 30 minutes after the story first broke.

Satyajit initially found himself at a disadvantage in the conversation. He had just retired to the bedroom for his usual post-lunch nap when there was an urgent knock on the door. Irate at being disturbed when he had left precise instructions to the contrary, Kumar first tried to ignore the knocking. When it persisted, he bellowed angrily, 'Kaun hai? Kya chahiye?' (Who is it? What do you want?)

Once it was made clear to him that a very angry Damyanti was on the line, demanding to speak to him at once, he reluctantly picked up the phone, and immediately held it away from his ear, so loudly was she bellowing into it.

Given that he hadn't been following the story, it took him a few minutes before he could make any sense of what the Dalit Morcha leader was saying. When he finally got the gist of what had happened, he was livid as well.

How could Yadav possibly be so foolish? First, to have a policeman take off his shoes for him in public. And then, to add insult to injury, choose a Dalit man to perform the service. Was the man out of his mind? Forget about the optics itself, surely he knew that this would incense Damyanti and she would be out for his blood?

In an attempt to placate the Dalit leader, Kumar offered up the most abject apology he could devise at short notice. 'I am truly sorry, Damyanti ji. This kind of thing is unforgiveable, I know. But all I can do is humbly ask for your forgiveness, both on Yadav's behalf and on behalf of my party. Please tell me what I can do to make it right, and I will do so right away.'

'Sorry? You are sorry?' Damyanti exploded yet again. 'What do I care about your sorry? Can I make a potion out of it and apply it on the fresh wounds that your man Yadav has inflicted on the whole Dalit community? What use is your sorry to me?'

'Well,' asked Kumar, keeping his calm with an effort, 'if my sorry is not enough, what would you like me to do? Would you like Yadav to call up and apologize to you? I was going to make him do that anyway . . .'

'I don't want to have to do anything with that man,' shouted Damyanti. 'He thinks that he can insult a Dalit man while he is a member of my government? He thinks he can show that Dalits belong at his feet? Is that the message he is sending me? That I might be the leader of a political party, I might be the leader of an entire community; but at the end of the day, people like me are only fit to tie his shoelaces?'

Kumar spent the next ten minutes trying to calm Damyanti down. And by the time the conversation had ended, he had managed to arrive at a compromise formula of sorts. Raghubir Yadav would send a letter of apology to Didi Damyanti, which would be released to the media. The minister would also hold a press conference at which he would apologize in person to Kamal Dev, and reiterate his commitment to upholding the rights and dignity of the Dalit community.

But if Kumar thought that he weathered this storm, he had another think coming. Hanging up on Damyanti and dialing Yadav, he came up against an intransigence that was as maddening as Damyanti's temper had been.

His call with Yadav started propitiously enough. Stricken by the thought that he had triggered a national controversy, the minister was full of apologies when his party leader called him. Even before Kumar could berate him, Yadav was stammering out his apologies.

'Satyajit ji, *mujhse bahut badi galti ho gayi. Maaf kar dijiye,*' (I have committed a big mistake. Please forgive me) he began. And then, without waiting for Kumar to respond, he went on a long tangent about how he had recently had a hernia operation and had been told not to bend forward under any circumstances. That was the only reason why he had asked his PSO to help him with his shoes. Otherwise, as Kumar knew well, he was a completely humble man, who even washed his own clothes at home.

There was a limit to how much humbug Satyajit Kumar was willing to take. Cutting into this long-winded justificatory monologue, he interjected, 'Even if you did need help, couldn't you at least make sure that there were no cameras around when you got someone to take off your shoes? And did you really have to choose a Dalit to do that? Your staff is crawling with men whose last names are Yadav. You couldn't ask one of them to do it?'

'Sir ji, mistake *ho gayee,*' said a dejected Yadav, who by now sounded close to tears. 'And how would I know he is Dalit? He is calling himself Kamal Dev. Does that sound like a Dalit name to you?'

Kumar knew that this was nonsense. A caste-conscious man like Yadav would have known what caste his PSO belonged to. And even if he couldn't tell by his name, he would have made it his business to find out. So, these excuses didn't really cut it with him.

But rather than get mired in the weeds, Kumar decided to plunge on straight ahead. 'Anyway, forget about all that,' he said impatiently. 'What's done is done. Now we will have to do some damage control.'

He explained to Yadav what Damyanti expected of him. But while Yadav was fine with writing a groveling apology and sending it to Damyanti, he balked at the idea of apologizing to his PSO in person and in public.

'Sorry sir ji, *par yeh toh mumkin nahin hai*,' (Sorry Sir, but that is not possible) he said firmly, once the idea was mooted to him. 'How can I apologize in public to a man like that?'

'What do you mean? Man like that? Are you saying you can't apologize to a Dalit? You do know that even Didi Damyanti is a Dalit, don't you?'

'It's not a question of Dalit, sir ji. It's a question of rank. He is only a policeman. How can I, a minister, apologize to someone like him? People in my community will not take it well. They will treat it as an insult. And I will probably never get elected again if I do something like that.'

'People in your community? And how do you think people in his community will react if you don't make amends to him? How do you think the leader of his community will react?'

But no matter how many arguments Kumar deployed, how many threats he made, and how hard he expostulated, Yadav remained unmoved. He would write a letter of apology to Didi Damyanti. But that was as far as he was prepared to do.

There was no way he was going to say sorry to a mere PSO. He had some standards after all.

* * *

While these negotiations were going on, the story—now duly dubbed Sneakergate—had taken on a momentum of its own. The visuals of Yadav having his shoes untied and then tied again by his Dalit PSO were running non-stop on all the national news channels, accompanied by the mandatory howls of outrage.

For once, Manisha Patel conceded, the anger was completely justified. The very fact that Yadav had thought nothing of being photographed and filmed in such a situation went to show how deep anti-Dalit prejudice ran in those parts. The minister was clearly so used to relegating menial tasks to members of the Dalit community that he had seen no problem in asking his PSO to be his personal shoe-bearer.

Quickly changing the run order of her show to lead with Sneakergate, Manisha tried hard to get Raghubir Yadav on the phone line so that she could get him to comment on the controversy. When that didn't work, she tried to get a reaction from Satyajit Kumar. But the SPP leader remained incommunicado as well.

So, Manisha had to be content with running a discussion with some Delhi-based Dalit leaders and the two journalists who had already been booked on her show. But even as she asked the usual questions of the usual suspects, she was sending off frantic texts to Didi Damyanti, begging her to come on the show—even if it was on the phone line for a few minutes—so that she could get her perspective. But she got no joy from the Dalit Morcha leader either.

Gaurav Agnihotri, churning his own outrage machine in his studio, was working the same phone lines as well. And he was coming up against the same wall of silence.

There was a good reason for that. Didi Damyanti was still spitting fire and in no mood to talk to anyone at all until Yadav had practically prostrated himself in front of Dev. And Satyajit Kumar, after failing to get Yadav to see reason, was gathering up the courage to call Damyanti and plead with her to dial down her expectations.

A public apology to Dev, he explained when he finally got her on the line, would be a humiliation for his minister. Surely it was enough so long as Yadav said sorry to Dev in private and made a public apology to her alone.

No way, responded an implacable Damyanti. It was Kamal Dev who had been insulted by the minister. So, it was only fitting that Yadav apologize to Kamal Dev.

A hapless Kumar now began working the lines with other SPP leaders in his Bihar unit, who were known to be close to Yadav. Perhaps one of them would be able to persuade Yadav to do as Damyanti had asked. But even though each of them tried his best, Yadav remained firm.

There was no way he was going to apologize to some Dalit policeman. He was a minister, after all. And ministers simply didn't do such a thing.

Now at his wits end, Kumar called up Damyanti yet again to plead Yadav's case. But instead of agreeing to a compromise, the Dalit Morcha leader upped the ante.

Fine, she said, if Yadav couldn't bring himself to apologize, he need not do so. But if he didn't, Kumar had to ask him to resign from the ministry.

A stunned Satyajit Kumar—who could not believe how a small incident like this had snowballed into such a serious matter—begged Damyanti to see reason. This was surely an overreaction, he suggested to the Dalit Morcha leader.

Yadav had made a mistake, there was no doubt about that.

But was it such a major mistake that he should lose his ministry as a consequence? Surely not? Maybe they should wait a day for tempers to cool, and discuss the issue again the following morning.

'Tempers to cool?' shouted Damyanti down the phone line. 'My temper will never cool when it comes to insults to my community. You can wait a day, a week, a month, or even a year, and my temper will never cool when Dalit pride is at stake.'

Satyajit Kumar tried to make soothing noises at the other end of the line, but Damyanti was having none of it.

Kumar had until 10 a.m. tomorrow. By that time, she wanted Yadav's public, in-person apology to Kamal Dev over and done with. If that wasn't forthcoming, then she wanted Yadav's resignation letter on her desk.

These were the only two options on the table. Now, it was up to Yadav—and Kumar—to pick one.

And that, as far as Didi Damyanti was concerned, was that.

* * *

In retrospect, that was the worst decision that Satyajit Kumar made: asking for time to resolve the issue. If he had prevailed upon Kumar to either apologize or resign that evening itself, he might have conceivably saved his government in Bihar. But by asking to postpone the matter, he allowed Damyanti the time and space not only to wallow in her sense of injustice but, more to the point, ruminate on her options.

And once she did that, the Dalit Morcha leader realized that she did not, in fact, need Satyajit Kumar and his SPP party at all when it came to staying in power in Bihar.

The more she thought about it, the more it made sense. In a 243-member Assembly, she needed 122 MLAs to form a majority. The Dalit Morcha strength stood at 110, so she could easily ditch the SPP, which had 66 members, so long as she could come to an understanding with Asha Devi's LJP, which had as many as 55 seats in the House.

But would Asha Devi be receptive to such an idea? Didi Damyanti realized that she had no idea how the Prime Minister would react to such a proposal. Damyanti had dealt with Asha's half-brother, Karan Pratap, on many occasions and had his measure. But even though she had met Asha a couple of times, it was just to exchange Namastes and smiles. She really had no special insight into how Asha operated as a politician.

Would she be pragmatic enough to accept an offer that gave her party a seat at the table in Bihar? Or would Damyanti's numerous personal digs against her, give Asha pause about aligning with the Dalit Morcha leader?

Well, there was only one way to find out. Damyanti reached for her phone and asked to be connected to the Prime Minister.

Asha Devi had just walked into Number 3 Race Course Road when her major domo came rushing up to say that Didi Damyanti was on the line. Canny politician that she had become, Asha declined to take the call, softening the blow by saying she would call back in five minutes. She needed that time to think things through clearly before she entered into any conversation with Damyanti, who was known to run rings around people.

The only reason Damyanti would be reaching out to her at this juncture was to use her as a pawn in her battle against Satyajit Kumar. Clearly the Dalit Morcha leader was livid about Sneakergate and itching to teach Kumar and his party a lesson. And what better way to do that than by enlisting the Prime Minister in her fight?

Asha, who had yet to recover from the hurt inflicted on her by Damyanti's jibes about 'dynasts' and 'naamdars', knew she had to play this carefully. Given that Damyanti was the leader of the Dalit community, she had to be properly respectful of her—especially at a time when Dalit pride had been hurt by the actions of Raghubir Yadav.

So, having settled on a few choice words of sympathy, Asha picked up the phone and called the Dalit Morcha leader. But even before she could get half-way through her prepared remarks, Damyanti dropped a bombshell on her.

'Asha ji,' she interrupted, 'I am a woman who likes to come straight to the point. So let me tell you why I am calling you today. I have a question for you. And I would like a "yes" or "no" answer.'

Okay, said Asha cautiously. She would try and give Damyanti what she wanted.

And what the Dalit Morcha leader wanted was both simple and startling. She wanted to dissolve her coalition with Satyajit Kumar's SPP and form a new government in partnership with the LJP.

Would Asha Devi be willing to do that? Yes or no?

Asha was flabbergasted. It was only a month since the Bihar government had been sworn in, and Damyanti was already so fed up with Satyajit Kumar that she wanted to end her alliance with him. Yes, admittedly she had had her patience tested by Sneakergate, but if that was really provocation enough for Damyanti to pull the plug on the SPP, it didn't bode well for any future allies of the Dalit Morcha leader.

On the other hand, here was a golden opportunity to humiliate her bête noire, Satyajit Kumar, provided to her on a platter. How could she possibly turn it down?

And then, there was the Sukanya factor. If she did ally with Sukanya's arch enemy, Didi Damyanti, to form the state government in Bihar, the Bengal chief minister was guaranteed to go ballistic. But would that be such a bad thing, wondered Asha. It would prove to Sarkar that the Prime Minister was not willing to be bullied by her main alliance partner. It would establish beyond doubt that Asha Devi was her own person, who took her own decisions, and didn't give a damn about whom she offended as a consequence.

So, after a pregnant pause, Asha Devi gave Didi Damyanti her one word answer. And the word she chose was 'yes'.

# 20

Asha Devi boarded the plane back to Delhi, and settled into her seat with a sigh. But it was a sigh born of relief rather than exasperation. She had just seen the new Bihar Cabinet sworn in, occupying pride of place in the front row next to Didi Damyanti. As sundry LJP MLAs strode up to the stage to take their oath of office as ministers, Asha had luxuriated in an unusual feeling: a sense of quiet satisfaction.

Not only had she managed to get into a power-sharing agreement in one of the more important states in the country, she had achieved this with minimal effort on her part. It was Damyanti who had made the initial overture, it was Damyanti who had bent over backwards to accommodate her every demand, and it was Damyanti who was trying her best to ingratiate herself with the Prime Minister.

Asha knew what it was about, of course. Now that they were allies at a state level, the Dalit Morcha leader wanted to take their alliance to the next logical step: an alliance at the centre.

And that's exactly what Damyanti had suggested when the two women sat down to have a cup of tea after the swearing-in ceremony was over.

For once, Damyanti had decided to forswear the large entourage that always surrounded her at such meetings. And in deference, Asha had asked her aides to stay outside as well. If Damyanti wanted a one-on-one meeting, that's what Damyanti would get.

Once the two women were alone in the room, Asha spent an inordinate amount of time choosing her tea-time snacks, loading her plate slowly with a chocolate biscuit, a soggy cucumber sandwich and a few spoons of namkeen, allowing the silence to stretch to uncomfortable lengths.

If Asha had learnt anything from her father, it was to be comfortable with a pause in the conversation. Don't rush to fill the silence in a meeting, Baba always used to advise her. Make it work for you. Don't feel pressured to initiate a line of conversation, allow the other person to do so. Not only will this give you an insight into their minds, but it will also grant you time to gauge what your response should be.

So, Asha settled comfortably in her armchair, plate perched on her lap, and chewed slowly on a biscuit, offering Damyanti nothing more than a beatific smile.

But that was all the encouragement that Damyanti needed. Taking a quick sip of her masala chai, she began, 'Asha ji, before we go any further, I just wanted to clarify any misunderstandings you might have.'

In answer to Asha's raised eyebrows, she continued, 'You know how it is. On the campaign trail, in the heat of the election, one has to say many things. And I admit that I said many things about you as well . . .'

Asha, who had crystal-clear recollection of every insult that had been heaped upon her, of every name that she had been called, of every slight thrown in her direction, nodded neutrally but refused to say a word.

After a pregnant pause, Damyanti went on, 'I just wanted to clarify that it was nothing personal. Election *kay time pey yeh*

*sab toh karna padta hai* (You have to do all this at election time).
I hope you didn't take it to heart.'

Damyanti looked at Asha questioningly, but all the Prime
Minister gave by way of answer was an enigmatic smile.

The Dalit Morcha leader went on valiantly. 'Asha ji, I
just want to assure you that I have nothing but the greatest
admiration for you, both as a woman and a political leader. You
have come back from impossible odds to lead this country. And
you have done a stellar job . . .'

Asha finally decided to put Damyanti out of her misery.
Holding up her palm as a signal to stop, she said, 'Damyanti
ji, please, you're embarrassing me. Of course, I know how
this game is played. And I know better than to take anything
politicians say on the campaign trail seriously. Believe me, there
are no hard feelings at all.'

Damyanti beamed in response, and reached across to
squeeze Asha's hand. 'I am so happy to hear that. Because
believe me, Asha ji, if the two of us get together, we can achieve
amazing things for this country.'

And with that, Damyanti laid out her master plan. Sukanya
Sarkar had proved to be a completely unreliable ally for Asha.
She had belittled the Prime Minister in the media, she had
made her dissatisfaction with the central government clear to
the people of India, and she had publicly broken with many
crucial decisions that Asha Devi had taken.

So, why did the Prime Minister feel obliged to stick with
such an ally?

Look at her own experience, Damyanti urged Asha Devi.
The SPP had humiliated her in just one instance, and rather than
ignore it, she had taken the bold step of breaking the government
and ditching Satyajit Kumar completely. That was the only way
of dealing with unreliable allies. You just had to get rid of them.

That was all very well, responded Asha, but she had a country to run. She could not afford to plunge all of India into chaos just because Sukanya Sarkar was up to her usual tricks. She had to be the adult in this relationship, because Sukanya clearly was an impetuous baby.

But why should she indulge Sukanya's temper tantrums, asked Damyanti, when she had a perfectly good alternative available? Asha could simply ditch the Poriborton Party and ally with the Dalit Morcha instead. And as for the shortfall in numbers, it would be simplicity itself to win over some Independents and smaller parties and be home and dry.

For form's sake, Asha pretended to give this proposal due consideration, assuring Damyanti that she would think about it and get back to her in a couple of days. But in her mind, she was clear.

Yes, it made sense to ditch the short-fused Sukanya Sarkar, and she had to do that before the PP leader went berserk on some non-issue and pulled the plug on her government. But only a fool would agree to substitute one mercurial, high-handed, bad-tempered, unreliable ally for another.

And whatever else she may be, Asha Devi was no fool.

\* \* \*

Ever since the news broke that Asha Devi's LJP was going to ally with the Dalit Morcha in Bihar, Sukanya had been in a massive strop. When the first murmurs began humming along the political hotlines, Sukanya had immediately called Asha on her mobile, only to find that the number was switched off.

Sarkar's office had then begun the excruciating—and in the end, embarrassing—task of tracking down the Prime Minister. They had tried her direct line at the PMO, but the phone rang out without anyone responding. Then, they had dialled Asha's direct line at RCR, but had no luck there either. Finally, they had been reduced to leaving increasingly desperate messages with the PM's various aides, asking that she call Sukanya Sarkar back as soon as possible.

The longer it had taken to track Asha Devi down, the worse Sukanya's temper got. And it didn't help that in a couple of hours it became clear that the Dalit Morcha and the LJP were going to be partners in the Bihar government, with both Damyanti and Asha releasing statements confirming the new arrangement.

Watching this on television, Sarkar had felt as if her head would explode. Asha knew perfectly well how Sukanya felt about Didi Damyanti. The two leaders of the Poriborton Party and the Dalit Morcha had been sworn enemies for years now. And as Sukanya had made clear to Asha's half-brother, Karan Pratap, when they were negotiating to form the central government, there was no way Sarkar would ever consent to being part of the same alliance as Damyanti.

So, how could Asha conceivably think that she could get away with allying with Sukanya Sarkar at the Center, and with Didi Damyanti at the state level? Surely, she should know better. And if she didn't, well then Sukanya would lose no time in setting her right.

But in order to do that, she had to get the Prime Minister on the phone first.

It wasn't until early the next day, though, that Asha returned Sukanya's many phone calls. Sukanya, who had spent the night seething sleeplessly, cut through Asha's pleasantries and commenced battle immediately.

'I am shocked, Madam Prime Minister, I am absolutely shocked by your behavior,' she began . . .

'I am so sorry Sukanya ji,' Asha cut in calmly, 'I simply could not get back to you sooner. I was stuck in meetings all evening yesterday. I am really sorry about that . . .'

'That's not what you should be sorry about, Asha ji,' interrupted Sukanya angrily. 'I am not bothered about how long you take to call back. I am insulted by the fact that you have entered into an alliance with Damyanti without bothering to check how I feel about it. You seem to have forgotten that we are allies. And that we need to consult each other before we take decisions like these.'

Asha was prepared for just such an argument. Affecting great surprise, she responded, 'We should consult each other before such decisions? But Sukanya ji, just last month you entered into an alliance with the Bhartiya Socialist Front (BSF) and joined the state government in Orissa. I don't remember you calling me and asking permission before doing so? So, why would I call and check with you before joining the Bihar government? Frankly, I am astonished that you would even expect that. Why should this even be an issue between us?'

Sukanya knew that this was a bald-faced lie. Like everyone else in the country, Asha was well aware of the history between Sukanya and Damyanti. Having begun their careers as budding political leaders in the SPP, the two had soon fallen out as they vied to be the chosen favourite of their party leader. And even after both had left the SPP and set up political parties of their own, that enmity hadn't withered and died. On the contrary, it had become even more entrenched.

So, Asha knew perfectly well that allying with Didi Damyanti was like showing a red rag to Sukanya Sarkar. The rules of the game were quite clear. When it came to Sukanya Sarkar and Didi Damyanti, you had to choose between them.

It was either Sukanya or Damyanti. And once you chose one, you had to eschew the other. It was as simple as that.

The whole world knew that when it came to Damyanti, it was personal for Sukanya. But how could she say that to Asha in so many words, without coming off as petty and small-minded? And why should she have to, given that this was common knowledge in all of India?

Livid at the Prime Minister for putting her in this spot, Sarkar resorted to bluster instead. 'You know it is not the same thing, Asha ji. It is not the same thing at all. The BSF is a small regional party. There is no conflict of interest here if I ally with them at the state level. The BSF is not a rival party as far as you are concerned. But the Dalit Morcha is a direct rival to me. How would you like it if I made the SPP a partner in the Bengal government? Would you still say that as allies we don't need to discuss these things?'

'Please be my guest,' replied Asha tartly, finally allowing a flash of temper to show. 'I could not care less who you choose to ally with in your state. That is your choice, your decision. Just as it is mine who I choose to ally with in Bihar.'

'Fine,' snapped back Sukanya, 'if that is how you want to play it, that's fine by me. Satyajit Kumar came to me months ago begging for an alliance and I turned him down out of loyalty to you. But if that is all the loyalty you are prepared to show me, then I will definitely take him up on his offer.'

'Yes, you should do that,' said Asha, assuming a tone of faux cordiality. 'In fact, from this point on, both of us should be clear what our duties and responsibilities are to each other. We are allies in the central government, and there, I agree, we should take all decisions after consulting each other. But other than that, we are the leaders of our own parties, and our parties can decide on what alliances we strike at the state level. I hope we can agree on that.'

And, with very bad grace indeed, Sukanya Sarkar had agreed.

But now, as she sat in her office, watching the swearing-in of the Bihar Cabinet and saw Asha Devi and Didi Damyanti sitting next to each other, talking and laughing together, she felt a fresh rush of blood to her brain.

This was nothing short of an outright insult to her; an insult that cried out for vengeance. And nobody knew how to exact vengeance quite like Sukanya Sarkar.

\* \* \*

The media, innured though it was to the instability inherent in coalition politics, had been taken by surprise at how quickly the Bihar government had collapsed. One minute, Raghubir Yadav was having his shoes taken off by his Dalit PSO and the next Satyajit Kumar had had his neck wrung by Didi Damyanti.

Whatever you might say about the temperamental leader of the Dalit Morcha, there was no denying her decisiveness. Once she decided on a particular course of action, nothing and no one could deter her. Which is why it had taken less than a day for Satyajit Kumar's humiliation at her hands to be complete.

But as TV news channels went back to their studios after running a live telecast of the swearing-in, the hot topic of discussion was not Satyajit Kumar or even the state of Bihar. The only thing that the anchors were talking about was what this DM-LJP alliance would signify at the national level.

Would the Poriborton Party-LJP coalition government at the Centre survive after Asha had humiliated Sukanya Sarkar by allying with her archenemy, Didi Damyanti?

Manisha Patel, who had a direct line to Sarkar, had tried hard to get her on the line. But while Sukanya was willing to rave and rant about Asha Devi on an off-the-record basis, she resolutely refused to come on air and say what she really thought of the Prime Minister.

This was not the right time to do so, she told Manisha. She needed to strategize with her party leaders on the way forward. Once she was clear on that, she would give Manisha an exclusive interview detailing her plans.

Manisha knew that this was nonsense. There were no party leaders that Sukanya wanted to strategize with. For one thing, she was the only leader of consequence in the Poriborton Party. And for another, she had zero respect for the opinions of others when it came to taking political decisions.

The only reason Sarkar was refusing to go public was because she was not ready to pull the plug on Asha Devi's government just yet. The decision had probably been made, but the timing was not quite right. No matter, Manisha was willing to wait for the scoop until it finally fell into her lap.

Until then, Manisha made do with the usual suspects in her prime-time debate show. The LJP spokesman refused to be drawn on whether the LJP-DM alliance in Bihar meant that the two parties would enter into a coalition agreement at the Centre as well. All he would say is that the government at the Centre was stable and would serve out the rest of its term.

The journalists on the panel were openly scornful of this claim. Rajiv Wadekar, a former editor turned TV commentator, laughed aloud at this claim. 'If Asha Devi really believes that she can string along both Sukanya Sarkar and Didi Damyanti at the same time, she is not just deluded but foolish. If you ask me, by getting into an alliance with the Dalit Morcha, she has effectively pulled down her government at the Centre. It's now only a matter of time before Sarkar calls time on this coalition.'

Much the same consensus prevailed in the debate conducted by Gaurav Agnihotri. Only in his case, bolstered by what he fondly imagined to be his 'special relationship' with the Prime Minister, the discussion quickly veered into examining the finer qualities of Asha Devi and the political daring, not to mention the chutzpah, she had displayed by displacing Satyajit Kumar and getting her own party into power in Bihar.

'Ladies and gentlemen,' said an ebullient Gaurav, 'you have to admire the sheer suddenness of the maneuver, the sheer unexpectedness of the move, the sheer unpredictability of the action, the sheer audacity of the decision. With this, Asha Devi has proved herself to be a politician par excellence. Today, I can say with complete confidence, that there is nobody in the entire political firmament who can compare with the Prime Minister when it comes to political skill and strategic sense.'

Only one panelist was brave enough to venture a contrary opinion. Surely, he asked Gaurav, this was a move fraught with danger. And was it really worth risking the survival of the national government just to get into power in one state? Did that make any political sense at all? Surely the move was, if anything, suicidal.

Gaurav fairly snorted in contempt by way of answer. And then, with a sneer on his face, he replied, 'That is exactly what real leaders do, my dear friend. They take risks, because they believe in pushing the envelope. They take risks because they have confidence in their decision-making. And in the end, it is only those who take risks who survive in politics. As the saying goes, nothing ventured, nothing gained.'

Reeling under the fusillade of clichés emanating from Gaurav's mouth at the speed of a sub-machine gun, the hapless panelist mumbled something unintelligible in agreement and retreated into silence. Gaurav looked challengingly around his horseshoe-shaped table to see if anyone else had the temerity to challenge him on this.

He nodded in satisfaction as everyone else stayed quiet, and then, with a triumphant flourish, turned to the camera to do his customary closing.

'Ladies and gentlemen, I am afraid that's all we have time for now. Thank you for watching. And thank you for choosing News Over Views.'

And with that little kick to irony, Gaurav Agnihotri signed off for the night.

\* \* \*

As her motorcade drove into the Race Course Road complex, Asha made a snap decision. She was not going to watch any of the evening's coverage of the events in Bihar. She had had enough of the media's constant sensationalizing of every event, not to mention the endless editorializing that followed. And she was tired of being bashed by TV anchors on a daily basis, no matter if she deserved it or not.

By any objective standard, this was one of those rare evenings that marked a triumph for the Prime Minister. But Asha knew that even on such a day, the loud-mouthed anchors of TV news channels would find an angle to pummel her yet again.

So, rather than punish herself by watching more of this nonsense, Asha would spend the evening with Alok Ray, who was already at Number 3 RCR, waiting for her to arrive. They would crack open a bottle of wine, have dinner, snuggle on the sofa, watch a bit of Netflix and then, well, chill.

Asha broke into an involuntary smile at the innuendo implied in that oft-repeated slogan. But jokes aside, if there was one thing she needed, it was an evening off from politics. She needed to spend a few hours away from the demands of her job or risk going insane.

She walked into the drawing room to find that Alok had already read her mind. The TV was switched off, and Ray was busy pouring red wine from a decanter into a couple of glasses. His eyes lit up the moment she walked through the door, and abandoning the wine, he strode up to Asha and took her into his arms. As she nestled against his wide chest, she could feel the tension leave her body. It was almost as if his touch was a magic potion that miraculously calmed her nerves, no matter how high her stress levels.

She raised her face for a kiss and it was duly bestowed upon her. But she could feel that Alok's heart was not in it. Asha broke away from his embrace and cast an enquiring look at him.

'What's the matter?' she asked. 'That wasn't really your best work. Is everything okay?'

Alok handed her a glass of wine and gestured that she should join him on the sofa. 'Everything is fine,' he said, pulling her towards him so that her head rested on his shoulder. 'It is better than fine. Today is the day we have been waiting for so long . . .'

'What's going on, Alok?' asked Asha, pulling away so that she could look at his face.

The excitement was apparent on Alok's face as he gave her the news. Dark Matters had called him an hour ago to say that they were all set to mount the operation to capture Madan Mohan Prajapati. They had managed to infiltrate a couple of their operatives into the close security cordon of Prajapati. Today, the task of escorting Madan Mohan on his morning walk had been assigned to these two men and they were going to ensure that their principal never ever made it back home.

Ray was a bit hazy on the operational details. All he had been told was that the moment Madan Mohan was a safe distance away from the main villa, the two Dark Matters operatives would overpower him and lead him to a vehicle that was waiting nearby. Once he was in the vehicle, they would send a picture to Alok Ray on his private phone to confirm that they had the former defence minister in custody.

From there, Madan Mohan would be driven to a nearby airstrip, where a Gulfstream jet was waiting, staffed entirely by Dark Matters operatives. This plane would take him on the long— fifteen hours or so—journey to Tel Aviv. That's where the plane would refuel before bringing Madan Mohan Prajapati back to Delhi.

Asha's mouth went dry as she contemplated all the many things that could go wrong with this plan. They had to capture Madan Mohan, spirit him to a car, drive him to an airplane, make the long journey to Israel, refuel and then fly to India. And every juncture of this journey, there was a real chance that someone could throw a spanner in the works.

Alok hastened to assure her that these people knew what they were about. Dark Matters did this sort of thing so often that they had a whole network of operatives at airports across the world to facilitate their flights. It would be child's play for them to smuggle Madan Mohan on board and fly him out.

But after her recent experiences with the Jamia Nagar disaster and the Kupwara operation, Asha Devi had lost all faith in the ability of security forces to mount an operation that didn't result in the death of the principal targets. What if Madan Mohan tried to escape, and was shot and killed instead.

That was never going to happen, said a sanguine Alok. These were professionals, he assured Asha, people who did this sort of thing day in and day out. And their payday depended on their being able to keep their targets alive. There was no way that they were going to kill Madan Mohan in the process of capturing him.

Asha took a huge glug of wine to calm herself. It was finally happening. The moment she had been waiting for so long was here. But it wasn't until half an hour later, when a picture of that familiar jowly face flashed on Alok's phone, that Asha finally allowed herself to celebrate.

Strangely enough, her joy manifested itself through tears, which first fell silently and then escalated into loud sobs. Alok said nothing to comfort her, just holding her close and caressing her back until her crying jag finally ended.

Wiping her tears, Asha said in shaky tones, 'I have to call Amma and tell her. She must be the first to know . . .'

'No,' said Alok, shaking his head. 'You can't tell anyone just yet. We have to wait until he takes off from Israel before we can break the news to the family.'

'Don't be ridiculous, Alok,' said Asha. 'Surely, you don't think that my mother or brothers will leak this information?'

But Alok was adamant. Dark Matters had insisted that nobody should be informed until Madan Mohan Prajapati was on the India leg of his journey home. And they had to comply with these instructions.

There was, however, one call that Madam Prime Minister had to make. She had to phone the Israeli Prime Minister and ask that the plane carrying the fugitive be allowed to refuel in Tel Aviv.

But she needed Nitesh Dholakia for that, objected Asha. He was the one who had all the contact numbers of world leaders on his system.

Not to worry, said Alok. He had already informed the Israeli Ambassador that Asha Devi needed a secure line to speak to the Israeli PM on a matter of great urgency. Alok would call the Ambassador and he would patch Asha through.

In the end, it took just a couple of minutes for the two PMs to get on a secure line together. And once Asha had laid out the scenario to her counterpart, he didn't hesitate for a second before granting her request.

Madan Mohan Prajapati would be making a brief stop in Tel Aviv. And then, he would head home to face justice.

# 21

Madan Mohan Prajapati had been in an unusually good mood that morning, as he rolled out of bed. Late last night, he had managed to transfer all the money from his two secret bank accounts in the Cayman Islands and Lichtenstein just hours before the Indian authorities had finally traced and blocked them, thanks to a tip-off from a source in the Enforcement Directorate.

So, he now had just over 225 million dollars stashed away safely, more than enough to keep him in the style to which he had become accustomed for as long as he lived. He had, on the other hand, lost around 127 million in all the numbered accounts in Switzerland that had been traced and frozen by the Indian government. But, as he told himself, pulling on his sneakers, easy come, easy go!

He walked down the staircase and made for the front door, which was guarded by four armed men, all of whom had come highly recommended from a local agency. They saluted smartly as he appeared and then two of them broke away to follow him at a discreet distance as he did his usual walk around the property.

Madan Mohan slid in his airpods and clicked on his playlist of Bollywood hits. That was the only way he could get through the forty-five-minute daily walk that his doctor had recommended on pain of death—quite literally. A bout of uneasiness a few months ago had led him to a local hospital, where tests had shown that his calcium score was 430. Before discharging him, the doctor had warned him that if he didn't adopt a better diet and incorporate some exercise into his life, he couldn't expect to last much longer.

Frightened out of his wits, Madan Mohan had immediately hired a dietician and trainer. And thanks to their joint ministrations, he had lost about ten kilos in the last three months. He felt healthier and lighter than he had for a long time. And with every passing week, he felt happier as well, feeling more and more confident that he had outwitted the Indian authorities, and that they could never trace him to his current hideout.

Lulled into this false sense of security, he ambled on, humming along to Yo Yo Honey Singh, completely unaware that his days of freedom were finally at an end.

The loud music in his ears meant that he was oblivious to the fact that his two security guards had caught up to him as he slipped off the road and headed inside the wooded area where he liked to take a break on a bench that had been carved out of an old piece of driftwood. But today, Madan Mohan did not make it that far.

As he slowed down his pace, one of the guards came right up to him and plunged a syringe into the side of his neck. Madan Mohan remained conscious just long enough to utter one cry of protest before he collapsed on the ground. The two men picked him up, one holding him by his shoulders and the other holding his legs, and carried him a few hundred yards along the road, where a car was waiting, hidden in the foliage of the trees, with two Dark Matters operatives in the front seat.

The trunk was opened, Madan Mohan was dumped unceremoniously inside, one of the men took out his phone and snapped a photo of the unconscious man and sent it off into the ether.

Then, the two guards got into the back seat of the car, which drove off at great speed along the deserted road, heading straight for a nearby airfield.

The Gulfstream was fuelled, fired up, and ready to go. The men in the car handed over their 'package' to the four-member crew on the plane and drove off. Madan Mohan was still unconscious but the Dark Matters agents were taking no chances. They slipped on plastic ties on his hands and feet and deposited him on the sofa at the back of the plane, buckling him up for take-off.

It was somewhere over the Atlantic Ocean that Madan Mohan Prajapati finally woke up. For a moment, he wondered if he was having a nightmare. But the sharp pain that shot through his wrists as he tried to loosen the plastic tie around them convinced him that this was no dream, but real life.

A quick look around confirmed his worst suspicions. He was on a private jet, and that could only mean one thing. He had been taken prisoner and was being flown back to India.

But Madan Mohan was not one to give up in a hurry. In his world, everything ran on money. And this situation too, he felt, could be 'managed' if he threw enough money around.

Swinging his legs off the sofa, he struggled to sit up. The moment he stirred, the two men seated opposite him rushed to prop him up. His mouth felt so dry that he could barely get a word out. He muttered that he needed something to drink. A glass of orange juice was conjured up and one of the men held it up to his mouth so he could drink.

Madan Mohan asked if he could have his restraints removed. After all, what harm could it possibly do? He was their prisoner on this plane. Even if he wanted to escape, where could he go? Out the window?

But no, the restraints stayed on.

By now Madan Mohan was convinced that these men—both of whom were Caucasian and blond—had not been sent by the Indian authorities. They were probably mercenaries for hire, who had kidnapped him on the instructions of some Brazilian gang, which was looking for a handsome ransom.

So, Madan Mohan tried his luck again. How much money have you been paid to capture me, he asked.

The men stayed silent.

It doesn't really matter, went on Prajapati. However much you have been paid, I will give you double the amount if you let me go. Just get me a mobile phone and I will transfer the amounts right now.

At this, the two men looked at one another. An unspoken message seemed to pass between them. Then, after an infinitesimal pause, one of the men reached into his pocket and pulled out a phone.

'Twenty million dollars,' he said tersely, cutting Madan Mohan's ties and handing the phone to him.

Madan Mohan's hands were trembling so much that it took him double the time to go through the four layers of security to access his account and transfer the money to the numbered account his captor provided. Once the transfer was done, he handed the phone back with an unctuous smile, and gestured to his feet, that were still shackled, indicating that it was time they were freed.

The man put his hand into his pocket. But instead of bringing out a knife to cut him loose, he took out another syringe, which he plunged into Madan Mohan's neck.

Madan Mohan fell unconscious again. And that's how he stayed for the rest of the journey.

* * *

Madan Mohan Prajapati's arrival in India was very different from his departure from the country. The only similarity was that private planes were involved in both instances. But while his departure had taken place in secrecy, under the cover of darkness, his arrival happened in full glare of the cameras.

Except that these cameras did not belong to the TV news channels, which remained in the dark about these developments. Asha Devi had taken a decision that she would not brief the press until Madan Mohan was on the ground in India and behind bars. The last thing she wanted was a media circus at the airport when he landed.

But that didn't mean that Madan Mohan's ignominious return to India in handcuffs would go unrecorded. Not a chance. The government would send out its own videographers to record the event—with the Prime Minister and her family watching in real time on a video link—and the clips would then be released to all the channels.

So, there were just two cameramen, one still and one video, who were at the Air Force Terminal of Delhi airport when Madan Mohan's plane landed. But what the welcoming party lacked in media attendance, it more than made up in security forces, which were blanketing the airport, some of them in full riot gear.

Madan Mohan was escorted off the plane, still wearing the track suit he had put on for his morning walk nearly a day ago, his face frozen in a rictus of embarrassment and, daresay, shame, as he was frogmarched into the terminal.

Asha, sitting in the living room at Number 3 RCR, squeezed her mother's hand tight as that familiar jowly face came into view. Both women found themselves in tears as they watched the fugitive who was behind the murder of the man they had loved most in the world finally brought to justice. At long last, thought Asha, Baba's soul could rest in peace.

She cast a quick look at the sofa on which her two half-brothers were seated and saw that they had tears in their eyes as well. Clearly, they were experiencing the same feeling of catharsis as Amma and herself. As their eyes met, the siblings exchanged tremulous smiles, semaphoring their relief that the hunt for their father's killer was over at last.

Asha took comfort from that little unspoken exchange, hoping that it meant that Karan and Arjun had forgiven her for keeping them out of the operation to capture Madan Mohan.

She had called them both over to Number 3 the moment Madan Mohan's flight took off from Tel Aviv to Delhi. The first to arrive was Karan, bristling a bit at being summoned by his sister. Asha had ignored his hostility and hugged him in welcome. She had still to disengage herself when Arjun came through the door, eyebrows raised at this little display of sibling love.

But if the Pratap Singh brothers had started off by being irritated, they soon progressed to full-blown anger as Asha began recounting the story of Madan Mohan's capture. How could she have kept them out of this, they asked, with mounting indignation. This was a matter that concerned their father's killer; his sons should have been kept informed about this from the beginning.

Asha tried to explain that the secrecy had been enjoined on her by Dark Matters. But her heart was not in it. She knew, at a visceral level, that she was in the wrong on this one, and her brothers were completely in the right. She had just gone along with Alok's insistence on secrecy because it was the path of least resistance, when she should have pushed for taking her family into confidence.

So, Asha had apologized abjectly, and after some pushback, had been forgiven. Amma, thankfully, hadn't made an issue of being kept in the dark. Having spent her entire life retreating from rooms in which business was to be conducted, Sadhana Devi was used to being the last one to know.

As for Radhika, she had greeted this news with the same indifference with which she treated the rest of life. Even now, as images of Madan Mohan in handcuffs flashed on the screen, and the entire Pratap Singh family grew emotional, Radhika watched in a catatonic stupor. Clearly, the wounds left by the time she had been captured by terrorists still lingered, so many months later.

Asha turned her attention back to the video feed, which now showed Madan Mohan being placed inside an armoured jeep, with two machine gun-toting security guards on either side of him. As the jeep began its journey to the army cantonment area, flanked by motorcycle outriders and two army trucks, there was a knock on the door.

Nitesh Dholakia popped his head around in answer to Asha's command to come in. It was time for her to prepare for her address to the nation later tonight. He had jotted down some thoughts if the Prime Minister wanted to cast an eye on them. Asha reluctantly turned away from the live images on the TV set, contenting herself with one last look at the sullen visage of her father's killer, and headed for the study.

Casting aside the notes that Dholakia had made for her, she opened a new file on her computer and began typing rapidly.

This was going to be the speech of her life. And she was damned if it was going to be in anyone's words but her own.

* * *

The clips of Madan Mohan's arrival in India were released to all the news channels in time for the 8 p.m. shows. And from the moment they flashed on TV screens across the country, the media went into meltdown.

Madan Mohan Prajapati had been captured and brought back to India, without a hint of this operation being leaked to anyone. How had Asha Devi pulled this off? Who had been in the know? Which government agency had been in charge of the operation? The questions piled up—but answers were scarce on the ground.

Gaurav Agnihotri had called his usual sources in the CBI, the IB, and R&AW but had drawn a blank. All he could gather was that Prajapati was now housed in a special prison block created for him within the army cantonment in the Dhaula Kuan area. There was a three-tier security cordon around him, to make sure that he didn't meet the same fate as his nephew, Sagar Prajapati. His close protection was in the hands of the army, which was guarding his cell and the immediate environs. The second layer of security comprised an entire battalion of paramilitary forces, while the third and last layer was composed of Delhi Police.

But that was about all the information he could gather. From what he could tell, no Indian agency seemed to have any knowledge of the operation that had resulted in Madan Mohan's capture. Gaurav knew the security agencies well enough to know that if they had had the slightest involvement, they would have been scrambling to take credit. The complete denials his questions met with meant that they really had had no clue.

So, that was the question that Gaurav Agnihotri addressed as he began his show. 'Ladies and gentlemen,' he began, in his usual overblown style. 'Today is a great day for this country. Today is the day that the death of our Prime Minister has been avenged. His killer is now in custody, and he will soon pay for his crime.'

Gaurav paused dramatically and then went on, 'But the big question still remains: how did Madan Mohan Prajapati end up in the custody of the Indian government? Our investigations have proved that no Indian security agency was involved in the operation that finally captured him. So, how did Asha Devi manage to track down her father's killer and bring him back to India?'

Gaurav turned to the former R&AW operative on his panel. 'What do you think? Did the Prime Minister use the offices of a foreign country to get Madan Mohan Prajapati? Do you think the Americans were involved in this? And where do you think Prajapati was hiding all along?'

The ex-R&AW man had been texting his contacts at his former agency frantically. And he had managed to extract one fragment of information after calling in some IOUs. The aircraft that had arrived in Delhi carrying Madan Mohan, he was told, had taken off from Tel Aviv. He presented this little nugget to Gaurav Agnihotri with all the pride that a cat takes in bringing a mangled bird back to its owner.

That was all the information that Gaurav needed to spin an elaborate conspiracy theory on the spot. 'Thank you for confirming that,' he shouted excitedly. 'I have always believed from the outset that the Prime Minister had tasked Mossad with tracking down Madan Mohan. That is why the Indian government chose to go with the anti-missile system that Israel had developed over the French and American ones. That must have been the quid pro quo for Mossad to find Madan Mohan wherever in the world he was hiding and render him back to India.'

Now that he had a hook that no other channel did, Gaurav doubled down on his theory, despite the complete lack of evidence supporting it. And in no time at all, he had fashioned a new narrative. In this telling, Asha Devi, the grieving daughter, had lost all confidence in the Indian agencies and had turned to Israel for succor. 'That is the mark of true leadership,' he enthused, 'the ability to think out of the box. I can say with full confidence that no other Prime Minister would have had the guts to use Mossad, like Asha Devi has done. And she has done her father proud in the process.'

In Manisha Patel's studio, the debate had taken an entirely different turn. In the absence of any real information on how and where Madan Mohan had been captured and by whom, Manisha had decided that the best way to approach her show was to turn it into an obituary of sorts for the former defence minister. Given that he was a dead man walking, it made a certain kind of sense to go back and examine his life to see why it had led to this day.

'Why do you think relations between Birendra Pratap and Madan Mohan went so wrong?' she asked the former editor on her panel. 'They were good friends all their lives, and such close political allies. How did it end up like this? With one of them dead, and the other charged with his murder?'

The editor smirked in his usual superior fashion. 'That's where you're wrong, Manisha. There is no such thing as "good friends" in politics. These are all opportunistic alliances, and they last so long as they are mutually beneficial . . .'

Not taking kindly to being condescended to in this manner, Manisha interrupted, 'Yes, yes, we all know that "friendships" in politics are opportunistic. But they don't usually end with one politician being charged for the other's murder, do they?'

The editor, not in the least bit abashed, smirked some more. But before he could patronize her any further, Manisha turned to the LJP spokesman on her panel. 'You have worked with both Birendra Pratap Singh and Madan Mohan Prajapati closely, you have seen their relationship from up close, how do you explain this?'

'You must understand, Manisha ji,' he began earnestly. 'Our respected late Prime Minister was a man known for his honesty. If there was anything that he could not stand, it was corruption. And if he got to know that Madan Mohan was making money from defence deals, he would have ensured that Prajapati ended up in jail for life. Maybe that's why he had to die . . .'

The voice in Manisha's ear interrupted at this point. Sukanya Sarkar's office had called. The Poriborton Party leader wanted to join the show and give her reaction to the arrest of Madan Mohan.

Manisha immediately cut to the link and went into split-screen mode, so that only Sarkar and she were visible to the viewer. Sukanya was in a rare good mood, smiling and congratulating the Prime Minister on getting her father's killer to justice. This was a great day for the country, declared Sukanya, their Prime Minister's assassination had finally been avenged. And it was all down to Asha's Devi's grit and determination.

The moment Sukanya hung up on Manisha, she asked her PS to put her in touch with Asha Devi. There had been so much bad blood between them lately. This was an ideal opportunity to put that behind them, and bond over some good news.

Sukanya Sarkar had had time to mull things over—and she had come to the realization that for now she needed Asha Devi more than Asha Devi needed her. So, it was time for some damage control. And what better time to do that than when the Prime Minister was in a euphoric mood over getting her father's killer to justice?

There was just one problem with this plan. It was impossible to get Asha Devi on the phone. The Prime Minister was getting ready to make an address to the nation, her office said. And she simply could not be disturbed.

On the face of it, this seemed a reasonable enough excuse for not taking her call. But it still left Sukanya Sarkar with an uneasy feeling.

Had she taken things too far with Asha Devi? And if she had, was there any way back now for the two of them?

* * *

Asha had asked Doordarshan to set up their cameras in Number 3 RCR rather than in Number 7, as they usually did. Number 3 was the house that she had shared with Baba. So, on the day that his killer was in custody, there was a certain poetic resonance to addressing the nation from the very room in which she had shared so many loving moments with her father.

She walked into the room to find that Alok Ray was already there, checking out the shot, and asking for some lighting changes. Asha's heart lifted to see him there, and with a gesture she asked him to stay while she read out her address.

Her heart was thumping as Nitesh Dholakia uploaded her speech on to the teleprompter. His mutinous expression made his misgivings clear; he thought that she was making the biggest mistake of her career. He had tried hard to convince her of that, but Asha was adamant—it was her political life, and it was not up to anyone else to tell her how to live it.

She had always operated on her own instincts, and they were yet to let her down. And today, with Baba's killer finally in custody, her instincts told her that this was the only path forward.

The red light began blinking on the camera and the DD producer began counting down. Asha took a deep breath and began reading off the screen.

'*Mere pyare deshvasiyon, Namaskar,*' she began. 'Today is a blessed day for me, as indeed it is for every Indian. My father, the father of our nation, can finally rest in peace. The man behind his death is now behind bars. And Madan Mohan Prajapati will pay with his life for taking the life of Birendra Pratap Singh.'

Asha paused to control the quiver in her throat and then resumed: 'Now that his killer is behind bars, where he belongs, we can finally begin to celebrate the life of my father. The man who made India the shining example it is to the rest of the world. The man who moulded me into the woman I am today.

'The life lessons that my father taught me are the rules by which I have lived my entire life. He taught me that public service is the highest calling of all. He taught me that staying true to my principles is more important than staying in power. And, most important of all, he taught me that the people are supreme in any democracy.'

Asha could see a dawning comprehension in Alok's eyes, as she came closer to making the announcement that would leave India—and Sukanya Sarkar—gasping in disbelief.

Smiling slightly, as she imagined Sukanya watching her address, her jaw dropping with every sentence, Asha continued: 'That is why today, on the day that my father's death has been finally avenged, I am turning to the people of India and asking them to give me a fresh mandate to run this country as it deserves to be run.'

There were a few subdued gasps in the room, as the TV crew grasped the import of what the Prime Minister was saying.

Asha continued, 'Over the last few months, the limits of coalition government have hemmed me in and forced me to deny my own instincts and go along with the judgement of other people because I had to keep my government afloat.

'I did that, not because it was the convenient thing to do or because I wanted to stay in power at all costs. I did that because I felt I owed it to the people of India, to all of you watching at home, to provide a stable and secure government in which everyone would prosper and thrive.

'But today, as I sit before you, a daughter who has finally brought her father's killer to justice, I realize that this is not enough. Instead of doing what others consider to be expedient, I should be doing what I consider to be right. But that, I am afraid, is not possible in the coalition government that I currently run.'

Asha paused and drew a long breath. 'So, it is time to go back to the people of India and ask them for a fresh mandate, a fuller mandate, so that I can serve them without all the pulls and pressures that currently operate on me. Which is why, earlier today, I sent a letter to the President of India, asking that Parliament be dissolved and fresh elections announced.

'And after these elections, if I am privileged enough to win your trust, I hope to be back at the helm of a majority government, that will allow me to govern in a manner that would make my Baba proud.

'The people of India deserve no less. And in a democracy like ours, it is only the people who matter. And, by the grace of God, I hope to dedicate the rest of my life to their service.

'*Namaskar. Jai Hind.*'